crowd of lies

book 2

LISA HELEN GRAY

crowd
of lies

Believe,

Melany x

prologue

KAIDEN

From the moment I learned of Ivy Monroe's existence, I knew vengeance would finally be mine.

Someone had to pay for her mother's sins, and she was the next best thing.

I hated her before I met her, wanted to shred the ground she walked on and make her wish she had never been born. I wanted to break her, piece by piece, until there was nothing left to scrape off the floor.

Then she stormed into my life, blowing up everything around me.

I forgot about my plan, my game.

I forgot about the promise I made to myself when I was just a kid, when my world was ripped apart: to destroy anything and everything her mother cared about.

I forgot it all.

Because I let her in. I let her into a place where only my mum and brothers and best friend were.

I took my eye off the ball. And now the sky is falling down on me, shattering my world into a thousand pieces.

I now have a new promise to fulfil.

To find out the truth and protect *her*.

Blood will be shed.

Lives will be ruined.

And I will get what I want.

I'm Kaiden Kingsley.

chapter one

KAIDEN

THE MUSIC IS THUNDEROUS AS I MAKE my way downstairs, louder than what it was forty minutes ago, when I went upstairs to send an email to the Kingsley Academy Education Board.

My mother, Nina, owns the Academy. She owns the Kingsley name; my dad choosing to take her name instead of his own. It was a power play on his part, and a clever one. My mum's family were notorious for networking, and they were rich. Rich enough to own whatever their hearts desired.

Right now, I desire Ivy. I want to find her, drag her to the closest room and fuck her senseless. My need for her is so strong I don't even care if people are in said room.

My gaze travels across the sea of people, drinking and dancing, when my gaze locks with Ethan's. He grins, but then his eyebrows furrow as he glances over my shoulder. I turn but see no one behind me. Anyone who comes to one of our parties knows not to go upstairs. They know what we would do to them wouldn't be worth it.

I head over to him, ignoring a few Academy students on my way. "What's wrong?"

It's Lucca, Ethan's twin, who answers me. "You're becoming a let-down, bro. Over already?"

"What are you going on about?" I grit out, my look slicing through him, still annoyed over the party.

"Where's Ivy?" Ethan asks, not at all bothered with my mood. "She went upstairs to find you."

"Ivy?" Grant asks, joining our huddle. We've been friends since we were born, but his actions of late are beginning to worry me. He's always had a darkness about him—it comes from being raised by a loveless father—but recently it's been different. Having Ivy here is fucking with his head. Though he does seem to be better than when she first arrived, over a month ago.

Still, he needs to be watched.

"Yeah, you seen her?"

"What are you going on about, Ethan?" I bite out, agitated about everyone being inside our home. I just want it to be us, Ivy and Grant. I don't want all these leeches here.

"Like I said, she was here and we sent her upstairs to find you. Did you not see her?" Ethan asks.

I look to Grant, raising my eyebrow in question. "The only person I've seen is Dad. He rushed out of his office fifteen minutes or so ago, looking thunderous over something."

"I didn't see Dad," Lucca comments, sharing a secretive look with Ethan.

I ignore them, pointedly staring at Grant. He looks sheepish, glancing to the door.

"She ran out of here thirty minutes ago, looking like she'd seen a ghost. I thought it was because she was pissed about Danielle."

That can't be right. She would have come to me before leaving. Since the night of the fire, her walls have come down and she's let me in. We've grown closer throughout the week, and it's not just me who's become addicted. She's nothing like I expected.

Something doesn't feel right, though, so I head outside, leaving my brothers and Grant to follow me. Our housekeeper, Lenore, always hires men to blend in and guard the house, in case we step out, so I know nothing will happen with us all gone. I may have asked the twins to get Danielle here without being too obvious, but a party isn't something I'm in the mood for.

Nova is running out of her house like it's on fire, and an overwhelming feeling that something bad is about to happen, creeps up my spine.

"Where's Ivy?" I yell out to her.

She jumps, clutching her chest. "Have you seen her?" she asks, hope flashing in her eyes.

She's been crying, which means she's probably had another argument with Ivy. I'm kind of surprised, though, since Ivy said they were getting along better. Another thing that doesn't add up.

"What's going on, Nova?"

"I-I—it's private family stuff. I need to go look for her."

My jaw hardens as I walk towards her, and she takes a step back, looking scared, unable to meet my eyes. The twins notice too and watch her warily.

I love Nova, think of her like an aunt, like a mother really, but I can also tell when she's lying. She might be a damn good lawyer, but she isn't a defence attorney. She deals with land and other crap, so lying isn't her strong suit, not when it comes to those she's closest to.

My phone rings in my back pocket, and I pull it out to see an unknown caller ringing me. "Yeah?"

"Don't hang up," Rhys, whose voice I instantly recognise, rushes out, and I look back down at the phone, wondering if I'm hallucinating.

"Please tell me you have a good reason for calling me, Rhys." Our beef with the Remington's is long lasting, but for us, it's not about some old feud that happened many generations ago. It's personal. It's an act of disobedience, neither side wanting to submit to the other.

And we'll never submit. I'd rather die than have a Remington tell me what to do.

"I do. I do," he rushes out, and for the first time I notice he sounds nervous, not cocky and so sure of himself.

The guys pay close attention when they hear who I'm talking to. They gather closer, listening intently to the one-sided conversation.

"Spit it out," I snap harshly.

"Carter called me from his bike. Man, it's bad. You need to get to the hospital. I told the paramedics to take them to Farley Hospital."

I laugh, seriously thinking the guy is high. "Why the fuck would I care?"

"Because he had Ivy on the back of his bike."

My back straightens, and I feel the blood rushing from my face. "Talk! And start from the beginning." I look over at Nova, who's glancing down at the phone clutched in her hand, her face pale. "Nova, hand Grant your keys. He's driving us to Farley Hospital."

She looks up, white as a sheet. "It's Ivy, isn't it?" she asks, passing the keys in her hand to Grant.

Why doesn't she sound surprised? What the fuck is going on? I've never been scared in my life, not even when my mum overdosed and was rushed into hospital. Right now, I'm fucking petrified of what Rhys is about to tell me.

"He said someone was trying to kill them, and told me where they were. By the time I got there, they were loading them into an ambulance."

"Who was trying to kill them? And why the fuck was Ivy with him? If this is some fucking sick game you're playing and it got Ivy hurt, I'll slit your throat first, then make my way through your entire family," I growl as we get into the car, causing Nova to whimper.

"It's not, I swear. And I don't fucking know. I'm doing you a fucking favour here. He didn't say. Just fucking get here."

I end the call as Grant pulls off, glancing at me through the rear-view mirror. "What's going on?"

I run down everything Rhys said, noticing how tense the twins get either side of me, their hands clenched on their knees.

"Nova, you want to explain why Ivy was with Carter Remington?"

"You'll need to ask Ivy," she whispers.

A phone rings in the car, and Nova jumps, reaching for her bag. I notice she doesn't answer the phone in her hand but the one she pulls from her bag.

"Sam," she cries. "Are you with her? I don't know. Oh my god. Please, no! This is all my fault."

I share a look with Grant in the rear-view mirror, both of us confused as we wait for her to get off the phone. "Nova?"

A small sob escapes her. "It's Ivy."

My heart stops at those words, and I break out in a cold sweat.

No!

"Sam said she wasn't breathing when they brought her in."

I punch the back of the driver's seat to let out the anger and fear bubbling inside of me. When that doesn't work, I lean over Ethan and punch my fist through the window, shattering the glass into a thousand pieces.

"Calm down," Grant yells from the front.

"Fucking drive. And fast," I bite out, gripping the ends of my hair.

Blood seeps from my knuckles and trickles through my fingers, but I don't care.

Ivy!

I'll fucking kill Carter for getting her hurt. He's gone too far by going after her. When we gate-crashed his party, I told him she was off limits. We'd gone there to throw punches, but when I saw him hovering over her, trying to work his slimy charm, I felt like I was the one who'd been hit in the gut.

He clearly didn't get my meaning.

He will though.

Soon.

WHEN WE REACH the hospital, I don't bother to wait for Grant to park. I push Ethan out of the car before jumping out myself and rushing through the hospital doors.

I know from experience that if you're brought in by ambulance, you are treated on the first floor, so that's where I start searching, not caring if I look like a wild animal.

The second I lock eyes on Carter, rage boils through my veins. I rush up to him, grip him by the T-shirt he's wearing, and slam him against the wall. A picture frame falls down, smashing on the floor.

"What the fuck did you do? What did you get her into? I'll fucking kill you," I roar, pulling my fist back.

He laughs when I punch him in the jaw, spitting out blood. His gaze hardens, and he pushes me back. "You should be thanking me. It wasn't me they were trying to kill. It was her."

"What?" I ask, stepping back.

"Yeah. I was heading to a mate's house when I saw her getting run off the road by a black Mercedes with blacked out windows. When it spun back to finish the job, I stopped and got her on the back of my bike. It didn't stop until we crashed."

For the first time, I take a good look at him, noticing the road rash and head injury. His clothes are torn up. My stomach sinks. If he's this bad, with his experience in how to land and what to do during a crash, then I dread to think what Ivy looks like when she has no fucking clue what to do.

"Where's the driver?" I can't even think of anyone we know who has that car, but my head isn't thinking straight right now.

He shrugs, running a hand over his face. "According to guy who stopped to help, some man stole her bag and took off."

What?

I turn to the sounds of my brothers coming down the corridor, my gaze zeroing in on Nova, who's whispering something to Sam, a man she's hated since he cheated on her.

That tingling sensation, a feeling that tells me something big is about to happen, runs down my spine, and I know, without a doubt, Nova has the answers.

"Is she okay?" Ethan and Lucca ask, their gaze narrowing in on Carter.

"Hey, I fucking helped her," he snaps, holding his hands up. He moves away, giving us privacy. I look away when a nurse starts fussing over him, trying to get him back into his room.

"I'm going to look for her," I tell the twins, just as Sam steps up.

"No, you aren't, son."

"I'm not your fucking son," I grit out, pushing past him. He grips my arm, pulling me back.

"They're trying to save her life in there. They'll come out with news once they can."

I push at his chest, knocking him into Grant. "Do you really think you can use now to worm your way inside her life? You can't play dad now. You don't get that chance."

Sam laughs in my face. "You have no idea. I don't want her near you. She isn't safe."

I rear back before punching him in the face. He staggers into the wall, and Nova screams, going to his aid. "Kai!"

"I'd never hurt her."

He wipes blood away from his lip, glaring at me. "You think I don't know what you planned to do to her?"

"That was before," I tell him, stepping back in shame.

He's right though, Ivy wasn't safe around me before. I was going to ruin her, break her. But then it changed. I can't even pinpoint the monumental moment that killed all my plans, but something, at some time, did. I no longer hate her. I don't fuck her like I hate her.

She's mine.

"Miss Monroe?" a nurse calls, and Nova turns to the door the woman stepped out of.

"Is she okay?"

The nurse watches us warily, picking up on the tension before turning back to Nova. "She went into cardiac arrest for a few moments on the way in."

I spin around and punch the wall, bowing my head as I tune everyone out.

I'll kill whoever did this.

A hand on my shoulder has me spinning around. Ethan.

"Woah, Kai, hold the punches. She's fine. She has a collapsed lung, a broken arm and a few broken ribs."

"What else?" I ask, resting my hands on my bent knees as I slide down the wall, relief filling me.

She's okay. She's breathing.

"She has a mild head injury, but nothing serious. She's still out cold, but Sam and Nova have gone in."

"Guys? What are you doing here?" Selina asks, casting Carter a wary glance when she sees him leaning against the wall, his cousin Rhys next to him. I watch as she drops the sleeve of her dressing gown, covering her burnt arm. "Did you lot succeed in killing one or the other? Is Ivy here? I was just going to get some decent food."

When no one laughs at her attempt of a joke, she looks around at all our weary expressions. Ethan is the one to step forward.

"Selina, it's Ivy. She was in an accident."

Her accusing eyes come to me. "What did you do?" she snaps, and I feel like I've been stabbed in the chest. Ethan said accident, but it didn't matter. She still assumed it was me. "Where is she?"

"Calm down," Ethan warns her, stepping closer.

"Get away from me! Where is she? She told me what you guys did to her, what you've said, and I didn't say anything because she didn't want me to. I thought you were past it. I thought you were together," she yells, drawing attention from other visitors and nurses.

"Calm her the fuck down," I bark at Ethan, ignoring her insults.

"Calm down? Are you for real? Where is she?"

"Selina, why don't you go back to your room?" Carter speaks up.

"Don't fucking talk to her," Lucca snaps.

Carter pushes off the wall. "Or what, Kingsley?"

"Watch it," I warn him. "I'm still thirsty for blood."

Sam steps out of the room, completely ignoring me. "Selina," he murmurs, and she rushes over to him.

"Is she okay? What happened?"

"She's going to be fine. She can't have any more visitors, but as soon as she can, I'll come get you."

"I'm not leaving," she screeches, looking at him like he's crazy.

"She needs her rest. I'll come by your room and explain everything in a little while."

She watches him for a moment longer before reluctantly nodding. "I'm going to call—" She pauses, her eyes glistening with tears. "She doesn't have anyone for me to call. I take it Nova is already here?"

Sam pats her shoulder, comforting her. "She has all of us."

I snort, glaring at him. She has us, not him. She wouldn't want him here. She doesn't need him.

Grant's phone goes off and he looks down at the screen, his eyebrows scrunching together. He glances up at me before throwing Nova's keys my way. "I need to go. Dad needs me back at the house."

Sam flushes with anger as he bares his teeth. "Why?"

Grant curls his lip. "None of your business."

Sam turns back to Selina as Grant leaves. "I need to go."

I thought he'd leave to go back into the room, but he doesn't, instead heading for the exit.

I snort. "Why am I not surprised?"

Selina glares at me. "Shut up! He loves her. He might not have shown it, but he does."

"Right!"

Nova steps out before Selina can say anything else. "The doctors said she needs to rest. You guys should go home."

"I'm not going anywhere," I tell her.

She sighs. "All right. But she can't have visitors due to risk of infection. She has a collapsed lung and other open injuries."

She's not telling me all of it. Instead of arguing, I nod. "I'll wait."

Selina looks torn as she stares at the closed door. "Why don't you go back to your room, Selina. We'll keep you updated if anything changes," Lucca offers.

"Promise?"

"I promise."

She looks down at me, sitting on the floor. "If I find out you did this to her, I'll run you over and make it look like you committed suicide. Don't test me. I'm crazy enough to do it."

I listen to her walk back down the hallway, her slippers flopping across the floor.

I need answers, but when I go to ask Carter a few more questions, he's gone, and so is his cousin, Rhys.

"What do you think they're all hiding from us?" Ethan asks, sitting down on my left while Lucca sits on my right.

"I don't know. Is this my fault?" I ask, glancing down at the floor.

"How? You weren't driving the car."

"What if it was Danielle?" I mention, ignoring how Ethan is trying to make me feel better.

"Nah, this is something else. You saw Nova outside ours. She was scared of you. She's acting weird."

"Yeah, she is."

"We'll find out who was driving that car and deal with them ourselves," Lucca tells me.

I turn to him, feeling numb inside. "When I find out who was driving that car, I'm going to slit their throat. I don't give a fuck if it's Danielle." I pause, running a hand over my face. "Lucca, start looking deeper into Ivy's past. Start with her mum. Whoever did this succeeded in killing her for a few minutes. I want to know who. Ethan, start looking for any cameras in the area the crash happened. I want to see the car."

"On it," they say, getting up from the floor and leaving.

I clench my hands into fists as I stare at Ivy's door. I'm going to make this right. What I did to her, what was done to her and what happened today... I'll make it right.

No one fucks with mine.

Ever.

chapter two

KAIDEN

*I*T'S BEEN TWO DAYS SINCE IVY WAS BROUGHT IN, and they won't let us fucking see her. We've been camped outside her room the whole time, refusing to leave. Lenore, our housekeeper, brought us a change of clothes and the hospital let us use the family room shower.

We managed to get into her room yesterday—her eighteenth birthday—but she was still out cold. I wanted to touch her, but Sam would only let us so close, threatening to get us removed if we didn't obey. And I believed him.

As much as I didn't want to listen to him, he held the power in the hospital, so I took what little they would give.

She looked weak, pale, and had bruising. It was hard not to say 'fuck it' and go to her. It killed me to see her looking so small and lonely in that bed. I wanted her to know I was there, that I hadn't left.

The only reason we've not charged in there since is because they haven't let Selina in either. Yet, I'm still confused over the hostility.

Something is going on with Nova and Sam. They're hiding something big.

I'm not worried. I'll find out what it is and what it has to do with Ivy.

The twins are getting edgy too. They went through Cara Monroe's background, but there wasn't anything we didn't already know, same for Ivy's. Whoever tried to kill her, they weren't from her past.

Which begs the question, who is after her now?

"Where the fuck is Grant?" Ethan barks, sitting forward.

We'd dragged chairs out from the waiting room to right outside Ivy's. All of us wanted to be close.

"He's not picking up?" I ask, turning to Lucca.

He turns his phone around, showing me the screen. "He's not picking up."

"I wonder why his dad wanted him?" Ethan muses.

"Probably to give him a list of shit to accomplish at the Academy."

"I still can't believe we go back next week."

I grunt. He's right there. This summer has gone too quickly. Dad had promised we could finally visit Mum, but he broke it, saying she had another relapse. Who the fuck smuggles drugs into a rehab facility?

After I've found out and dealt with who hurt Ivy, I'm going to look for Mum. She needs to get home, take control of her companies. Dad has already sold one off and the funds have disappeared. I've had a few people look into it, and they've all said the same thing. That it was all legalised and somewhere in one of our many accounts. I don't trust it. It was like they rehearsed their speech. I know Dad got to them, which is why I need to find someone who can't be paid off.

"Try Grant again," I order Lucca.

I need him to go look at the crash site. Ethan and Lucca have refused to leave Ivy, and I can understand that. They've grown close. All the work they've done to find out what happened was done in the hospital after Lenore brought all our stuff.

Grant, however, is still unsure about her. He's not been himself for a while now, long before Ivy arrived.

His dad has been on his case a lot more about getting into the family business. When Grant refused to start a work placement so he could spy for his dad, he got a beating that night, and I'm sure more since. I've seen the bruises.

"We're supposed to be a team and he fucks off?" Lucca snorts, shoving his phone back in his pocket when there's no answer. "He's been acting shady as fuck for weeks. I'm still pissed at what he did to her in that pool. He should have been arrested for what he did."

I give my brother a dry look. "And what you did was better?"

Ethan growls under his breath. "We would never have taken it that far. We just wanted to see if she'd fight back. You might have forgotten, but *we* didn't want to cause her shit in the first place. We never blamed her for Mum. You did. We wanted to make sure she was strong enough. He's lost the plot, Kaiden. You know it; you just won't admit it."

I grit my teeth at them mentioning Mum. "Her mum is the fucking reason ours is the way she is. And give him a break. He has shit going on."

I don't know why I'm sticking up for him. He has been a dickhead for a while, acting out of character.

And Mum… She barely remembers who we are most of the time. Life broke her, and it all started with Cara. It's the reason I was going to break Ivy. I wanted revenge for what was done to her.

At the moment, Mum is in another rehab centre, has been for almost two years. Dad has been keeping her there, which is another reason why I hate him so much. The twins need their mum, whether they wanted to admit it or not. She's been absent most of their lives. At least I remember parts of her.

"Listen to yourself, Kaiden. Mum made her own choices. Dad made his own. *We* make our own. Grant has changed and it's time you see that."

"I'm not mad at Ivy anymore. I never really had a reason to be. I know that." I haven't been since I heard her talking to Nova that morning about her life, about her mum. When she questioned if her mum was raped, I had to know more, that feeling in the pit of my stomach twisting into knots. I knew then something didn't add up. I was just too stubborn-headed to do anything more about it.

"We know," Lucca assures me.

"And as for Grant, you know what his dad is like. Whatever is bugging him, he'll come to us eventually."

"Right, because he's so fucking chatty," Ethan mutters dryly. "I just think you should talk to him."

"I will," I assure him, and I will. I've been meaning to have another talk with him for a while.

Lucca stands, kicking his chair against the wall in the hallway. The duck-egg walls are starting to get to me too.

The hallway isn't small, but when you have basically been living in it for two days, it starts to get smaller. There is nothing to look at but blank walls, and I think it's getting to the twins.

Lucca bangs his fist against the wall, a growl tearing from his throat. "This is stupid! Why won't they let us see her? The nurses said she'd be awake soon."

I scrub a hand down my face, exhausted. It's only early evening, yet it feels like the early hours of the morning. "I don't know. I'm giving them another hour before I go in."

"I don't like how they're guarding it, like we're the ones who ran her off the road," Ethan comments.

I think about his comment, wondering the same thing. The way Nova has been treating me and Sam, you'd think I was the one who had put her in hospital.

And Sam… He left the same time as Grant the other day and didn't get back until late last night.

I don't trust him, not one bit.

"I'll sort it," I promise him. "I'll find out what this is about."

"Has Selina been here today? I went to her room to see her when I went to get us drinks, but she wasn't there," Lucca adds.

"Wasn't she meant to get released today?" Ethan asks.

"Yeah, but her stuff was still in her room and someone's jacket was left on a chair."

"She'll be here soon. It's Ivy. She loves having her here."

I look up at the sound of footsteps angrily stomping towards us. At first, I'm worried it's Dad, coming to demand we go home. Nova has asked us to leave a few times but hasn't taken it any further when we've refused. She could have had Sam kick us out completely, but she didn't. Dad, on the other hand, won't give a fuck. He'll get security to escort us out.

I'm surprised to see Grant. I'm instantly on alert when I get a look at his thunderous expression. I get up from my chair, taking a step towards him.

He pushes me out of the way, taking me off guard.

"What the fuck?" I growl, glaring at him. He tries to push through Ivy's hospital room door, but I block him, pushing him back. "Start talking!"

"Get out of my way," he barks, his face red with anger.

"Not until you tell me what is going on. Where have you been? We've been trying to get hold of you."

His lip curls in disgust. "I want to fucking see her. Is the slut awake?"

"Hey!" the twins call out, stepping up beside me.

Grant forces out a laugh. "I should have known you two dogs would stand beside her."

"What the fuck is your problem?" I grit out, getting in his face. I don't want to hit him, but I will. He's pushing, and the way he's going, it won't be long until he's knocked out.

"My dad is gone."

"And what does that have to do with Ivy?"

"That slag has something on him. She's been blackmailing him."

I step back, shaking my head. I don't believe him. I've been friends with him since we were in nappies and only known Ivy for weeks, yet I know what he's saying is a lie. She doesn't care about wealth, fame or fortune. She cares about having somewhere safe to sleep, a roof over her head, and food. She hates it when we let it go to waste.

She has no reason to blackmail his dad. There's nothing she'd want to gain.

She doesn't.

"You're a fucking liar," Ethan growls, stepping closer.

Grant laughs again. "Is she spreading her legs for you too? Has she got that cunt squeezed around your cock so tight you can't even feel your balls anymore?"

I reach out to grab him, but Lucca beats me to it, punching Grant in the jaw, knocking him backwards.

I pull Lucca back, ignoring his glare. "What is she using as blackmail, exactly?"

"You don't know, do you?"

I glare at him. "I wouldn't fucking ask if I did."

"She's been blackmailing your dad too. They're gone. They've had to. She's fabricated some sick fucking story to get them arrested."

"Wait a minute, what story?" Ethan asks.

I turn to him. "Call Dad!"

He nods, stepping out of the way with his phone in his hand. I turn back to Grant, watching him.

"What did your dad say?"

"He wanted me to go with him, said she'll take me down with them."

"That doesn't answer my question. What does she have on them?"

"You don't believe me?" he asks, curling his lip. "Why am I not surprised. She's got her claws so far into you."

"Watch it," I warn.

"This is your fault. I warned you she was just like her mum. You said you didn't think she was and cancelled what we had planned. Now I've got to see that smug bitch's face everywhere. I want whatever she has over Dad, over my family. I won't let some dragged up whore bring down my family's legacy."

I punch him, knocking him to the floor. He wipes the blood away from his lip, narrowing his eyes at me.

"You're a fool," he curses, getting to his feet. "Is she really that good of a lay you'd believe her over me?"

"You want to watch it, Grant. Don't make me hit you twice," I warn him. "You might want to fill us in on what is happening."

"He wouldn't tell me what she has, just what she'll do if they don't give her money. She wants everything. She told them she wouldn't just share whatever it is she has, but she'll get me done for rape. You lot too. She's had this planned from the beginning."

I look to Ethan, who glances up from his phone. He frowns, shaking his head.

"That story sounds fabricated, even to me," Lucca says.

Grant glowers at Lucca. "She's going to get us fucking done for rape. I'm not letting some washed up tramp who doesn't even own her own clothes, ruin my life."

"You don't even know if it's true," I warn him.

None of it makes sense. At all. But something rings true in his words, and it's bugging me that I don't know what.

"Wait, is this why Ivy was run over? Why someone tried to kill her?" I ask, feeling my blood begin to pump.

Grant shoves me backwards. "You blaming that shit on my dad, on yours?"

"Touch me again, mate, and I'll break your fingers."

"Dad didn't do this," he tells me, shaking his head. "We arrived at the house at the same time."

"That doesn't mean shit," I tell him.

"Are you seriously fucking accusing my dad of this? You'll throw years of friendship away for that slag?"

"She's not a slag. Stop acting jealous and get your head out of your arse," Lucca warns.

Grant ignores him, turning to me. "She's ruined our lives, and you're going to let her get away with it? You're still going to stand there and stick up for the bitch?"

I run a hand down my face, tired of all this bullshit. "What did your dad say, exactly?"

Grant groans, looking up to the ceiling. "He was in a rush, not making much sense at first, just kept telling me to pack my bags, that we had to go somewhere they couldn't touch us. He was talking about your dad, the business, but nothing really stuck out. He said she was coming for us all, to ruin them after they ran her mum out of town. She's out for revenge, on all of them."

"Wait up," I tell him, holding my hand up. "Revenge? What for? Her mum made up lies, saying she slept with our dads. There was more, but I can't remember all of it. I know that much is true. Mum would cry, and said it started with Cara Monroe." I pause, truly thinking about it. As a boy, it's all I could think about. My mum was the way she was because of Cara Monroe, because of something she did when I was a baby. As a young boy who just wanted his mum's love, I placed all the blame and hatred on Cara. I never really stopped to actually think about it. "Wait, if by some miracle her mum was telling the truth and they did sleep with her, why would my dad care? He's cheated on Mum for as long as I can remember."

"I don't know, and I don't fucking care. She was a slut, and everyone knew it. People still gossip about her and what an embarrassment she was. She ruined lives, Kaiden. She made up shit to drive a wedge between them all. She couldn't stand the fact they were all happy. Growing up, every single night Dad would get drunk and tell me she killed Mum."

"So why would Ivy want revenge?"

"Because she's pissed she wasn't given the life we had. They ran her mum out of town after Mum died. Even her family cut her off. Ivy somehow managed to get something on them, something that has them scared, and has threatened to get us arrested if they don't pay her. She'll not only destroy their businesses, but our lives."

"Ivy didn't even know about Nova until her mum died, Grant."

"Dad's still not answering," Ethan interrupts, stepping into our little circle. "And you might not want to hear it, but I don't think Ivy has anything on our families. Whatever is going on, it's not because she has some grudge."

"He's right," Lucca adds before we can speak up.

"One way to find out," Grant bites out, daring me to stop him when he moves towards her door.

I'm too fucking torn to stop him. I want answers, and the only one who can give them to us right now is Ivy.

Nova's going to have to get in line, because I'm not leaving until I find out what is going on.

If I'm about to break a life-long friendship for a girl, it had better be because he's in the wrong.

I won't be made a fool of.

chapter three

IVY

I wake up to raised voices, confused and disorientated. I recognise Kaiden and Grant immediately, but their voices are muffled.

I open my mouth to call out to Kaiden, but memories come flooding back. I scrunch my eyes closed, clamping my mouth shut.

I'd prayed being chased by a mad man was all just a bad dream, but as I wake up in my hospital bed, that dream is crushed. It was all real, the whole damn lot.

I'm past angry. I'm livid. He tried to kill me. It doesn't take a rocket scientist to figure out it was Royce who ran us off the road.

I tilt my head to the side, scowling when I see Sam and Nova sitting side by side on the sofa of the grand room I'm in.

This place isn't a hospital. It's more like a hotel room.

The walls are a light grey with landscape paintings of mountains covered in snow. It has a recliner in the corner, and a blanket has been thrown over the top, like someone has been using it to sleep on.

I shut my eyes briefly, breathing through the pain throbbing through my head. Everything hurts, and as much as I want to cry, I know now isn't the time. There will be time for that later.

I ignore the arguing going on outside the room and turn my attention to my so-called dad and aunt, who miraculously decide now is the time to become best buds.

"Get out!" I grit out, losing my voice towards the end. I clear my throat, wincing through the sharp ache in my chest as I try to sit up further. Pain shoots up my arm and my eyes widen at the white cast that spans from my hand to just below my elbow.

Nova rushes to my side, relief pouring through her. "You're awake."

"No thanks to you."

"Ivy," she whispers, her tone pained. I look away, trying to be unaffected.

I thought we were getting close and it was all a lie. She made me think I could have a family, a life, and she lied.

Her betrayal stings, and I force myself to look at her. "I said, get out!"

"Listen to her," Sam warns me, and I narrow my eyes at him.

"Why are you even here? Come to gloat?"

His jaw clenches. "You know that's not true."

"I don't know what's fucking true anymore. Someone keeps lying to me. I would have been safer back in the flat." Remembering my bag filled with the truth, I look around the hospital room in a panic. "Where's my bag?"

"Bag?" Nova asks, taken off guard from the change of subject.

"Yes, it had everything in it," I tell her, glancing at Sam from the corner of my eye. I don't know what she's told him, or if she's lied to him too. I wouldn't put it past them to be in on it together.

"Oh, um, it's gone. Whoever ran you off the road, they took it," she explains.

I close my eyes as anger consumes me. The monitor beside me starts beeping a little faster, and I try to calm my breathing.

I don't need any more proof to know it was Royce.

And she can't be that stupid to believe it was an accident.

"You know who's got it, don't you?" I ask her, a bite to my tone. "He's going to get away with it."

She nods, her bottom lip jutting out as she crosses her arms in front of her chest. "It's why I lied to you. He's dangerous, Ivy."

"So why live next door to him? Why bring me into the lion's den?" I bark.

"Because you're my niece, my family. I didn't know he had your mum killed. I didn't know any of it. I thought that as long as you were kept in the dark, he wouldn't go after you. Then he showed up the first day."

"He mentioned money," I tell her, remembering when I listened in on them the first time I met him.

"Yes. He was worried you'd liquidate the company they co-share together. I swear, I didn't know he had your mum killed, Ivy. I would never have brought you back to Monroe Manor. I would have sent you to live with your uncle."

I shake my head in disgust. "But you knew what he did to her and let him get away with it."

"He would have gotten away with it regardless, Ivy. As sad as it is, he would have. He had a family with a wide range of connections. He had money. And she acted out after, doing drugs, sleeping around. They wouldn't have taken her seriously."

"She was pregnant with her rapists' baby," I tell her, angry all over again. "If that wasn't cruel enough, she had to live with them, knowing they'd gotten away with it. She lost a part of herself, and in the end, had no one. She didn't even have me, because she never let herself get close. And I can see why. I understand it all now. Everyone she loved betrayed her, so why get close to anyone else?"

"Ivy, you have to understand—"

I turn to Sam, arching my eyebrow at his condescending tone. "Understand what? You have no idea what life for me was like, but I'm willing to bet my life it was worse for her. I can't even hate her anymore. I don't even know how to feel, because if that hadn't happened to her, growing up, I would have had a mum, a dad, a family. Instead, I spent my life around drugs, a drunk mum, and men who would get handsy. So, don't sit there and tell me to understand." My throat burns as my voice rises. It's so dry my tongue feels rough against the top of my mouth.

A flicker of guilt flashes across his face. "Royce knew how to play the part, Ivy. He's always been sick in the head, but he hid it well with his looks and charm. He was different and everyone knew it, could sense it. He was as cunning and evil as the devil."

"And that makes it okay?"

Nova shakes her head. "It doesn't make any of it okay."

Sam runs a hand across his jaw. "Our fathers and their fathers' fathers have been in business together for many generations. We grew up together, but Royce was groomed early, ready to take over when his dad went into politics. But his dad made a wrong business decision and they were on the verge of losing everything, and with his campaign around the corner, he couldn't afford to, so he needed to get the other families onboard."

"That's peachy, but I don't see what that has to do with anything," I tell him.

He sighs, pulling a chair closer to the bed. "Hear me out. I'm telling you everything so you understand where we're coming from.

"The rest of us were groomed from high school, all of us learning the family business. Royce has always been about money, wanting more than he'd ever need in a lifetime. It was never enough for him.

"Nina, Kaiden's mum, was going to break up with him. He was controlling, manipulative, and when his dad started punishing him at home, he'd take his anger out on her. We'd see the bruises on her arms at school, in places he thought we couldn't see. He'd always been a bully, always cruel to those he thought were less than him. She loved him and kept forgiving him until it got too much, I guess. His dad was on his back to marry her or a Monroe, to connect their families by blood, since they were pushing him out of the company."

"So, he raped my mum," I finish, the words from the tape coming back to me. "He was meant to get her pregnant, to become a Monroe?"

"Yes. Not even your grandfather or great grandfather would have been able to refuse marriage then. They would have forced them to marry if a child was involved. It would have looked bad on the family if they didn't.

"The Monroe's and the Kingsley's are the richest families in the UK. They have businesses or investments in pretty much everything. To our community, they are gods, the people you want to have connections with. Royce's dad, and Neil Tucker's dad, made a wrong move and it cost the company millions. From what I remember, they were cast out, fired by the board. They lost money, too much money, and their dads were furious with what they had done with their legacy and demanded they fix it. They came up with a plan. They would get one of their sons to marry into one of the two richest families and connect their wealth to theirs. They knew Nova and I were very much in love, and Royce knew Nina was going to break up with him. He'd been secretly trying to get her pregnant for a while and it wasn't working. Neil was with Flora, Grant's mum, at the time, and he didn't want to break up with her like his father told him to. But he knew he'd have to if he wanted to be successful in life. They needed the money. Flora's family was wealthy, but nowhere near the same level as a Kingsley or a Monroe. They'd joke about it to me, how they were going to toss a coin, like it was some sort of game.

"That night, I didn't know what I walked in on. Your mum was out of it—moaning or whimpering, I don't know. I was weak, and I'm ashamed to admit it, but I was scared about what they'd do to Nova."

"What?" Nova asks, seeming surprised by the news.

I feel sick, and I have to look away for a moment, trying to catch my breath.

Sam nods sadly. "Did you never wonder why I kept quiet, why I didn't tell anyone? If I spoke up, you'd have been next. They cornered me the next day and kicked the living shit out of me, saying they'd tell people I was there, that I thought it was you. I knew then that I had to get stronger, not only to stick up for myself, but for you too. Cara never said anything, and I didn't want to bring it up. I'm ashamed of what I did, and I'll never forgive myself for my part.

"The night before she left, she told everyone what they had done to her, but they didn't believe her. Flora had just died, so I was having a drink, then two, then three, then four. I knew it was my fault. I should have spoken up. Cara came around that night, and I was so out of it, drinking away my sorrows. I don't remember—"

"I don't need to relive this," Nova mutters, looking away.

"I do. Go on. I want to know everything," I tell him, clenching the sheets.

"As I was saying, I don't remember any of it."

Nova snorts. "So you say."

"I don't. Why you won't believe me, I don't know. One minute I was on the verge of being drunk, the next, Cara was on top of me, and I was too out of it to realise it wasn't you. I should have known by the different coloured hair. She begged me to tell her the truth about what happened that night, but I couldn't find the words." He pauses, turning to me. "Nova walked in, and that's when I realised what was going on. I told Nova everything after she left, needing her to know what Cara said was true and to stay away from Royce, since he was living next door at this point. I was worried he'd take advantage of me not being there and get revenge for the storm Cara had caused."

Nova nods. "I didn't tell you because I wanted you to be safe, Ivy. You would have looked at Royce differently, and he would have known. I couldn't risk that, not after what he did to your mother. I may not have known the Cara she became, but I knew who my sister was, deep down, and she wouldn't have wanted you to be put at risk. Not like that."

Wait, something she said a while ago comes back to me. "You said he likes young girls. Was that to warn me away or the truth?"

"Sadly, the truth. He's made accusations go away before they've even gotten to the police station. But I've heard the rumours. He's also not shy about showing the world who he cheats with."

"I don't get it. Why try to kill me? He'd already gotten away with it."

"Because you have the power to destroy what he has left," Sam announces.

"What do you mean?"

"He doesn't have full access to the Kingsley empire. He has what he's siphoned from profits, but he doesn't have full control, only temporary control until Nina is well enough to take back her position. Nina has full authority, and when Kaiden turns twenty-one, so will he. A few months ago, Nina slowly started making changes through her director, freezing accounts when they started noticing money disappearing.

"Since then, he's been doing everything he can to get more from our start-up business. We have a clause in our agreement, which we put in place when I bought a percentage from him a few years ago. It states that if I don't have an heir to the business, it gets left to him."

"But he had to know what was in my bag before he took it," I mutter, not understanding. "This couldn't have been about that clause."

"Something like this getting out… He'd lose everything, they both would. They have a lot to lose, and something tells me that Royce stealing from mine and Nina's companies means he has the most to lose. He'd lose his partnership with us. He wouldn't be able to claim they are false allegations, not with the proof Nova said you had. And you've seen how the media works; one story gets out and thousands more will appear. It would have been a mess he couldn't fix with money."

"Has he been arrested?" I ask, arching my eyebrow when they share a look, their foreheads creased as they seem to be in some kind of conflict. "What?"

"He's gone, and so is Neil Tucker."

"What do you mean, gone?" I ask, swallowing past the lump in my throat.

"Gone. I've been watching Neil for a while, had a PI looking into his businesses, and he's been stealing, along with Royce, and forwarding shares into an offshore account in a different name. I was waiting on more evidence before taking it to the police. I've informed them he's trying to leave the country and have a team looking for him and Royce."

He looks away and I go on alert. "What aren't you telling me?"

A weary sigh escapes him. "I don't have any concrete evidence on him, Ivy. Even if the police were to bring him back, they have nothing to hold him with."

"You have the phone with the evidence on," I tell Nova, getting frustrated.

But then the door bursts open, and I jump, looking away from Nova.

chapter four

KAIDEN

My eyes land on Ivy the second Grant bursts through her door, and my chest constricts at the sight of her. She doesn't look better. In fact, she looks worse. On the left side of her face, she has a bruise, and road rash covers her arms, neck and chest. And that's only what I can see. Her arm is in a cast, propped up on some pillows, and she has dark circles under her eyes.

Something isn't right though, and it's not because of her injuries. Something inside of her has shut off.

I'm not sure what I was expecting, but her aloof demeanour wasn't it.

She scans the room, looking right through me—which has my back straightening—before her attention goes to Grant, who's foaming at the mouth, wanting to strangle her.

I'm instantly on alert, wondering if Grant was right in what he said outside and she does have something on our dads.

In my head, I don't believe it. I've gotten to know her over the past five weeks and she doesn't have a cunning or manipulative bone in her body.

Still, something isn't right, so I step back and let Grant do the talking.

My brothers share a look with me, and without words, I know they've noticed her reaction to us.

"No grapes or flowers?" she teases tightly, her lips pressed together.

"I wouldn't piss on you if you were on fire, let alone bring you fucking grapes," Grant barks, stepping forward.

Sam gets up from his chair, ready to intervene. Not that he'd be able to do much. I bet the guy hasn't been in a fight in his life. If Grant goes to touch Ivy, I'll step in.

"Watch your mouth, Grant, before I have you escorted outside and banned from the hospital," he warns.

He ignores Sam, scowling at Ivy. "I knew you were fucking trouble the minute you rolled into town. Whatever fucking game you're playing, it ends now or I'll end you. Whatever you're using to blackmail my dad, I want it. It ends today."

I see a flash of confusion when her eyebrows pinch together, before she masks it, putting on a bored expression as she plays with the sheet on her bed. "I do love to make an impression."

"This isn't a fucking joke," he barks, taking another step.

The twins step forward, also ready to intervene if need be. I stand back, watching Ivy closely. This isn't her, that much I know.

"Pray tell, what, exactly, am I meant to have?" she asks dryly, grimacing a little when she shifts to get comfortable.

He grasps the end of her bed, leaning forward. "Your mum was a mean fucking drunk, spread her legs just as much as she spread her lies. And now you're following in her footsteps. For a second, I was beginning to think you were different. You nearly had me fooled. I won't let you do this to us."

"Grant," Nova whispers, stepping forward to reach for him. He slaps her hand away and Sam steps forward, pushing him back.

"Don't fucking touch her."

"Looks like I'm not the only one who follows in their parents' footsteps," Ivy spits out, grimacing as she sits forwards.

"What is that supposed to fucking mean, you dirty cunt?"

"Maybe you boys should go and calm down," Nova tries.

Grant glares at her. "Why don't you shut the fuck up. Your family did this, Nova. And now you bring her into our lives, after everything her mum did."

Ivy begins to laugh, and all our attention turns to her. "Listen to yourself. You're just some scared little boy crying for his dad's approval and love because he didn't get it from his mum."

"My mum was ten times the woman your mum was. It should have been her who died that night, not mine. Your mum deserved everything bad that happened to her, so don't fucking bring my mother into it."

"No, let's talk about how *your* dad, *and* theirs," she bites out, pointing to Grant and then me and the twins, "raped *my* mum, got her pregnant, and ruined her fucking life."

I turn to stone, studying her closely to see if her words are true. She doesn't even flinch, staring right at Grant.

The room is silent, all of us processing what she just said. A million thoughts run through my mind; the diary Ivy mentioned—though only she had seen it when she first arrived—and the way Nova had gone pale, not looking at her when she told her it was a lie.

"Not got anything to say?" she baits, deliberately looking at Grant, who has had a lot to say until now.

In the blink of an eye, I watch as Grant unfreezes, swiping everything off the table at the end of her bed.

"You fucking liar! You sick, fucking liar. How fucking dare you!"

I step forward, grabbing his jacket and pulling him back. Whatever the fuck is going on, we won't get answers this way.

Her gaze turns to me, and I can see she's putting on an act. She's angry, pissed, but this isn't her, not the real her. Her emotions are running wild, something she rarely lets go of, and right now, she has no control, no matter how hard she's trying to act like she does.

"Ask Kaiden. He knows everything."

I arch my eyebrow at her, speaking up for the first time. "I have no fucking idea what you're going on about, Ivy, but you need to start talking. We're clearly the only ones in the dark." I pointedly glance at Nova and Sam, who have the nerve to look away.

Her face twists into a scowl. "Short version? Your grandfathers thought they could play Pinky and the Brain and take over the world. When they fucked up, they used their sons to make it right. Their two sons happily followed the rules like good little boys. My mum was an easy target, it seems. They raped her to get her pregnant, so they'd have to marry, and it worked. They took a gamble on who the father would be. She got pregnant by one of them. The jury is still out on whether she had an abortion, but I'm guessing she wanted the spawn out of her. When her own parents warned her to keep quiet about it, she turned to drugs and alcohol. She came back and must have seen how happy you all were and decided to share your dads' dirty little secret. And now, here we are. Royce had my mum killed and tried to have me killed." She turns to Nova, frowning. "I didn't leave anything out, did I?"

"Ivy," she whispers, her voice filled with anguish.

"How do you know all of this?" I ask, trying to remain calm, when all I want to do is punch my fist through a wall.

I glance at the twins from the corner of my eye, noticing how pale they've gone. They shouldn't have to listen to this. Dad has never been a good dad to them, never really been anything, but he is still their dad. I couldn't care less. In my eyes, he'll always be a piece of shit.

"I listened to them rape her through a recording I found in your dad's office," she tells me. "But you know that, don't you?"

"My dad isn't a good person. He's a prick, Ivy, but this… this is extreme," I admit, torn over what to think.

Could he do this?

I wouldn't put anything past my dad, but rape, murder… it's a little much to wrap my head around. If he did this, I'll turn my back on him for good. I've never loved him, never cared, and often wished he'd die, but for the twins, I put up with him. But he's still my father.

For a moment, I wonder why I'm not going ballistic, why I'm not screaming she's a liar and leaving.

I try to think back, to pull a memory of any sign of this behaviour, but I'm coming up blank. I'm not sure if I blocked it out, or if it was never there. Or maybe I don't know because I never paid that much attention to him. He wasn't worth my time.

However, he is still my dad and this doesn't just impact those accused. It impacts everyone in this room.

"She's telling the truth," Nova whispers, pulling a phone out of her pocket. "This is the phone she found, and it has evidence on it that proves he had her mum killed."

"She could have planted that herself after killing her mum," Grant barks. "This is all fabricated so she can get her claws into my family's money."

Nova shakes her head, her eyes filled with pity. "What money, Grant? Your dad has been stealing from Sam's company for a while now. Sam found out last week."

"What?" he asks, taking a step back, paling further.

"She's telling the truth. I have all the evidence," Sam admits, stepping closer to the bed.

"And where's yours?" I ask Ivy, ignoring Sam. My voice is raspy with shock, yet gentle. I don't want to upset Ivy further.

She looks down at her lap, fiddling with the blanket. "It's gone."

Grant laughs. "Sounds about right."

She looks up, glaring at him. "Yes, because getting run off the road and nearly killed was my plan all along. The bag was ripped from my body, you fucking dipshit."

I stagger back, glancing to the floor. When we arrived, Carter told me the witness said a bag was stolen from her.

I don't want to believe my dad could do something like this. I've done some fucked up shit, even threatened to kill people, but the thought of committing murder the way Ivy is telling me he did… I could never, *would never* do that. As for the rape allegation and why he did it—only the worst of humankind could do such a thing, men on death row. My games with Ivy were just that: games. Yes, I'd wanted to hurt her, make her suffer for her mother's crimes, but not once had it entered my mind to do something so evil. My plans had been child's play compared to this. I would never have physically harmed her. I'd never have forced her to do something she didn't want to do. I knew right from the beginning that she wanted me. I could feel it the first time I laid eyes on her as she watched me fuck Danielle.

And Ivy is mine. If he tried to kill her, he will pay for it.

I stare at Nova, and when she feels my gaze on her, she looks up. "Is this true?" I ask, keeping my tone even.

"Yes. I didn't believe it until Sam told me," she explains.

I look to Sam, arching my eyebrow questioningly. "I walked in on them the night they raped her. I saw it." He bows his head, unable to look at us.

I rub my tired eyes, blowing out my cheeks. Why had he never brought this up before if what he's saying is true? I'm even more disgusted that if it is true, then he kept it quiet all these years. I didn't think much of the man to begin with once I found out who he was. I think even less of him now.

"You're lying," Grant bites out. "She's your daughter. You'd say anything to win her over."

"If you really believed that, you wouldn't just be standing there, Grant. The night your mother rushed out of the house was the night Cara told her what they had done to her. Your mum must have known something the others didn't, because she left your father without questioning him. She packed her bags and left."

"That's not true," he whispers brokenly.

"It's true. She called my mum, who was her godmother, and asked for a place to stay. She believed it. She crashed before she even left Cheshire Grove. She was on her way to my mum's cottage in Devon."

"This is bullshit!" he yells, picking up the chair and throwing it across the room. The twins duck, barely dodging it.

Grant storms out, and a part of me wants to go with him, but another needs more answers, more than what they've given me.

"How did you find the stuff?" I question Ivy the minute he's gone.

She rolls her eyes at me, but I can see the flash of hurt in her gaze. "Don't stand there and pretend you didn't know any of this. This is why you wanted me gone, isn't it; to keep my mouth shut, to break me? That's what you said, right, that you were going to enjoy breaking me?" she yells, slamming her fist on the bed. "You can't break what's already broken, only shatter it further. You've got your wish, so get the fuck out. I never want to see your face again."

"What?" I ask, my heart in my throat. "I swear on my life I didn't know anything about this. I assumed it was something else, that she slept with Dad and it broke my mum. I didn't know he fucking raped her! We're just as innocent in this as you. If what you have told us is true." I look away briefly, catching my breath. I didn't mean to lash out, but we've been through so much, and as much as Ivy likes to believe what we have is just sex, it isn't. I've given her more of myself than any other person. It grieves me to know she thinks I'm capable of this.

She screams, her entire face turning red with anger. "Get out! I've told you the fucking truth, all of it. Your dad is a monster." She forces out a laugh, yet it sounds broken as she pushes the hair out of her face. "I'm so stupid. He wasn't offering me money to get me away from you, he was offering it to me to pay for my silence. He didn't want me getting close to the truth."

"What money?"

"It doesn't matter. I trusted you, Kai. I let you in, and you did exactly what you said you were going to do. Now go fucking gloat somewhere else."

"I'm not fucking gloating," I snap, stepping forward. "You're talking in fucking riddles and I'm just trying to get answers. It is my dad you're accusing of rape."

"It's not accusing if he actually did it," she snaps. "And welcome to my world. You've been talking in riddles since I first met you."

"Ivy," Ethan starts, but she glares at him.

"Don't! I don't trust any of you. I want you to leave."

"We didn't know," Lucca adds.

I can tell she's torn on what to believe, but right now, it's fresh, and she's livid. "It doesn't matter. I don't trust you. You've played games from the very beginning, and it ends now."

"I've not been playing you. You know that," I tell her, getting frustrated. I had no idea about any of this, not even an inkling. I assumed whatever Cara had said was bad, but not this.

If it turns out to be true, I don't even want to think about it. I feel sick now.

"There's no need to keep lying," she whispers, anguish covering her features as she starts to tremble.

"I'm not fucking lying!" I roar.

She jumps, her monitors next to the bed going crazy. "Ivy, calm down," Nova warns.

"Tell them to leave," she bites out, looking away.

"Ivy, don't do this. I didn't know." Silently, I plead with her to look at me, to see that I'm telling her the truth.

"Goodbye, Kai," she whispers.

I turn to Nova, fighting hard not to yell at her. She's known my hatred for Cara, the blame I wrongfully placed, and all this time she let me, knowing it was all a lie. It makes me wonder just what else she has been keeping from me. Where my mum is, for example. They are best friends. I asked her if she knew where she was and she said she didn't know. I should have listened to my instincts back then. Because she had lied to my face. I can feel it in my gut. "Do you know where my mum is?"

If someone can fill in the blanks, it's Mum.

She looks to Sam briefly before flicking her gaze back to me. "I do."

"Is she really sick?" I ask, feeling bile rise in my throat.

Do any of our parents give a fuck?

"Not anymore. She's been clean for two years."

"Why hasn't she come back?" Ethan asks, a hardness in his tone.

"Because your father wouldn't allow it. Any time she tried to get clean, he'd spike her food or drink with a prescription pill and she'd be back to square one. He was trying to take over as beneficiary for the Kingsley empire, so your mum disappeared before he could," she tells him, and I can feel the tension in the room begin to rise.

I grit my teeth together. "Call her. Tell her to come back," I order, before turning and leaving the room.

Outside, we stop in the hallway, and I scan the twins, gauging their reactions.

"We'll figure out the truth," I assure them.

Ethan glares over at me. "Who the fuck cares? He's not even our dad. You've played that role for as long as we can remember."

"Ethan," I warn, hating this for them.

"Don't!" Lucca growls. "It's true. In there, while you were debating whether Dad did all of those things, me and Ethan didn't even question it. We've only ever seen the bad side to him."

"What do you mean?" I ask, clenching my fists.

Lucca shares a look with Ethan, and they silently communicate with each other. Ethan nods, giving him the go ahead before he turns to face me. "Remember the time he missed our game and you took us to the office to have it out with him?"

"Yeah," I ask, confused as to where they are going with this. They were, like, eight or nine at the time.

"We went to go find the bathroom, but instead, we walked into a conference room and found him, his hand over a young woman's mouth, fucking her."

"He was raping her?" I bite out. "Why the fuck didn't you ever say anything?"

"We don't know if he was or not. But at that age, seeing a half-naked woman and your dad balls deep inside of her, was fucking gross. Neither of us wanted to speak about it."

"Fuck!" I roar, slamming my hand against the wall. I turn to the twins. "We need to go back to the house, find Dad."

"What about Ivy?"

I look to the door, my chest tightening. "She doesn't believe we didn't know about this."

"So, what are we going to do about it?" Lucca asks.

"We need to find Dad."

Ethan glares. "Are you seriously going to believe him over her? He'll never admit it, Kai. And you saw her in there. That was fucking real."

I narrow my eyes at his tone. "I know that. But we need proof."

Lucca sighs, shaking his head at me. "She's never going to forgive us."

I smirk. "She's mine, whether she likes it or not. She can't avoid us forever. She starts Kingsley Academy once she's well enough, and I'll make sure I get in some of her classes."

"You've already done them," Lucca reminds me.

I shrug. "I've only got a few classes to attend this year, a few extra won't hurt. But right now, we need to track down Dad and see what we can find. He must have left some kind of clue as to what is happening."

"Let's go then," Ethan orders, clasping his hands together.

chapter five

IVY

I'VE SPENT THE PAST FOUR WEEKS RECUPERATING. My ribs still hurt, but the pain is nothing compared to the scabs I got from the road rash. I wanted to pick and scratch those fuckers like nobody's business. It drove me insane. I'm glad they are finally gone.

My cast won't come off for another four weeks—if I don't take the thing off myself beforehand.

I'd rather be covered in scabs and have both arms in a cast than be in that hospital bed, forced to listen to Sam tell me about himself. He'd tried to get to know me, but I don't think there is anything worth knowing, so I made it difficult for him, acting like a complete bitch.

It had taken me that time to calm down and understand Nova's reasoning. I couldn't yet forgive her for her part in it all. But being in that hospital, nearly dying, made me realise how much I needed someone right then.

Finding out the whole truth had been a wakeup call, not just for me, but for everyone.

The day the doctor came in to discharge me had been a relief, yet scary, because I knew there was no way I could go back with Nova to Monroe

Manor. I had a few reasons as to why, but mostly because I had been weak, and with Kaiden living next door, I didn't want my guard down. I couldn't take the risk of him sneaking into my room. I just couldn't. And a part of me worried I'd never be able to say no to him.

Then there was Nova. I thought time apart would do us good, give us a chance to really be alone with our thoughts.

When I broached the subject in the hospital room, she automatically assumed I was running away and began to panic. Once I explained why I couldn't leave with her, she paused, actually taking in my words and my fears. She surprised me by agreeing yet wouldn't agree for me to stay on my own in a hotel.

And with Royce still out there, she didn't want to make it easy for him to track me down. He hadn't been seen or heard from since the day I was run off the road. If he had a brain, he'd have run to the other side of the world by now and not stuck around trying to finish the job.

I'd be ready for him this time.

Sam offered for me to stay with him in his home twenty minutes away from Monroe Manor. However, Nova took one look at my expression and fixed the awkward situation, pointing out Sam worked a lot and couldn't be there. He went to argue, but when Nova mentioned Elle and her husband, Ed, I practically screamed *yes*.

Which is how I ended up staying with Elle and Ed for the past three weeks. They had been more than happy to nurse me back to health and watch over me. It had been blissful having this time away from everyone, having the time to truly think. It was also a monumental moment for me. I finally got to feel what a home felt like.

Ed isn't as stiff and grumpy as he liked to make people believe. He's a huge teddy bear and I've loved our time playing cards together. It would have been chess, but all the pieces confused me.

My time is coming to an end though. I need to move back to Nova's and get back to reality. I don't want to leave. My chest hurts as I shove clothes into my bag.

Being here has not only made me feel worthy and cared for, but it has taken my mind off the clusterfuck that is my life.

Having Elle and Ed had been great, but it was her two Beagles that helped heal the pain missing Kaiden had caused. They were beautiful and made me feel at ease.

I still don't know how I could miss Kaiden, want him, when all he's done is lie to me.

He hadn't even seem bothered at the hospital. When he walked in after Grant, my heart nearly burst from my chest. I wanted to forget how angry Grant was, how angry I was, and just have him hold me. But he seemed aloof, not at all affected by my condition. He'd had no reaction to the news that his dad was a rapist, or that he had tried to kill me. It just cemented the fact he knew all along, no matter what he tried to tell me.

I shove the last of my clothes into my duffle bag, shaking thoughts of Kaiden away.

A floorboard creaks behind me, and I turn to find Ed leaning against the doorframe. "You could stay another week," he grouches.

I grin at him. "Are you going to miss me?"

He rolls his eyes at me, but he can't hide the twitch of his lips. "It's definitely going to be different without you here."

I look around the guest room that has been mine for the past three weeks, and sigh. It's going to be hard not being here. They didn't treat me like I would break and had me helping with chores after just over a week of being here. I liked that they didn't look at me with pity and just got on with their lives, not overcrowding me.

"I'm going to miss it here too," I admit.

"I've not asked why you didn't go back to your aunt Nova's, but I will ask if you're okay going now."

I tilt my head, beaming at him. "Aww, are you worried about me, Mr W?"

"Just want you to be safe, kid."

"Nova isn't the reason I was run off the road," I tell him.

Nova couldn't lie about the accident; it was already in the paper and

Carter's cousin didn't keep his mouth shut, telling all his mates we were run off the road.

But to keep Elle and Ed safe, Nova didn't disclose who had ran me off the road. Or our suspicions.

Nova had told them someone deliberately ran me off the road, but we didn't know who as of yet. I agreed to the lie, knowing it would keep Elle and Ed safe.

"I didn't think it was," he explains, then pauses, watching me closely. "Was it the Kingsley boy, Kaiden?"

"Kaiden?" I ask, looking away. Just hearing his name hurts. "Why would you think it was Kaiden?"

"He showed up a few times the first week you arrived, looking for you."

"What?" I practically screech.

"Don't be dramatic. We sent the boy away. What I want to know is whether you're safe in going back there."

I soften a little inside at his affection. "I will be. And it wasn't Kaiden."

He doesn't look like he believes me, but after a moment, he makes a gruff sound before stepping further into the room. "Let me take your bag downstairs."

I let him pick it up before following him down the stairs.

Elle is rushing around the kitchen, shoving containers into a bag. She spins, startled when she hears us. Her gaze goes down to the bag in Ed's hand and her eyes glaze over.

"You're really going?"

"You know I need to start school. I've already had enough time off. I don't want to be there longer than I have to."

"I'm going to miss you," she tells me, getting teary.

"Don't you dare cry on me," I warn her, making her laugh.

She wipes under her eyes before grabbing a bag off the counter. "I've made your favourites. I know you have that fancy schmancy cook up there, but I couldn't let you go without them."

"Meatballs?" I ask, licking my lips. Elle is the best cook and puts Annette to shame.

She chuckles, handing me the bag. "Of course. And chocolate cake for later."

She runs her hands down her apron, and I laugh, putting the bag on the floor before stepping forward and pulling her into my arms.

I'm not a hugger, and if anyone else tried this shit, they'd get a broken nose. But it's Elle, and living with her the past three weeks has been what I imagined living with a real family would be like. I've never felt so at peace. She helped stem the anger boiling inside of me.

"I'll be back Saturday morning to help you in the garden."

She pulls back, clearing her throat. "No, we have the church market Saturday."

I swallow the lump in my throat before talking. "How could I forget. I'll be here bright and early to help with loading the crates."

"Does that mean I get to go to the cider stand?" Ed asks happily.

Elle smacks his chest lightly. "No, it doesn't. You know what the doc said about your cholesterol."

He grunts. "There is nothing wrong with me. He doesn't know what he's talking about. He's barely out of nappies!"

I giggle lightly at his gruff tone. He loves his wife, which is the only reason he went to the doctors in the first place a few months ago. He's had to go every two weeks since, and each time they tell him his cholesterol is too high, he hates it, because Elle has him on a diet, and the man loves his grub.

She rolls her eyes at him. "Don't make me book you in early," she threatens.

He swallows, looking away. "I'll go get these bags outside."

I reach forward, taking my bags from him. "I've got this. I'll wait outside for Nova to arrive."

He scrunches his eyebrows together. "We can wait with you."

I feel my cheeks heat. "If it's okay with you, I'd rather wait on my own."

I'm too embarrassed to tell them I've never had to say goodbye before, not like this, and it's hard. What they've done for me—practically a stranger—means the world to me.

"We can—"

"Ed, let the girl leave," Elle interrupts, giving him a pointed look.

He sighs, giving me one last look over before nodding in agreement. "Don't be a stranger."

"I won't, I promise," I tell him, hefting the duffle bag over my shoulder and lifting the bag of food with my good hand.

I swallow past the ball in my throat and give them a small smile that probably looks more like a grimace.

"Be good and take care of yourself," Elle warns softly.

"I'll see you both soon. Thank you—for everything."

"You're welcome," she tells me.

Ed makes a sound under his breath before turning away from us. "Get with you, girl. I'm going to check on the chickens."

I smile at his retreating form. "He's such a softy."

"It's why I snagged him. Big enough to make grown men piss themselves but a teddy bear where I'm concerned."

I laugh at her apt description of Ed. "I'll be seeing you, then," I murmur, still struggling to find the strength to leave, and not just because I love being here. It's also because I know once I step outside, what's happened will become real again. I've been able to pretend it didn't happen, that missing Kaiden was okay because really, we'd only had a disagreement.

Leaving here… it's going to be a slap of reality and I'm not ready for it.

And yes, I'm going to miss Elle and Ed.

"You won't get far standing there, girl. Get going," she orders, though her expression is soft.

I nod, clearing my throat. "See you Saturday," I tell her, before turning and leaving.

The second I step outside, I tilt my head up to the bright blue sky and close my eyes, basking in the heat of the sun beaming down on me. I suck in a lungful of fresh air, and the weight of reality, of what I know, what I had, and what happened, hits me. There's no more escaping, no more hiding.

"Looking good for someone who was roadkill a few weeks ago."

I snap my gaze to the end of the path, relaxing when I see it's Carter

Remington leaning against his bike, his shades covering those deep, piercing blue eyes of his.

I smirk, eyeing the shiny black motorcycle behind him. I don't remember much from that day, but I'm pretty sure his bike was red.

"Nice bike. You sure are brave bringing it around me," I tease him, walking to the end of the path to meet him.

His expression breaks out into a smile, and he laughs. "The bike was totalled, but I'm good with the new one."

"What brings you out here?" I ask, watching him warily. My first encounter with this guy wasn't the best, but then again, none of my first encounters with the people in Cheshire Grove have been great.

"I've been looking for you, wanted to see if you were okay. Any word on who ran us off the road?"

I place my bags down on the floor before shrugging. I don't gossip, and I don't trust Carter Remington to be here for anything other than that.

He won't be getting answers from me. I tell myself it's because it's none of his business—which it's not—but I know that deep down, my loyalty is still with Kaiden.

"Why have you been looking for me?"

His lips twist into a smirk as he pushes his shades up on the top of his head. "All right, so you won't tell me who was after you. That's okay. I really did come here to check if you were okay. When we arrived at the hospital, you went into cardiac arrest."

"What can I say, not even the devil wanted me," I explain. "But I'm good. You didn't need to come here." I pause, thinking about it for a moment. "How *did* you know to come here?"

His smirk spreads, and he really is a good-looking bastard. I can see why Selina has a crush on him. "I have my sources."

I brush his comment off, not needing to know. "How are you? They said you were pretty banged up yourself."

"Good. I've had worse."

I inhale, putting my pride aside, and say, "Thank you—for what you did."

I was really grateful. He didn't have to stop that day. For all he knew, I was just a piece Kaiden was fucking. I meant nothing. And yet, he stopped, risking his own life.

"It's not your fault," he tells me, rubbing the back of his neck. "I need to get going, but if you ever need anything, let me know. You know where I live."

"Thank you, but I won't."

He shrugs as he swings his leg over the bike. "Offer's there, babe."

I step forward, holding my hand out to stop him putting his helmet on. "I really am sorry you got hurt, and about your bike."

He stares, searching for honesty, before shaking himself out of it. "Like I said, not your fault. Do you have a phone?" he asks, resting his helmet in front of him.

"Um, yeah, why?"

He holds his hand out, and I reach into my back pocket for my phone before giving it to him. He types something in before I hear a beep coming from his pocket. "Call me if you need me. Be careful, Ivy, not everyone is who they seem to be. You can't trust anyone."

Before I have a chance to argue, he hands me my phone back. He puts the helmet on with those parting words, revving his bike. He speeds off, and I watch, wondering how much he knows about what really happened.

A car pulls up behind me and I turn, greeting Nova with a small wave. She gets out of the car, pulling her sunglasses up.

"You okay?"

I nod, grabbing my bags off the ground. "Yeah, I'm good."

She continues to survey the area, her lips twisting together. "You really shouldn't be out here alone."

I don't bother putting my stuff in the boot. Instead, I throw my duffle in the back and keep the food safe in the front with me. "I'm fine. And if you haven't noticed, Ed is peeking from behind the curtain."

She looks over to the house and waves. She gets in the car after me, shutting the door. When she doesn't drive, I look over at her, arching my eyebrow.

"Are you sure you want to do this? I feel terrible for everything that has transpired. Maybe going to the Academy isn't the best idea."

"Now you tell me," I groan, but I know this is something I need to do. I don't break my promises. "But no, I'm fine. You were right in the sense that I need a better education, and Kingsley Academy can give me that."

"I'm worried it will be too much for you. I know what some of the girls can be like. I was once amongst them. They are horrid to the girls they think don't belong."

I give her an evil smirk. "Then they are in for a rude awakening. I'm not going to let some uptight skank tell me what to do."

"Then there's the Kingsley boys. You know you won't be able to avoid them. They attend the school and their mum owns it."

"I'll be fine."

I look out of the window when she pulls off, not saying anything else. It's hard to imagine that nine weeks ago we followed this same road. A lot has happened in such a short amount of time.

Tomorrow will be a completely different challenge, one I plan on conquering.

I'm not going to let the Kingsley's get to me. I'm going to turn up at that fancy-arse school and get a fucking degree in something so I can get a high-paying job and get the hell out of here.

No one is going to stand in my way.

chapter six

KAIDEN

I'VE BEEN SLOWLY GOING OUT OF MY mind for four weeks, punching anyone who's dared to look at me wrong.

I'm angry at everyone, at the world.

Dad is still MIA, but I couldn't give two shits at this point. He can stay gone. We found papers proving he had been stealing and selling land owned by our companies. The second I got back from the hospital, I trashed his office, trying to look for anything that could prove whether or not Ivy was telling me the truth. There was nothing, but it didn't mean what she'd said was true.

Leaving the way he did makes him guilty in my eyes. I'm not some naïve little boy who only wants to see the good in people.

There are a lot of snakes in our world, all out to get what they can or seek out who they can use to get where they want.

Mum still isn't home, even though Nova told me she was making plans for her return. The whole situation is fucked up. She's been gone for years, making us believe she was this broken woman who couldn't be trusted to look after her own kids. Instead, she's been hiding, okay with leaving her sons with a man who only cares about himself.

Do I believe my dad, who's been a money grabbing, power hungry knob for most of our lives, or the girl I have known for only a short amount of time?

I want to believe Dad didn't do it, that he wasn't sick enough to do something so degrading and twisted, but I can't. The doubt is there and it's eating away at me. I'd seen how ruthless he could be, how cruel when it comes to his own sons.

The twins aren't handling it much better either, both drinking and partying when they should be concentrating on their first year at the Academy.

If they don't calm down in a few weeks, I'm going to step in and put a stop to it, or at least warn them to slow down.

"Have you seen her yet?" Lucca asks, sitting on the picnic bench beside me.

I know he's asking about Ivy, who got back last night from wherever Nova had been hiding her. I'd looked in hotels, at Sam's house, and even Elle White's, the old lady who lives near the outskirts of the gated community. She wasn't anywhere.

I've never been attached to anything, even sports I can go without, and the only people I care about are my brothers and Grant.

Then she walked into our lives, and slowly, I questioned everything I ever believed was true. And it wasn't even her natural beauty; it was her, the way she saw the world, our world. It had been refreshing. She wasn't some chick who wanted to bed a millionaire, hoping one day I'd wed her. She didn't have an ulterior motive. She didn't want or need anything from me.

She was real, and it was hard to find that in our world.

I'm addicted to her, there is no other way to put it.

I wanted to go around last night, to question her further about what she found, but a part of me was scared about why I really wanted to see her.

Did I want to hurt her or fuck her? I blame her for what my brothers are going through. It's driving me insane from the inside, so I've left her alone. I'm torn in a way I can't describe. I'm loyal to my family, and even though she might be telling the truth, that damn loyal part of me wants to say she's wrong anyway. It's messing with my head.

It still doesn't stop me from looking for her as I scan the field.

The school is surrounded by forests, hidden well into the trees, and if you don't know where to go, you probably won't find the entrance.

The place is built on acres of land, spread out and divided into sections. They have a medical department, science department, and even a sports department. Whatever career you want to follow, you can learn here.

Most students who attend Kingsley Academy come for the business course. It's one of the best in the UK and can teach you to run a multimillion-pound company and then some. It helps young minds start up their own businesses.

The school is different from your average college or university. It has a variety of courses and teaches you more than the basics. You leave here with connections, with partners, but only the best of the best or the richest can attend. It's exclusive, invitation only, apart from a selected few who make hefty donations to get their son or daughter in.

We even have scholarships, but they are only granted to those with the highest grades and glowing recommendations.

Me and my brothers are legacies, along with a few other attendees this year. I didn't care. I didn't thrive off a name like many others do. I might use it to influence people. I always get what I want. But I didn't care for the attention that came with our name.

Ethan steps up to the bench, rubbing his temples. "Grant is fucking some random in the front seat of his car."

"How'd that happen?" Lucca asks, and when Ethan arches his eyebrow, he puffs out a breath, continuing. "Not the fucking part. I meant him being with someone."

"He talking to you?" Ethan asks me, ignoring the ridiculous question.

Grant hasn't been himself, drinking more than the twins. The only difference is, he's not been fucking everything in sight. He hasn't even touched any of the new girls. He hasn't done much of anything and gets angry at anyone who tries to approach him.

"He's still licking his wounds," I comment.

"Have you seen her yet?" he asks.

"Already asked. I think his silence was a no. I was afraid to ask again in case he punched me. *Again*," Lucca growls.

"I said I was sorry," I snap, getting up from the bench. I grab my bag from the ground, swinging it over my shoulder. "She'll be here."

"How do you know?" Ethan asks.

I shrug, walking off and letting them follow. "Because I saw her getting dressed this morning." I've lost count of how many nights I've sat staring out my window and into hers, wishing that night was the night she'd return.

"Stalker much?" Lucca teases.

I stop for a minute to glare at him, and he swallows.

"Does she know you switched classes?"

"No, but she will. And I didn't switch. I just added them to my regular classes."

"It's still stalking," Ethan mutters.

"I don't give a fuck. She needs to be watched," I tell them.

"You still can't believe Dad's innocent? He did a runner right after Ivy got run down. If that doesn't scream guilty, I don't know what does."

I let him believe that's why I want her watched. But it's not. I'm worried what the bitches in this place have planned for her. I know Danielle, know her friends, and they aren't going to let Ivy's ride here be easy.

"Are you coming up to the rec room?" Lucca asks, high-fiving a mate who walks past.

The rec room is our place at the school. No one other than me, the twins and Grant have a key. It's our home away from home, a place we can hang out between classes, or if we don't want to drive back after a long day, we stay there. It's also convenient when there is a party. It means we don't have to leave our cars or drive drunk.

We're above the main entrance of Kingsley Academy, yet others stay not far away, in a separate building of the school's, called Kingsley House.

When it first opened, they had a high list of responses, so they decided to build their own accommodation. The building was separated into two blocks, one for the guys and one for the girls, separated by a reception and security room. House Captains and members of staff helped run it.

"Not yet. I want to wait on Grant, see if he's heard anything from his dad yet."

Ethan grunts in acknowledgement but doesn't say anything more. They're having a hard time trusting him since he went off the deep end, but I'm not ready to give up on him. Not yet.

He had it worse than all of us growing up. His dad was abusive and angry. And having people tell him his dad wasn't always like that, that losing his wife did something to him, made Grant angry, bitter.

We all lost something vital growing up, and it shaped us, made us into the men we are today, but Grant… Grant somehow lost his way over the past few months.

"Fuck," Lucca growls before pasting on a fake smile.

I look up, inwardly groaning when Danielle and her group of friends walk up to us.

I scan her, wondering how I never noticed how slutty she was before. She might not have spread her legs for anyone while we were fucking, but looking at her now, I don't know why that mattered. She's hot, don't get me wrong, but until Ivy, I hadn't realised how fake Danielle looked. I guess getting my dick wet took precedence.

We have uniforms here at the Academy, all designer and required. Danielle and her friends, however, wear theirs differently to the rest. Their skirts are rolled up to become shorter, their ties loose and a few buttons on their shirts undone to reveal their cleavage, and instead of the basic black shoes, they have high heels to make them look taller. The rules are strict, but somehow, Danielle gets away with it.

"Kai," she breathes out, her voice sultry and low.

I want to tell her to fuck off, but I need to find out who set that tent on fire, and if this bitch did it, she's going to get what's coming to her. She was warned to leave Ivy alone and was warned by the twin's multiple times to not go near Selina when we were all in high school together.

She crossed a line and went too far.

"Danielle," I greet, giving a chin lift to the others.

She runs her finger up my blazer, fluttering her eyelashes at me. "Are you still having a party this weekend?"

Movement from the side catches my attention, and I subtly look at Lucca, who nods once, confirming there is still, in fact, a party.

I grit my teeth together. I told them not at the house, not with Dad MIA and Mum returning any day now. Whatever she has to finish up is holding her back.

News about my dad hasn't been revealed, and I was surprised. I know Nova contacted a detective friend of hers and gave him what she had. They're still looking for him, but if my dad wanted to disappear, no one will find him.

I don't want the news getting out, not because I care what people might say about him, but because I care what people might say to the twins. I could also see others turning on Ivy, the outsider, and she has better things to deal with.

I know I'm still protecting her, and I have no idea why. I should hate her for causing my family pain. I've hated her before for far less.

"Kai?" Danielle calls, her voice harder.

I glance down at her with a bored expression. "Looks like."

"Do you want me to stop by before the party?"

Whoever told her about me and Ivy is getting fucked up. She has been coming on strongly ever since, and I'm getting tired of it.

Ivy and I aren't done.

Not by a long shot.

I just have to figure out whether I want to fuck her or hate her.

It still doesn't mean I'm going to go back to Danielle. I'm bored, and now I've tasted perfection, nothing will ever taste sweeter.

"No thanks," I tell her, gripping her wrist when she slides her hand down my chest.

Her jaw clenches, her eyes hardening as she stares up at me. "You could never go long without a fuck, and no other girl will touch you. I made sure of it."

I lean in close, and I watch as her pupils dilate, her breathing escalating. "If I wanted to fuck Jenny," I start, glancing quickly at the girl in question next to her. Her shoulders straighten and her face lights up, like she thinks I mean it. "I'm pretty certain she wouldn't tell me no. In fact, I'm pretty sure she'd beg."

"You're a pig," she curses, trying to shake off my grip.

I smirk. "I was good enough for you. Don't think you have the power here. You aren't the only cunt I can use to get my dick wet."

"I'm going to make you swallow those words," she grumbles, glaring at me.

"You're the only one who swallows, love."

She screeches under her breath, and this time, when she tries to get loose, I let her.

Selina's car pulls into the drop off point and the hairs on my neck stand on end. Everyone stops what they're doing the second a tanned leg slips free of the car, right before Ivy emerges.

My breathing stops at the sight of her gripping the top of the car door, scanning the area, her mouth slightly parted.

She looks different, hotter, and I force myself not to go to her.

Her ink black hair is shorter, chopped off below her shoulders. I hadn't noticed when I saw her getting dressed. The loose, wavy curls are pinned back, giving her a Catholic schoolgirl look, especially paired with her uniform. I can't see her eyes because they're covered by her sunglasses, so I can't tell if she's spotted us.

She clears the car, and the breath leaves my lungs in one *whoosh*. Hundreds of girls wear the uniform, but none of them look as hot as Ivy right now. I'm already imagining pushing the red and black, tartaned pleat skirt up around her waist and pulling her knickers down.

I'd make her leave on the grey, knee-length stockings and black shoes with their inch-high heels and ties around her ankles. Fuck, she looks hot.

Her grey blazer fits her perfectly, showcasing her perfect curves. I take in the cast, remembering how close I was to losing the one thing that had brought me peace, something I hadn't felt in a long time.

"Holy fuck!" Lucca curses, sounding turned on. I turn, seeing him outright checking her out. I growl under my breath, and he quickly looks away, concentrating on his phone.

The second Selina steps out of the car, the wolves descend, and I know I'm not going to make it through the day without killing someone. I know the minute Leeroy grins at her, he's flirting, and if the rugby player doesn't back the fuck up, he won't have an arm to play with all season.

Danielle's laughter cackles through the air. I glance down at her, finding her looking up at me with a calculated expression, her lips tipped up into a smirk.

"Just remember, it doesn't have to be this way," she warns me. My gaze hardens as she steps closer, rubbing her body against mine before leaning up to whisper in my ear. "You'll come running back the minute I prove she's weak. And I'm going to enjoy every minute of it."

I clench my jaw as she steps away. "If anyone touches her, you'll answer to me."

She shrugs. "But I don't answer to you, not anymore." She waves, grinning like a maniac. "See you around, boys."

Ethan shudders, stepping closer to me. "I'm trying to figure out what I found hot about her. She creeps me the fuck out."

"It was her tits," Lucca answers before taking a sip of his water.

Ethan sighs. "Yeah, it was the tits."

"Fucking idiots," I growl, stepping away from them. When I look up to try and find Ivy, she's gone. I search the grounds, not seeing her or Selina anywhere. "Fuck!"

chapter
seven

IVY

I GLANCE IN THE MIRROR, BARELY RECOGNISING the girl staring back at me. I promised myself I wouldn't turn into one of those snotty-nosed bitches, however, looking back at me is a replica of the very person I didn't want to become.

It's going to take a lot of getting used to.

When I got back from Elle's yesterday, Nova had a team of people waiting for me. Selina didn't let me refuse, saying it was a late birthday present arranged by the both of them.

Selina is still going through the trauma of nearly being burned alive, so I couldn't say no to her. It would be like telling your puppy he couldn't have a treat. And she's still getting used to the faint scars they tried to minimalize after her skin graft.

For four hours I let them cut my hair—something I usually did myself—wax and tint my eyebrows, curl and tint my eyelashes, and give me a manicure and pedicure. I even had a full body massage, which was the only thing I didn't complain about—mostly because I fell asleep.

Now, my jet-black hair is just below my shoulders. It feels foreign, lighter somehow, and because I can't do much with one hand, I let Selina have her way this morning and do my hair. She blow-dried it so it had a wave to it and then pinned it back from my face. The second she tried to put a tartan hairband on me, I put a stop to it and told her it was enough.

I'd applied some foundation, mostly to cover up the dark circle under my eyes. If I don't get a good night's sleep soon, I'm afraid they'll permanently be there.

I run my palm down my uniform, inwardly groaning. I thought I saw the last of a school uniform when I left high school, but no, the prestigious Academy has to go and have a strict dress code.

The grey blazer with a black trim isn't so bad. I just feel fake wearing it. It's not me. The pleated red and black tartan skirt, however, is ridiculous, something a porn star would wear. It was a choice between this or a grey skirt. The grey one was more flowy, and one gust of wind would have the whole school seeing my underwear. At least the pleated one had weight, but to be safe, I'd pulled on a pair of tiny gym shorts that could be classed as boxers.

But the clothes, the hair, the makeup, none of it matters. I still feel like an intruder, a girl playing dress up.

"You ready for your first day at the Academy?" Selina calls, and I step away from the mirror and walk out of my walk-in wardrobe to greet her.

She looks up from her phone, whistling when she sees me. "Damn, girl, you look smoking hot! Last night did you some good. You look a lot better."

I roll my eyes. "I'm wearing the same thing as you," I remind her, not commenting on her compliment.

"Yeah, but I don't rock it like you do. The guys are going to blow a nut when they see you. You look like an innocent Catholic schoolgirl."

"Great, I really do look like a porn star."

She laughs. "You don't. You coming down for breakfast?"

"Yes, I need coffee to deal with your chirpy behaviour. It's eight in the morning. No one should be this hyper."

She rolls her eyes, grabbing her bag off my bed, but she pauses when she looks into my wardrobe.

LISA HELEN GRAY 62

I peer over my shoulder, sighing at the small pile of presents I dumped in the corner before going to bed last night. I've not opened them, and I don't feel like doing it any time soon. They're presents from the twins, Selina, Sam and Nova. Even Annette got me something, but I don't feel comfortable accepting them.

They were left on my bed for me to open when I got back yesterday, but I just haven't brought myself around to opening them. I've never received a present before, and I don't know how to feel about it.

For all I know, the twins could have put a dead animal in a box after what I revealed to them. It hurts not seeing them. They'd become what I imagined having brothers would feel like.

And forcing myself not to care, when really I do, is killing me. I don't want to let it get to me, but it's hard when, for the first time in my life, I know what I'm missing.

"Are you not going to open them? I promise it's nothing girly," she tells me, sounding a little hurt.

I grab my bag off the back of the chair and turn to face her. "No, it's not that. I'll open them when I get back, okay?"

She beams up at me. "All right."

I groan as I follow her out of the room. "Please tell me there's coffee downstairs."

She laughs, a bounce in her step. "Of course, there is."

I roll my eyes. Every time I've spoken to her or seen her since leaving the hospital, she's been in this mood. Last night I heard her screaming out, yelling, "It burns. Help me!". It killed me to listen to her in so much pain, but I had no idea what to do to make it better. I'm not exactly the cuddling type.

I fucking hate this 'feelings' crap. It's inconvenient and annoying as hell.

I want to help her, to show that her façade of being bubbly and okay doesn't work with me. I know she is still hurting.

♡

I DON'T UNDERSTAND the nerves flitting through me as we drive through the open iron gates. I'd been the new kid in a school before, more times than I could count. This shouldn't be any different.

My palms begin to sweat. I wipe them down my skirt as I glance out the window, scanning my surroundings.

"Why is it hidden away?" I murmur as we pass more trees.

Selina laughs, finally glancing away from her phone. "We have celebrity children, politicians' children, and the rich and famous attending the school and Academy. They pay for privacy, and privacy is what they built."

I gasp as we drive towards a huge stone building that has to be two-three storeys high. "Holy shit!"

When Selina said the school was big, I hadn't expected this. I knew it was split into different departments and they were all connected by hallways or an overpass, but I never expected it to be this substantial.

"How do you find your way around?" I ask in amazement.

"This is Kingsley Hall, the main area of the Academy. Its where basic classes are taught and where we will be for the most part all year round. You won't be walking all over the school. I think most first and second year students are in this part."

"How many buildings are there?"

She shrugs as she shoves a book into her bag. "I don't know, but they're broken off into six areas. Then you have Kingsley House, which is accommodation."

"Nova said she has a room here for us if we ever need it."

"Yes, it's above Monroe Hall. The place freaks me out, so I never stayed there. I guess it wouldn't be bad if someone else was there."

When the car pulls to a stop in the drop off point, I take in a deep breath. "Let's do this."

"That's the attitude," Selina boasts, just as her phone beeps with a message.

I pull down my sunglasses, covering my eyes, and push open the door before the driver walks around to do it. I slip out of the car, scanning my surroundings in wonder. It's a lot to take in.

I'm glad my eyes are covered, because my emotions would be on display for all to see when my gaze lands on Kaiden and the twins. The betrayal feels fresh all over again, and I force myself not to react to the sight of them.

They'd known. They had to. No one treats someone the way they treated me if there wasn't a valid reason. They'd just wanted me gone, so I didn't spill their dad's secrets.

But my time with Kaiden hadn't felt fake. That's what hurts the most. He was never anything but real with me; the good and the bad. At least I think he was. It's why I'm so torn up inside. I want to believe they didn't know, desperately, but I've been made a fool of one too many times.

They look good. I wasn't expecting them to be in disarray over the news I shared, but I expected some sort of emotion. It seems they really didn't care about me to begin with.

I don't know why I keep torturing myself. It not like we were in love. At least, I don't think we were. I know my feelings were—are—strong, but how could I know the difference between love and lust? My mum was emotionless and never showed me how. And it's not like he told me he loved me.

I finally force myself to look away from Kaiden, and my blood boils for another reason. I don't know how I didn't notice that stuck up cow the second I got out of the car, but there she is, her paws all over Kaiden like she owns him. Danielle's so close to him I can taste the bitterness on my tongue. I want to rip her away, tell her he's mine.

But he's not.

I slowly look away, pretending I didn't see them. I don't show how much it hurts to see he went back to her so quickly.

I guess he got what he wanted in the end.

I still have plans to prove she was the one who set fire to my tent with Selina inside.

"You okay?" Selina asks, but before I can answer, a group of lads walk over to us.

The one in front swaggers towards us, a cocky grin on his face. I inwardly roll my eyes when he hooks his blazer on his finger, throwing it over his shoulder. He is everything I pictured a preppy rich kid to look like.

He tucks a piece of his thick, curly blonde hair behind his ear as he starts to undress me with his eyes.

"Sabrina, do you want to introduce me to your friend?" he asks, never taking his gaze away from me. "I'm Leeroy DeCamp."

I smile at his ridiculous name, and the fool thinks I'm smiling at him, like I'm charmed. His grin spreads.

I tilt my head and in a sweet voice, say, "Her fucking name is Selina, and no, *she* doesn't want to introduce her friend."

"Feisty, I like it." His friends laugh as he takes another step towards me. "There's a small party in Kingsley House tonight. You should come."

"Will you be there?"

"Oh God," Selina whispers behind me, but I ignore her, still staring up at Leeroy.

"I most certainly will," he tells me.

"Then I'll pass," I tell him, inwardly smirking when his smile falls. I grab Selina's arm and pull her towards the large wooden doors. "Come on. We have people to see."

The minute we're out of earshot and inside the building, Selina leans into me. "Do you know who that was?"

"Leeroy Denkins?"

She laughs. "Decamp. His father was a footballer until he got a knee injury. Now he's this big British actor."

I arch my eyebrow. "You say that like it's meant to mean something to me."

She rolls her eyes. "I know, I know. But at least try to play nice. He's captain of the rugby team and there are whispers he's going to go far. He had scouts come to a game in high school, but he turned them down, saying he wanted to do two years of school. Personally, I think he just wanted to party a lot before he has to take life seriously."

"He looked like a player. I don't care how rich they are, you stare at me like I'm another warm body, I'm going to say something."

"All right. But please, tone it down when we go to see Principle Hackett.

I've only met him a few times, but he's a hard arse. He's been here for ten years, and from what the rumours have said, Kaiden has tried to get him fired more than once."

"Why did he try to get him fired?" I ask, trying to come across unaffected by the sound of his name.

She shrugs. "I don't know. There were too many rumours, but they did get one thing right: he is a sleaze."

"Great," I mutter as we walk up a marbled staircase.

It's as dull as I thought it would be. Browns and beiges everywhere. The artwork hanging off the walls are set in gold frames. If they had them in my old school, they'd have been robbed and either pawned or used for scrap metal.

As we walk down another hallway, I look out of the window at the view. There's a large field behind the school before the forest begins.

I squint my eyes as we get further down the hallway and spot something in the trees. "What's out there?" I ask Selina, pausing for a moment to look closer. It looks like house, but from this far away, it could be a well-built shed.

She stops a few steps ahead of me and looks out. She shivers. "That is the groundskeeper's house. He's creepy as hell. He's been here for as long as anyone can remember."

"Weird. Does he live there all year round?"

"Yes. It's his home, I guess. Come on, we don't want to be late."

I look away and follow behind her, glancing at the pictures on the walls. They're all portraits, and I wonder if anyone knows who they actually are.

A shiver runs up my spine when I notice the eyes in the pictures following me. I stop, walk back a few steps, and my eyes widen. Holy crap! Is this place Hogwarts? They're definitely following me.

"What are you doing?" Selina asks incredulously, standing outside an open doorway.

I feel my cheeks heat and wave her off. "Nothing. He in there?" I ask, pointing towards the room behind her.

She rolls her eyes. "Yes. Please, just… try not to offend him. He can make your life hell."

I step past her and into a reception room. They must really like their creature comforts, because there are sofas on either side of a coffee table and a coffee and tea counter along the wall to my left.

In front of me, a lady sits behind a mahogany counter. She peers up, above her glasses, almost sneering at us.

"Yes, Miss Farley?"

"Miss Crapper, we're here to report in with Mr Hackett."

I glance at Selina to see if she's serious, and she is. I start laughing, which earns glares from both of them. It only makes me laugh harder.

Selina's eyes widen, and she shakes her head at me, silently telling me to shut up. I can't though. Who keeps a last name like that?

"Something funny, young lady?"

I try to sober, feeling my cheeks heat. "No, nothing. Nothing at all."

She curls her lip and turns back to Selina.

"Go on in," she tells her before pressing something on her desk. "Miss Farley and her friend are here."

We leave Miss Crapper to her own devices and head down a smaller hallway. Selina knocks on the door and waits.

"Come in," a voice rumbles.

The office is all dark wood, shelves lining the room, filled with books. Thick, square pieces of glass make up a window, some frosted so people can't see through.

Mr Hackett swivels around in his large leather desk chair and gives us both a stern expression, his brows lowered, mouth set in a hard line. He's a middle-aged man, probably in his forties, with greying hair. He's not large, but he's not skinny either. And if it wasn't for his sneering expression, he might actually come across as approachable. There's just something about him that screams arsehole.

"I told you to report to me by eight. It's now half past."

Selina fiddles with the zip on her bag nervously. "We were late leaving this morning."

He stares at her for a moment longer, and it's awkward and uncomfortable, before he turns to me, his gaze flicking to my chest briefly. "I guess you are Miss Monroe."

"Yes, sir."

His lip curls as he flicks through a folder on his desk. "I hear you like to get into trouble. I won't tolerate it at this school, nor you becoming a bad influence on the students here."

"I—" I start, but he holds his hand up, glaring at me.

"Don't interrupt whist I'm talking," he snaps sharply. "We shape young minds here at Kingsley Academy, do not disturb that. I understand you aren't used to the finest education, but here, we don't tolerate impudent behaviour."

When I don't say anything, Selina steps forward. "We understand. We've come for her class schedule."

I narrow my eyes a little at the older man. He could have left my schedule with the receptionist but ordered to see me first. I guess the man wanted to put me in my place.

I grit my teeth when his gaze goes back to my chest and he licks his lips.

"Very well," he states, handing me a large envelope. "Your locker is in the west hallway. There's a map inside your packet, as well as your lunch code. You will be in the Manor dining hall. You're dismissed."

He gets up from his chair and it groans in protest. He doesn't seem the type to leave it, too fired up on the power he has in this school.

Selina was right though, I didn't like him, and it's taken everything in me not to say something to him. Life here isn't going to run as smoothly as I thought.

Selina walks out first, and just as I reach the door, a hand on my arm stops me. I startle a little, glancing back at Mr Hackett. "Get your hand off me."

His grip tightens, and I wince a little. "Mr Kingsley told me all about you, how you've caused trouble for his sons. Unfortunately for us, we can't cancel your acceptance to attend here. It was verified by Mrs Kingsley herself. That can change if you step out of line. I have the power to have you removed. If you want to last here at Kingsley Academy, I suggest you think of ways to make me happy. One click of my fingers, and you're gone, Miss Monroe."

I purposely glance down his crotch before looking back up at him. I arch my eyebrow and lean in closer. "I don't think so. Try it with someone who cares."

I shrug his arm off me, and too stunned by my reply, he lets go. He probably thought I'd bend over backwards to please him, but if he had read my file, then he should have known I rolled over for no one.

chapter eight

IVY

THE STARES I GET AS SELINA AND I MAKE our way down the hallway are becoming tiresome already. I know most are just curious as to who I am, others I've seen at one of the twins' parties, but if one more girl looks at me wrong, I'm not going to be held responsible for my actions.

Selina snatches the envelope out of my hand. "Let's take a look at what you've got."

I move closer and watch as she pulls out a timetable. "Urgh, technology. My basic skills for a computer don't go any further than knowing how to turn it on and start up a DVD. I'm going to come across thick if they ask me to do something more than that."

Laughing, she bumps my shoulder with hers. "You'll be fine. You'll have to use your own today though, the computer room is getting an upgrade thanks to someone's dad." She pauses, looking a little closer at the page. "You've got art, is that right?"

"Yes, why?"

She glances up at me, her lips parted. "Really?"

I sigh. "Yes, what's wrong with art?"

She shakes herself out of it, smiling wide. "The art programme is really hard to get into. You have to truly have talent for them to even consider you. I didn't know you could draw. When did you give them your entry piece?"

I stop in front of her, backing her up. "What do you mean, entry piece?"

She raises her eyebrow. "Um, to get in you have to show them pieces of your work. They usually select one. Didn't you apply?"

"No, Nova applied for my extra classes and I never gave her anything. I didn't even tell her how much I liked art."

She sucks in her bottom lip and looks away. I groan, grabbing my phone out of my back pocket.

"If you're calling Nova, I'm going to head to class. Your first one is in the last room on the left," she rushes out, looking guiltily at the phone. I roll my eyes and hit dial, waving Selina off.

"Is everything okay?" Nova greets.

"Did you get me into the art programme here?"

"Of course. You're very talented."

I close my eyes, walking towards the classroom. "Did you not think to ask me first? And how did you even know I could draw? Did you get hold of one of my paintings?"

She clears her throat, clearly thinking of a way to answer me. I still don't forgive her, but at least I can be in the same room with her without wanting to hurt her. It's a work in progress.

"I asked your old school for reports, and when they said you were an exceptional artist, I asked for some of the pieces you did. You'll go far with that talent."

I pinch the bridge of my nose, stopping to lean against the wall. "I'm also an exceptional skateboarder, but I wouldn't take it up as a career."

"That's a kid's toy, Ivy. This will take you so far in life."

"You've clearly never seen me on a board. I'll go far, trust me," I reply sarcastically.

"Ivy, take it seriously. It's a very hard programme to get in to. Even your father struggled, and he's really good. He has an architecture business."

"Peachy. Look, I've got to go. First class starts soon."

"Okay. Call me if you need anything, anything at all."

I end the call, not bothering to answer her. She's been feeding me more information on my father and what he was like when they were together. Sam has done the same, forcing me to get to know him. It's like he believes if I make him a person in my mind, know things about him on a personal level, I'll begin to care. However, all I care about right now is getting justice for my mum. She might not deserve my help, but she deserves to have justice for what was done to her.

I let out a deep breath, dropping my phone into my bag. I don't know what step to take next. I'm not a mastermind. I'm just a girl. To find Royce, I need connections, connections I don't have or know how to get. And I don't trust Nova, Sam or the police to find him and deal with him. I can't trust any of them, no matter what they've said.

I've barely stepped down the hallway when a hand clamps around my waist, pulling me into a room.

I freeze for a terrifying moment before I finally open my mouth to scream. A hand clamps over my mouth, muting the sound. Visions of Royce coming to finish the job hit me. He could have me killed, just like my mum, and there's not a person in this world who could do anything about it. Why would they? They didn't help my mum, and she was someone to them. I'm no one, not really.

My body shakes with adrenaline as I struggle to get out of the person's hold. I'm not going down without a fight.

My nails break skin as I claw at the arm wrapped around me. A smile lifts at my lips when I feel I've drawn blood. The only reaction I get in return is a light grunt, and the satisfactory smile is wiped from my face.

The tension is palpable, and panic begins to set in. I scan the area, finding myself in a bathroom, looking for an escape, but when Lucca steps out of a toilet cubicle, zipping up his trousers, my gaze widens.

The person who has me also seems to be taken off guard, dropping me to my feet slowly.

I inhale, exhaling slowly to catch my bearings, when a girl steps out behind Lucca, flustered and nervous as she does up the buttons on her blouse.

What the hell?

"Um, really, bro? I thought you were past sexually harassing Ivy."

My body goes slack in his arms the second I realise Kaiden is the one who grabbed me. Now that my mind has stilled somewhat, I can smell his scent. My chest tightens as I remember all the nights we fucked, how intoxicating he smelled and how I couldn't get enough. He always smelled manly, like the outdoors with a hint of musk and spice.

"Leave!" he orders.

At the sound of his voice, I close my eyes for a brief moment. It's commanding and deep. A shiver runs down my spine, and I inwardly try to shake it off.

Lucca glances away from me to focus on his brother, various emotions running over his face. He looks torn, conflicted. I just don't know why. It's not like any of them cared about me, not really.

"Bro, maybe we should just go to class."

"Leave!" Kaiden barks, his voice harder.

Lucca goes to talk but shakes his head, glancing down at the girl beside him. "Come on, Leana, let's get out of here."

Automatically, I glance over at Leana, stunned when I see her gazing longingly up at Kaiden, fluttering her lashes.

"Really?" I mutter, feeling awkward for her.

When Lucca sees what I see, a laugh spills from his lips. He's not at all bothered his latest screw piece is checking his brother out.

"He's not interested," he tells her, not an ounce of anger in his voice.

She flushes, glancing at the floor. I'll never understand girls like her, ones who can freely share their body with one man to the next. I'm all for fun, but it can't be safe or healthy. I guess sleeping with Kaiden the way I did doesn't seem so bad when there are girls out there who don't care who they share their bed with. *Or bathroom.*

When she doesn't move, Lucca takes her arm gently, pulling her towards the exit.

The second I hear the bathroom door shut, I finally become unglued and shove Kaiden's arms away from my waist.

As I turn to face him, my heart in my throat, I see his back is to me. He pauses by the door, and for a moment, I'm pissed that he's going to leave. I knew I would have to confront him at one point. I just didn't expect it to be so soon.

The lock clicks into place and I freeze, stepping back to put more distance between us. I've got no idea what he's up to or what he has left to say.

He slowly turns to confront me, and I know I was wrong when I saw him outside. He doesn't just look good; he looks fucking hot in his uniform.

I scan him, head to toe, and immediately, my damn traitorous body reacts. I hate that he can still elicit this kind of reaction from me. I hate that I want him, crave him.

I open my mouth to snap a retort, but instead what leaves my lips is, "I thought he only had threesomes with Ethan?" I inwardly groan the second it spills out, but I won't deny it was bothering me.

He watches me closely, tilting his head in that intimidating fashion. "It's mostly a rumour. They think it's cool and gets them laid more if they tell people that. Most of the girls have self-respect at this school, but there are some who want to rebel from the strict and suffocating upbringing they've had. Lucca and Ethan do participate in threesomes, but it doesn't mean they don't sleep with other people separately." He takes a moment to let me digest the information. It makes sense. The day of their birthday party, I had a feeling they were flirting with the girl to get a reaction out of me, to see if I'd be disgusted if they slept with the same girl.

Kaiden taking a step forward shakes thoughts of the twins out of my mind, and I become alert.

"But that isn't what you wanted to ask me, is it?"

Knowing prick.

I exhale, crossing my arms over my chest. "What do you want, Kai?"

"To talk."

"I have class," I bite out.

"Like you care about class," he retorts. "I want to know what you have on my dad."

My stomach sinks. It didn't occur to me that this was why he'd pulled me aside. I'd assumed this would be something to do with us, but I guess that had been wishful thinking.

"Why, so you can destroy it?"

He crosses his arms, taking a step forward. "No, Ivy. I just want to know the truth. I want to find him. I'm not the bad guy here. I didn't know about any of this until that day in your hospital room."

I snort. "He's your father. Don't tell me you didn't know what he was like."

He raises his eyebrow at me, taking another step closer. "I told you what my father was like. I've never been anything but openly honest with you, even when I was prick and treated you so poorly."

"It doesn't matter," I lie. It does matter. "He's gone. What we do have is worthless until he's captured."

He steps closer, growling, and pins me against the wall using his hands and body. A small gasp passes through my lips. I freeze on the spot, squeezing my eyes shut like it will somehow shut him out. It doesn't, and the pain of having him so close only increases when he leans in, breathing onto my neck. Goose-bumps break out over my skin when a feather-light touch of his lips whispers along my skin.

It hurts.

It all hurts, and as I try to build those walls back up, to force down my emotions, I realise it doesn't matter. It's Kaiden. He'll always find a way to break them down or stir them up, and I can't let him. I can't let him in again.

"It does fucking matter. You won't even answer my calls. I've been trying to find out where you've been staying for weeks. I needed to see if you were okay." He sighs, shaking his head. "I've been trying to find my dad, to find out if he was the one who ran you off the road. You aren't the only one who needs answers."

I open my eyes and push him back, anger pumping through my veins.

"News flash: not everything is about you. When I wanted answers, you didn't give them to me. You just had me running in circles." I push him further away, blowing the hair out of my face. "And please, don't act dumb. It doesn't suit you, Kai. You know it was your dad who ran me off the road. You also know, deep down, that I wasn't lying in that hospital room. This didn't happen to you, it happened to me. My mum died, and I then I was here, fighting a new fight, surviving in an entire new world. I fucking had no one, Kai, and just when I thought I had you and the twins, I found out it was all a lie. My life was turned upside down. So I'm sorry if I didn't stop to answer the fucking phone to the son of who caused it all."

"Is that how you see me? As his son?"

I sigh, already knowing my answer. "No, because I'm not you. I'm not holding your dad's sins over you. I'm holding your own over you. You lied to me. I don't trust you didn't know about it all."

"I didn't fucking know about it," he snaps.

"I guess I'll never know," I tell him, leaving him to stew on those words as I head for the door. I reach it, twisting the lock to open it. I pause with my hand on the door handle, looking at him over my shoulder. "I didn't come here to wreck your world, Kaiden. I didn't come here for any of this. I came for a new start, a chance to forget the life I had growing up, and maybe a chance of not becoming my mum and the bitter woman she had become. This mess… I wasn't the one who started it. It was men in suits who let power go to their heads. Don't let that be you."

I leave him standing there, not saying another word as I leave the toilets. Lucca is standing outside, leaning against the wall opposite me. I roll my eyes. "I didn't kill him, if that's what you were worried about."

"Ivy," he starts.

"Don't," I warm him, and walk in the direction Selina pointed me in earlier, groaning over the fact I'll have to make a late entrance.

A tall, slender girl with honey-coloured hair steps out of another hallway, nearly bumping into me. Her forest green eyes lock on mine, and she smiles.

"Please tell me you're the new girl." She grins, and I see a flash of a tongue piercing. I also notice a colourful tattoo peeking out of the collar of her shirt.

I roll my eyes. "Is there a bulletin board with notice of my arrival?"

Her laugh is musical, husky. "Nope. You've just been a hot topic of conversation around here. Don't worry, they'll get bored in a few days. Most don't even care. It's only the girls who want to get into Danielle's clique that do."

"Because she's such a role model," I announce dryly.

She laughs again. "I'm going to like having you here. It's about time some of these snobs had the brooms ripped out of their arses."

I arch my eyebrow. "Aren't you rich?"

She shrugs. "Touché. Yes, my parents have money. But they aren't like other parents. I've worked for what I've got. I'm not a spoilt princess. I don't let status or popularity define me."

I grin at that. "You mean you didn't get a pony as a child?" I tease.

"Nah, I did get a Savannah cat."

"Aren't they really large house cats?"

"They are big. It freaked my neighbour out, who happened to be Danielle. I had a snake before that, but once I lost it after sneaking it into her house, I knew I needed a pet that would come back. And I love cats."

I grin, picturing Danielle freaking out over a snake. I look at the door to the classroom I'm in and inwardly groan.

"This is me. It was nice chatting to you."

"This is my stop too. No one fucking told me they changed classrooms. I'm Clarissa, by the way, but call me Clary."

"Ivy," I mutter back and let her walk through first. I step inside, hiding the fact my stomach is doing somersaults.

The teacher looks up from where he's just about to hand out papers. "Take a seat, Miss Whitmore."

He's a lot younger than I thought a teacher here would be. He can't be much older than us.

"Are you Miss Monroe?"

I nod, pulling the strap of my bag further up my shoulder. "Yes."

"Take a seat. I'll bring the class assignment booklet over to you."

I take a seat nearest to the door, opting for a quick escape route rather than being furthest from the teacher.

I grab my laptop from my bag, knowing I'll need it. Since Selina helped set up my school email account, I've been flooded with emails. One told me I'd need to bring my own laptop for today's lesson.

It's not long before the teacher makes his way over to me. "Morning, Miss Monroe. Welcome to Kingsley Academy. I'm Mr Wilson."

I give him a brittle smile and lean in. "Please, can you call me Ivy?"

He smiles and nods. "Of course. I know you've missed some work but it won't take long for you to catch up. I'll email you a list of study materials to help you. I hear you didn't have this lesson at your old school, so I'm not sure what level you are at. I don't want you to feel behind or overwhelmed by all of the work, so I've taken the liberty of making this," he explains, handing me a folder. "It will have step by step instructions to help you navigate this course. If you have any questions, please don't hesitate to ask. My email is on the first page, along with a list of students who partake in tutoring."

"Thank you," I tell him, feeling my cheeks heat a little.

"You're welcome." He smiles, tapping my desk. The door opens and a stormy-faced Kaiden steps inside.

My heart races as he scans the room, briefly pausing on me before taking the seat a few aisles across.

Anxiety swarms through me when Grant steps inside, looking worse for wear. We've never been friends, never been anything really, and although I'm still going to watch my back where he's concerned, I'm hoping being hit with the truth is enough to get him to back off.

"Open your laptops and begin the Excel report you started last week. For those who are joining us, you should have the start-up material in front of you.

Reaching for my laptop, I can feel the heated glare Grant is aiming at me. I look away, opening my laptop.

The screen comes to life, and the sound that echoes out the speakers has the blood draining from my face.

It's my mum, pleading for her attackers to stop.

I look around the room with wide eyes, my body shaking when everyone gapes openly at me.

I slam my laptop shut, then grab my things and quickly shove them into my bag.

I have to get out of here.

chapter nine

KAIDEN

THOSE WORDS... PLEASE DON'T DO THIS. They echo in my mind. The realisation of what I'm listening to hits me, and bile rises in my throat.

There is no lingering doubt inside of me. What surprises me is that I'm not at all shocked by the realization that my dad did this. I guess deep down my subconscious knew he had this in him. I was just too stubborn and hopeful to believe he didn't. No one wants a rapist for a dad.

Anger fuels my veins as I think about everything I've done, everything I've said. I put an innocent girl through hell for no reason.

Every time I touched her against her will, every time I threatened or cornered her, I'd had to numb something inside of me, had to shut off a part of myself that made me human.

I'm no saint. In reality, I'm a prick who just hates most people, especially those who are fake and out to get what they can out of life without caring who they step on to get it. I can come across as curt, churlish and a hard-arse, but I've never once hurt a girl. I don't abuse the power wealth has given me.

With Ivy, all that went out the window. My lust mixed with the hate I had for her, confused all of that.

But it never stopped the little boy inside of me from wanting revenge for what happened to my mum. Pathetic, immature? I don't know. I didn't care. All I wanted was to avenge my mum. But all along, it was Ivy's mum who needed vengeance.

It wasn't me, Grant or Ivy. It was Cara Monroe. And when I truly grasp everything that has happened, all I want to do is throw up.

A flicker of movement from the corner of my eye snaps me out of it, and I rush to grab my bag from the floor, chasing after Ivy as she escapes the room, her face ashen.

Another chair scrapes along the floor behind me, and I know it's Grant. He's been my best friend all my life, but without a doubt, I know that if he tries to harm Ivy, I'll hurt him. He needs to be hit with the same reality I've just been hit with, because all our lives we were fed lie after lie. Maybe we wouldn't have turned out be the arseholes we are or done the things we've done to let out our anger if those things hadn't been an equation in our lives.

But they were. And now we have to deal with them.

I notice Ivy steer off to the right and rush into the girls bathroom we were in earlier. I follow her inside, finding her bent over the sink, breathing hard.

She looks up, wiping at the tears slipping down her cheeks. My chest tightens at the sight of her, and it takes everything inside of me not to go to her, not to comfort her.

She forces her expression to turn blank, but it's no use. I can see the anguish written all over her face, and how she's trying to conceal the pain she's feeling.

She grabs the laptop off the side, holding it to her chest, like I'm about to rob her. If it wasn't for the fact she has every right to behave this way, I would have scoffed.

"Play it," I rasp out, not sounding like myself.

The sneer on her face has my dick twitching. I love it when she gets feisty. Even under these circumstances, she still has the power to make my body react.

"So you can destroy it?"

Grant slowly steps up beside me.

"I need to hear it," he demands, breathing hard.

"I don't trust you not to destroy it."

It's the first time I've ever seen her look vulnerable. She's usually so closed off and sassy, not allowing anything to penetrate those walls. It's like she deems sadness to be weakness, and therefore locks it down before people can see it and exploit it.

I see her though.

At first, I thought she was a tough bitch, dragged up in a rough area where all she knew was violence. But she's so much more. She's not just physically strong, but mentally strong too. However, I see through her 'I don't give a fuck' attitude. It's just an act. She does care about those around her, and I don't think she chose to go with Nova because she wanted to get out of her living situation. After spending weeks getting to know her, I truly believe she just wanted a family, wanted the love she was neglected to be given as a child. She wanted what we all want; love, family and a home. The only difference is she was scared to want it, to reach for it.

"I can promise you right now that if I wanted that destroyed, it would already be in pieces around this bathroom. I want to help you, Ivy. If you don't want me near you, send a copy to me, Nova, yourself and anyone else you can think of who will keep it safe." My dad is still out there, and he's already proved he will do whatever it takes to get his hands on that recording.

"And why would you tell me to do that?" she asks, eyeing us both warily. "I don't trust you."

"Play it," Grant croaks, staring at the laptop like it's going to spring to life.

The moment she gives in, she takes a resigned breath, yet she's no less wary than what she was to begin with. I want to reassure her that she can trust me, but it will be a pointless plea to Ivy right now. I've never given her any indication that she can trust me, so why would she start now. It's frustrating, and all I want to do is make this right between us.

Slowly, she places her laptop on the counter next to the sink and opens it up. It automatically plays, and the breath leaves my lungs in one fast *whoosh*.

A scream startles us, the sound loud as it echoes off the bathroom walls.

"*Don't do this. Please, don't do this, Royce. I'm a virgin,*" a woman I assume is Cara, begs.

"*Good!*" Dad sneers, his voice louder than hers, like he's closer to the recorder.

"*Please! Oh my god! Please, stop! Neil, make him stop!*" I close my eyes, looking away as bile rises up my throat.

"*No,*" Neil states, sounding aroused. I take a deep breath, my hands clenched into fists. "*Hurry up, Royce. I want to take my turn.*"

Dad laughs. "*Don't worry, she's still got a virgin arse.*"

"*That won't get her pregnant, but I guess it will be fun to split her in two.*"

"*Please, no,*" Cara screams.

Grant staggers backwards, shaking his head.

"I'm a monster," he whispers, his gaze on the floor. He turns on his heels and leaves, slamming the door against the wall on his way out.

I want to go after him, to see if he's okay, but there is no way I'm leaving Ivy right now. I pull my phone out of the inside pocket of my blazer and type a message to the twins, asking them to go find him and check if he's all right.

The room fills with tension as I take a step towards Ivy. She takes another one back, just like earlier, and glances away from me.

And it doesn't hurt any less to have her pull away from me now than it did the first time. I deserve everything, if not more.

What my father has done, what I have done... it can't be forgotten, it can't be forgiven.

"Please, stop it," I plead, the sound of her mum's pleas forever embedded in my brain.

She bows her head. "I don't know how," she admits.

I step over, pausing the soundtrack, and take in a deep breath. I connect with the school Wi-Fi and quickly open my email account.

"What's your email address?"

"I only have the school one. I've never had the internet before."

I pause on the keys, closing my eyes. Every time I'm reminded of how little she's experienced or had growing up, it tears my heart wide open.

I clear my throat, pulling myself together as I quickly log out and open one up for her. It won't take much for someone with knowledge of computers to access her school email. It's all on one system and monitored at the school. It takes a minute to set up, and it's not long before I'm back on my account, adding Nova, Sam, and a few other trusted contacts to send it to.

Remembering the officer Ivy talked about when she was taken in, I ask, "Do you still have the contact information the policeman gave you at the station?"

Still in her own head, Ivy looks around the room like a cornered animal. I knew she would be shocked by the turn of events, probably still wary about me helping her.

I might be a dickhead to most people, but only to those who deserve it, and the quicker she gets that in her head, the better.

"Um, y-yes," she mumbles, grabbing her bag. Pulling out her purse, she opens it up and pulls out a small card. She hands it to me, and the brush of our fingers causes a jolt to shoot through my system.

Knowing this needs to be dealt with, I enter in his email address, attaching the recording with a short message explaining the details and that we'll be in touch soon.

Shutting the laptop, I hand it to her, and she's taken aback by the gesture. I sigh. "I told you, I don't want to destroy it. Believe it or not, this has been hard on all of us. I'm owning up to my mistakes, which is something I rarely do. I won't even fake it to placate someone, Ivy."

"But why?" she asks.

I shrug. "Because believe it or not, I do care about you. But even if I didn't, I wouldn't brush this under the rug. He's got a lot to answer for. At first, I thought he cheated on Mum because he didn't get what he wanted from her. She was broken, a mess, and I blamed your mum for it."

"It wasn't her fault," she says, tucking her hair behind her ear. She sighs. "And who blamed her? They had to have said something for you to react the way you did to me when we first met, for you all to do the things you did to me."

"I know that. I know you could have had us arrested for sexual harassment. Hell, what Grant did is classed as sexual assault. I'm not condoning or making excuses. What we did was fucked up."

"But you thought you were giving me a taste of my own medicine," she states, like she's finishing my sentence.

"I don't know. You know about the twins, but as for Grant, I've got no clue. What he did… he went too far."

"And my mum?" she asks, clearly wanting the subject closed.

"I've told you some, but what I didn't tell you was that I went to my granddad, on my father's side, and asked him about what I'd heard. He filled my head with so much crap, but I swear to you, Ivy, he never went into details about what she accused them of. He only said that she lied, tried to discredit our family, and that Mum was seriously hurt because of it. Everyone around us constantly blamed Mum's health on your mum. As a kid, it stuck inside my mind, and I've been feeding off the anger from that all these years. There were a lot of things going on that kept fortifying that anger, letting it grow, and I hadn't realised how much until I heard you and Nova arguing, and you let it all out about your upbringing."

"But we slept together. None of this makes sense. If you hated me that much, why? Why did you suddenly change how you felt?"

I arch an eyebrow at her, wondering if her question is legit. It is. "Simple. Because you are you. You don't realise how refreshing it is to be around you, to be with someone who doesn't have money signs in their eyes when they look at you. The way you see the world, how you look at the smallest things… I was drawn to it. And I didn't change how I felt about your mum until the second you revealed the truth at the hospital."

"But you didn't believe me."

I sigh. "You didn't exactly believe I didn't know, either. I guess we were wrong about a lot of things. And it wasn't that I didn't believe you, I just didn't want it to be true, because no matter how much I hate him, he's still my dad. I still share his DNA."

The tension in the air lowers, and she starts to relax somewhat, letting those walls she's built so high come down a little.

"I guess I should throw your words back at you and say you aren't your father."

"Aren't I?" I blurt out, surprising myself.

She looks genuinely confused as her eyebrows pinch together. "You might be a prick, but never once did you scare me, Kaiden. I'm not weak, but even the strongest can buckle when it comes to having that choice taken away from them. But I knew what you were doing. I just didn't know *why*. The only time I ever got worried and questioned myself was the night Grant pushed me into the pool. I don't think you're like your father."

"I don't know what got into him that night," I admit. Grant and I came to blows after that fiasco at my brothers' birthday party, getting in each other's faces. I warned him to stay away from her, that I'd sort it.

"I need to find a way to get back to the manor. Nova needs to see this," she explains, pulling me from my thoughts.

And just like that, she isn't wary around me. The offer to give her a lift home doesn't leave my lips. Instead, I ask, "It's that easy?"

Looking up from her bag, she raises her eyebrow. "Is what easy?"

"You aren't mad at me? You believe me?" I didn't realise how much it had bothered me to know she didn't believe me until now. I'm not one of those people who obsess about something until it drives them crazy, but I've found everything Ivy does drives me crazy.

She makes a guttural sound at the back of her throat. "Like I said earlier, I'm not you. I don't put blame where it doesn't belong." *Ouch!* I wince, wishing I hadn't asked. She sighs, looking at me in exasperation. "I'm still angry, but not like I was before. It's going to take time for me to trust you again, but I don't think you were keeping this from me. I saw your face when the recording played in the classroom. It wasn't one of shame, or anger at me for accidentally playing it, and you didn't care that other people heard. You genuinely looked shocked."

That's because I fucking had been. I still feel sick at the thought.

It still bothers me that we aren't together, not how we were before. I've never begged for anything, and even if I could push past my pride and beg her for forgiveness, it would only push her away.

Right now, Ivy needs to know I care, and I can't do that with meaningless words. She needs actions.

And she's going to get them.

No one has ever gotten under my skin the way Ivy does, not one person. She wormed her way inside, and although I should have been pissed, I wasn't. I found I liked having her there. The only regret I have is not seeing it sooner and instead had been a dick to her.

"Come on, I'll drop you back."

Her eyebrows shoot up at my offer. "That's not necessary."

I smirk a little. "Unless you want to call Nova, you'll be waiting until school finishes. Taxi's won't know where to look. We're kind of off the grid."

Although she doesn't look happy, I see the resolve in her expression. "All right, but this doesn't mean shit, Kai."

I gesture for her to leave the room. She doesn't move, pointedly looking at me as if to say I'm stupid. A small growl rumbles up my throat, and I turn, leaving the girls bathroom.

She'd meant it when she said she doesn't trust me, not even to walk behind her.

Nearing the exit, Principle Hackett cuts us off, glaring at us. He dismisses me easily, as is his way, but I don't like the look he gets when he eyes Ivy. It's a mixture of disgust and annoyance.

"Miss Monroe, skipping class on your first day?"

Ivy, still not herself, curls her arms around each other, staring at Hackett with a blank expression. "I'm just taking her home. She has to leave to see her aunt."

Eyeing me now, Hackett's lip curls. We've never gotten along, and more than once I've tried to get him fired. Not for the sole reason that we don't get along, but because I think he's a sleaze who preys on vulnerable girls. More so than not, a rumour will hit my ears that he's slept with another student. Or blackmailed them. I've seen his reactions, seen the way he looks at them, and I don't like it. Even if I didn't have the school's reputation to upkeep, I'd still want to fire him.

But he's easily controlled by the board, so they keep him around, and until someone makes a formal complaint, he'll stay. Or so they tell me. One day he's going to fuck up, and on that day, I'll be there, ready to get the proof they need.

He's also under my dad's thumb. The two had known each other before he started here at the school, and I've often wondered if Dad got him the job so that if Mum ever left him, he still had influence and control over the school. And I wouldn't put it past him to use Hackett as a way to keep an eye on me.

"It's her first day, and Miss Monroe hasn't called to say she needs her niece home."

"Why would she call you?" I ask, daring him to answer. It's not like Nova personally knows him.

He splutters a little, red-faced. "I'm the principle of the school."

"But calls go to the receptionist," I tell him dryly, purposefully not calling her by her name. No child should live with the last name 'Crapper'.

He turns his attention to Ivy. "I can't grant you permission to leave the school premises. If you do, I'll have no other option but to suspend you."

Ivy's back goes ramrod straight. "What?"

I quickly step in before she manages to get in his sights. One rant from her can make the strongest man feel inferior. It's how I felt every time she fought back, not seeming the slightest bit unnerved. She'll put him in his place, and he'll feel humiliated, and although that is something I'd love to see, it won't bode well for her. The rumours flying around Kingsley Academy mostly start with girls who had answered him back. Ivy wasn't going to be one of those girls.

"Respectfully, sir, you can't stop us from leaving and you can't suspend us for it. We'll be back for afternoon classes. Ivy has a family emergency at home. Why else would she be leaving this early in the day? She's not even had her first lesson. And you are capable of calling Miss Monroe. I can't say she'll be pleasant about you holding her niece up, but that's between you and her."

He hates that I'm confronting him, putting him in a position where he can't really argue. "And why are you leaving, Mr Kingsley?"

"She needs a lift as Miss Monroe is indisposed at the moment. If that is all, we really should be going."

"You can wait until I've spoken to Miss Monroe to confirm this," he tells me, the veins in the side of his neck popping out, no doubt picturing me dying a slow and painful death.

I grind my teeth together. "We're done."

Awareness spreads through my system as I take Ivy's hand, pulling her out of the exit doors. Mr Hackett begins to call us back, his tone becoming angrier and angrier by the second.

If I thought for one second that he wanted us to stay in school for academic reasons, or that we weren't allowed to leave, I'd obey his rules. I might be a dick, but I still respect figures of authority, even if it pains me to do so.

The sound of my car unlocking eases some of the tension. Not all, but enough for me to drive us back safely.

Ivy keeps quiet, off in her own thoughts. I desperately want to ask if she's okay—it was her mum on the recording—but I'm sensing she needs time right now. Time, I can give her. I just don't know how much until I take back what's mine.

chapter
ten

IVY

MY GAZE KEEPS FLICKING FROM THE ROAD to Kaiden. There's something sexy about watching him drive, seeing the concentration on his face. He'd taken his blazer off and rolled up his shirt sleeves the minute we got into the car, allowing me to now appreciate the pulsing veins in his arms as he grips the steering wheel. He is truly a sight to behold, and I wish I had time to see him drive in one of the races he takes part in.

Although my body still craves him, my heart and mind haven't decided whether they can trust him or not, which is why my attention has been divided between the road and him. I want to make sure we're actually heading to the manor, but I also need to keep an eye on him. There are many emotions you can decipher from a person's expression, and I guess I've been waiting for his to portray something that doesn't correlate with what he's been telling me. But I've found no anger, no cunning, sly looks, no flicker of emotion— other than the deep sadness I can see he's trying to hide. It's in the slight downturn of his lips, the barely perceptible tensing of the muscles beneath his eyebrows. It's like he got slapped with reality and doesn't know his place in the world anymore.

Which has been my life for so long; never feeling like I fitted anywhere. I've never belonged, not even to my mum.

The tension washes away the minute we pass through the community's gates, yet, my heart races in anticipation. I'm still sceptical about Nova, even if her concern has seemed honest.

Rubbing my hands over my pleated skirt, I keep my gaze locked ahead. I'm nervous about the recording. Listening to it again isn't an option for me. There is no way I could stomach it.

Putting the car into park, Kaiden turns to me, his expression grim. "For what it's worth, I am sorry you had to be brought into all of this."

I watch him closely, hearing only sincerity in his tone. "That's the thing, I wasn't *brought* into all of this, I was *born* into it. Born *because* of it." I take in a deep breath, my fingers gripping the strap of my bag until my knuckles turn white. I can't do this with him. He might be sorry, but it doesn't change what's happened. There isn't a way for us to forget. I don't know how to trust him again, how to see the man I used to after he got over being angry. Instead of voicing all that, I turn and say, "Thank you for the lift."

I exit the car, not bothering to look back at him when he calls my name. The reminder of what we could have been is too painful. I long to feel his touch, to have him hold me and tell me everything will be okay.

The second I enter the house through the side door, the sound of quiet sniffling reaches my ears. My heart stops and the bag slips through my fingers. I race through the house, searching for Nova, panic rising in my chest.

What if he's hurt her too?

"Nova?" I call out, quickly scanning the kitchen. I notice a steaming cup of tea sitting on the counter. She can't be far.

I don't bother telling Kaiden to get lost when I hear him following, not wanting to waste time arguing with him. Getting to Nova is the only thing that matters right now. I won't let what happened to my mum, happen to her.

I didn't understand it at first, the feeling inside of me, but I do care about her. I do care what happens. It was the same kind of feeling I got when I thought she betrayed me, when I thought I might lose Selina. It was a fear that I might lose them.

I'm scared to lose them.

Because you care.

The moment I hit the living room, I come to a sudden stop, my heart in my throat when I see Nova bent over a crate. Piles of books surround her; some open, some closed.

Diaries.

Mum's diaries.

I sag against the living room doorframe when I see there's no sign of physical injury. Hearing us enter, Nova sits back, tears streaming down her cheeks as she glances over at me. What I see is heart-wrenching. Deep, withering grief and despair pours out of Nova in waves, overwhelming me, to the point I nearly collapse.

A thousand things run through my mind as I wonder what has happened, but the sight of the diaries is just solid proof as to what this is about.

"I'm so sorry, Ivy. I'm so sorry I didn't help you, help her." She sobs, bringing a diary to her chest. "I wish I could go back. I wish I could have stood up to our society. I'm so sorry I failed you, Ivy."

As if approaching a wild animal, I slowly take a step into the room. She flinches, looking back down at an open diary.

"Nova, it's okay," I promise her, keeping my voice low.

I've felt emotions before—I'm not a robot. I've always known my upbringing wasn't conventional, that Mum wasn't like other mums. I've had to stand up for myself with a lot of people, learn to take care of myself, and over the years I hardened something inside of me, so I couldn't be left heartbroken. But those walls I built so long ago to protect myself, crumble the second her gaze locks with mine. She's filled with so much guilt and sorrow, it's suffocating. I want to run, to break free of this room and suck in air that isn't filled with grief. But I can't run, not from this, not from her.

From the moment I met Nova, I lied to her, to myself. I pretended I didn't care, that she was nobody, but deep down, it was all a lie. She does matter. I do care. And that scares me. She scares me. She has the power to run me down the same way Mum did. And it would hurt. I held onto hope the second she walked into my life, whether I choose to admit it to myself or not. I wanted a chance at a real family, a real life. And because of who I am, I wouldn't let myself reach for it, treasure it.

You wanted Nova to work for it, a voice inside my head whispers.

It hits me like a ton of bricks, and I stagger backwards a little, nearly losing my footing. All this time, it wasn't a lack of trust or my self-preservation coming between us, it was that I wanted Nova to want me, to work hard at keeping me.

I wanted someone to love me.

"I'm a terrible person," Nova whispers brokenly.

"No, you aren't," I tell her, because she's not. I've met arseholes in my life, and she's not one of them, not if I'm honest with myself.

"Yes, Ivy, I am. This happened to her, and she had no one. I'm her twin sister and I was never there for her. It was easier to accept what I was told. I could pretend that it was just a story. But these are her words, her thoughts and feelings. She must have been terrified. Cara was religious, just like our grandparents, and wanted to wait to lose her virginity until she found 'the one'. She lost more that night than anyone can really know. She lost her entire future—the one she writes about in these diaries."

"Calm down. It's going to be okay."

"I'm failing you too. I let you get hurt. He hurt you as well. Nearly killed you," she cries, losing it. I've never seen her like this. She's always so well composed. "I miss her. I miss the girl she was and grieve the woman she was supposed to be."

It's like it's all hitting her at once, and I grimace, wishing I knew how to comfort her. I'm angry at Royce all over again, wanting to run him down like he had done to me.

"Where did you get the diaries?" I ask quietly, sitting down next to her.

"From me," Annette says, stepping inside the room. She hands Nova a glass of water, guiding it to her mouth. "Drink," she orders shortly.

"You?"

Annette studies Kaiden for a moment before placing the glass onto a tray. She bends down next to Nova, watching her worriedly. "Yes. I found them not long after I was hired. I knew the rumours, heard the stories, and I found—" She stops, looking at Kaiden again, biting her bottom lip.

"Found what?" I ask.

She shakes herself out of it but seems to withdraw a little. "I found Mr Kingsley looking for them. He asked for them rather adamantly, saying they were important. At first, he was charming. He made it seem like he was doing Cara a favour. I didn't know what I know now, but I could see in his eyes that he was no good. And he's not. He got so angry when I told him I couldn't help him," she explains, sadness glittering in her eyes.

"He hurt you," I guess, then remember the day Royce presented me with a cheque. "And he hurt you that day he corned me in the kitchen, didn't he?"

She nods. "Yes. He can be very forceful," she explains. Her hands begin to shake, and I want to reach out to comfort her. "I'm sorry, Mr Kaiden, but it's the truth."

"Kaiden?" Nova whispers sharply, looking up, her eyes glazed over. She grabs my hand tightly, almost making me wince.

"I'm not here to hurt her, Nova. I want to help," he explains, unable to meet Nova's eyes. He tilts his head up, looking at Annette. "Don't be scared of me, Annette. I'm not my father."

"I know," she whispers, but she still looks hesitant.

"What happened in the kitchen?" Kaiden asks.

I wave him off, dismissing him. "It doesn't matter."

"It does."

"It really doesn't," I grit out, and he sighs, knowing he can't force me to explain. I'm too emotionally drained to try.

"What are you doing here?" Nova asks, quickly piling the diaries up in the black crate. I notice her movements are sluggish and begin to help.

"Ivy has the recording."

The sound of a diary dropping into the crate echoes around the room. Slowly, she turns to us, eyes wide. "I thought Royce had the recording?"

I shake my head, reaching for her hand. "He does, but I must have saved it to my computer. We've sent it to you and a few others, for safe keeping," I tell her, glancing at Kaiden. "It was Kaiden's idea."

"Why do I feel funny?" Nova asks suddenly.

Annette smiles gently. "I've given you a sleeping pill. You've had a stressful morning and need to rest. You've not slept in weeks, Nova."

"Annette," Nova grits out.

"I wouldn't have done it if you had just gone back to bed."

"Let's get you to bed," I tell her, but she clings to the box.

"We have to protect it all. We have to. I won't let him hurt you again. I never got to have kids, Ivy. I couldn't. But I have you, my niece, and he's not going to hurt you like he did your mum."

Kaiden steps forward, bending down and tucking an arm under her legs and another around her back. "No one is going to touch her, Nova. I promise."

"You know where her room is?" Annette asks, finishing clearing the diaries away.

"Yeah," he rasps, not looking at me.

Drowsy, she drops her head onto his shoulder. "It should have been me. Cara was a gentle soul, a loving person. It should have been me. She should have grown up in this house, raised her children here, raised Ivy. Not me. I'm alone. And Ivy hates me."

"I don't hate you," I whisper as he carries her out of the room, but she doesn't hear me.

"She knows," Annette says, startling me. "It's weighed on her a lot over the years—wanting to find and help Cara. She wanted to know you, love you."

"My mum didn't allow anyone she couldn't manipulate or profit from into our lives. She might not have been a prostitute, and yes, she slept with a lot of men, but she never asked for payment. It didn't stop her from taking what she could from them, but sex was never exchanged for it. Anyone else, she ran from. She stayed away from men who would try to control her. She was never going to be well enough to accept her family back into her life. And can you blame her?"

Squeezing my hand, she shakes her head. "Not even a little. But I can blame her for letting those people into *your* life. I'm going to check on Nova."

I need to get out of here, to do something. If I had my skateboard, I would go out and relieve my stress on that, but it broke not long before Mum died. My only other outlet was to read or draw, and neither of those feel the least bit enticing. I need concentration to do that, and right now, my mind is overflowing with thoughts.

I could go see Elle and Ed.

"Wait," I call out as Annette reaches the door. "Could you call Kingsley Academy and explain there was a family emergency and that I'll be back tomorrow, please? I can't go back today, and the principle has it out for me."

Her eyes soften. "Of course."

"And let me know when Nova wakes up. I'm going to go out and get some fresh air, but I want to know she's okay. We need to send that recording to the team of police you allocated as well as PC Sullivan."

"Don't worry about Nova. She'll be fine. I'll watch over her and call you as soon as she's awake."

"Thank you."

Needing air and out of this house, I head for the front door, ignoring Kaiden, who's on his way down the main stairs.

"Ivy," he calls out.

Without looking back, I keep walking, breathing in the fresh air as a light breeze fans my face. It won't be long until the sun reaches its peak and makes the heat unbearable.

"Stop!" he orders sharply.

"I need to get away from here, Kaiden. Don't bother trying to stop me," I warn him.

I nearly collide with him when he steps in front of me. "Go get changed."

"Again with the orders?" I mutter dryly.

His lips twitch. "Okay, think of it as a request. I mean, you don't want to go anywhere in your uniform, do you?"

He's right, I think sourly as I glance down at my attire. There's no way I'll be able to get on my bike with this skirt on, not unless I want to flash all of Cheshire Grove.

"Why are you still here?" I ask, somewhat harshly.

"I'm taking you somewhere."

Suspicion leaks into my veins. "And why would I go anywhere with you?"

"Because you're angry, because you need an outlet. I know what that's like—to want to lash out at everything and everyone around you, even though they aren't the issue."

Lip curling, I take a step back. "I've seen your form of release, and unlike you, I'm not into beating someone to a pulp. And if you're talking about sex, you're barking up the wrong tree."

His grin is wide, mischievous. "As hot as it would be to see you wrestling with another chick, that's not where I'm going with this. And neither is fucking you—though that would certainly relieve some of your tension." He runs his fingers through his hair, sighing when I don't move. "I'm not going to take you somewhere to kill you. I'm going to take you to a place my mum took me to let off steam when I was younger."

I'm not going to lie and say I'm not curious—deep inside, I do want to know more about him, more about his upbringing—but going with him is a bad idea, and not just because of who his dad is, but because of how my body still reacts to him. He must read the indecision on my face, because he growls. "I'm not going to hurt you, Ivy. I know saying sorry won't make up for all the shit I've done. You have no idea how badly I'm kicking myself for mistreating you to begin with. Nothing can make up for that, but let me help you."

"And what do you get out of it?" I muse.

"I just want to help you," he explains, but I don't believe him. This could be a trick so I owe him a favour. "Just get dressed. What have you got to lose?"

He's right. I look back at the house, biting my bottom lip worriedly. His expression is blank when I turn back, but the need to let go of some of this anger is compelling.

"You touch me, don't think for a second I won't rip your dick off and shove it up your arse. And no, it won't be enjoyable."

I can't stop the grin that spreads across my face once my back is turned, his slight flinch filling with me glee.

chapter eleven

KAIDEN

THE TWENTY-MINUTE DRIVE FEELS LIKE thirty because of Ivy's constant silence. She isn't giving me an inch, knowing I'll take it and beg for more. I'm selfish when it comes to her. I'm not going to give up though. I want her to open up.

"When do you get your cast off?"

"Four weeks."

Blunt. Curt. Crisp. Like all of her answers since we left the manor. I sigh, gripping the steering wheel harder as we near the factory.

Her phone beeps with another message, but I don't take my eyes off the road long enough to see her expression. Jealously is an emotion I'm not accustomed to, but I do feel it. I want to know who she's talking to; is it a male, an old friend, a new friend?

Instead of asking—because I know she won't tell me, anyway—I force my gaze to stay ahead.

"We're here," I announce, a bite to my tone. I sigh, closing my eyes briefly. "Sorry, I didn't mean for it to come out like that."

She puts her phone back in her bag, her gaze on me. I can feel the heat of her stare burning the side of my face. "Don't change who you are, Kaiden. I never wanted that. I still don't. How can I know if you're being fake or real if you apologise and bottle shit up?"

I switch the car off, turning to face her. "I don't want to push you away."

Her expression softens a little at that, but it's gone before I can blink. "I'm not made of glass, Kaiden. I've handled a lot more. Honesty won't break me. I get you want to make it up to me, and I know I've said this before, but I don't think I can go back to how things were, like shit hasn't happened between us or around us."

"They did happen. I'm not asking you to pretend they didn't. What I'm asking is that you give me another chance. Give me a chance to show you the real me. I need you, Ivy. I don't know how or when I needed you happened, but it did. You've been under my skin from the moment I met you. I like you in my life, in my bed."

"No, you liked the sex; the fact I'm a different flavour to all the other girls you fuck."

Frustrated, I grip the steering wheel until my knuckles turn white. "I'm not being big-headed when I say this, but I can get a new *flavour* in my bed any time I want. I've had variety, but none have been you. Never you." I take in a deep breath to compose myself. I don't want to scare her away. "Have you even asked yourself why I'm trying? Do I come across as someone who begs, who chases after girls?"

"No," she whispers, hesitant as she looks away.

"No, I'm not. I've never done any of those things, Ivy. You need to understand, and understand quick, that this isn't about having someone in my bed. This is about you, you in my life. I don't just want you, I need you."

With a tired sigh, she reaches for the door. "Can we just do whatever this is? I can't talk about this, not right now."

Knowing that's the best I'm going to get right now, I nod, letting her leave. I follow behind, locking the car before making my way up to the factory entrance.

"What is this place?"

A smile reaches my lips when memories of the first time I came here, surface. "When I first came here, Mum had not long come back from her *spa* vacation. Dad had been hard on the twins and me the entire time she was gone, and he decided to get drunk at a work's party the day before she returned. He came home with one of the many women he had an affair with. The twins were bummed because he missed their tennis tournament and were acting out. I knew they were upset but didn't want anyone to see, so they tried to hide it. I had it out with him when he rolled in drunk, the woman hanging off his arm. We went to blows, things were said and done, and I was angry. Angry at how he treated the twins," I explain, running a hand through my hair. It's hard to talk about emotions—I'm not that kind of guy—but she needs to understand. "Mum came back and I told her everything, even about the woman. She didn't seem fazed, but she was worried about me. She could tell I was angry. She told me to get my shoes on, that we were going somewhere. I was just glad I was spending time with her."

"Here?"

I grin at the dubious way she says it and pull her through the door. I step up to the guy at the counter, handing him the money. He nods, giving us a slip of paper stating our cubicle number and two sets of goggles. The second we step into the main building, Ivy gasps.

"What on earth?" she murmurs, looking up and down at the row of cubicles where the sound of ceramic smashing gets louder.

I thought the same thing when I walked in and heard the sound. It was deafening.

"She wanted me to get rid of my anger in the safest way possible. She handed me a plate and told me to throw," I explain, stepping into a cubicle and handing her a plate.

She holds it, looking at the wall ahead of us. "People really do this?"

I chuckle at her expression. "Yes. There's hatchet throwing on the other side. Give it a go. It's therapeutic."

"I don't know," she whispers.

Taking a pair of the goggles, I pull them over her head before leaning in close. "You've been fucked over too many times. By your mum, your dad, everyone. You were run off the road," I tell her, inwardly smirking when I see her face flush with anger.

"Fuck you, Kai."

"Any time, love." I wink, giving her a smirk. "But you enjoy being fucked, don't you?"

She turns and lets the plate fly, watching as it smashes against the wall. Breathing deeply, and without being compelled, she takes another plate and throws it.

Stepping up behind her, I lean close to her ear, whispering. "Come on, Ivy, let out that anger. Think of all the people that have hurt you; what they did, what they've said."

"Fuck you, Kai," she growls louder, throwing the plate with so much force, I have to step back.

The sound of ceramic smashing echoes along the walls of the factory, but in this cubicle, it's louder, angrier. But she needs to get it out, set it free.

"Fuck all of you who thought you could hurt me," she screams, and I step back, leaning against the bench, watching in pure fascination as she throws another plate. "I'm not a toy, a game you play with and throw away when you get bored. I'm a person." She keeps throwing, heading to the second pile. I watch when she turns, noticing the sweat beading on her temples and across her chest. I stand straighter, ready to go to her.

"Ivy?" I call out softly, but she doesn't hear me as she swings out her arm, throwing the plate harder than all the others.

"I hate that you couldn't get your shit together, I hate that you weren't like other mums, and I hate that I wasn't enough for you to sort your life out and learn to love again."

My heart clenches at the sound of misery and hopelessness in her voice. She's never let go like this. When I brought her here, I thought she'd get angry about my dad, but she's still angry at her mum.

And I don't know how to help with that. This is beyond what I thought was brewing inside of her.

"Ivy!" I call out again, this time harsher.

She pauses, dropping the plate on the floor as she gasps for breath. Her hands fall limply to her sides. I step forward, reaching for her, but she takes a step back.

"I can't keep doing this."

"Doing what?" I ask, my gut clenching.

"Pretending this isn't bothering me," she explains, lifting her head to meet my gaze. "I hate that I need to be strong all the time. I hate that I was dealt this life. I watched my mum go through men like a hot knife through butter, using her body to get what she wanted. I saw things no child should ever see. Those parts of my life were unfair, cruel, but I got through it."

"Ivy," I say gently, but she shakes her head, still refusing my comfort.

"When I reached an age where I understood what I was seeing, I was disgusted with her, disgusted with the men. I kept telling myself it wouldn't always be like this, that she'd stop or change. It didn't. And as I got older, the worse it got. Knowing it wouldn't be long before I was old enough to leave, I stayed quiet, telling myself after I finished school, I'd leave the day I turned eighteen. I promised myself I'd get out of that environment the second my birthday came around, and I was going to stick to it. Even when one of her boyfriends taunted me, telling me he wanted to keep it in the family, that I'd enjoy him being in my bed, I stayed. I stayed because I had nowhere to go. No one to care. No one to love me. She didn't get mad over the fact he was getting in my bed uninvited, she got mad because he wasn't paying attention to her. She heard him promise he'd buy me some shoes and a pretty dress if I let him sleep in my bed. Then she died, and I hated her even more. I felt nothing. Just a sense of relief and numbness. Then Nova," she says before taking a deep breath.

"What about Nova?" I ask, wanting her to keep talking to me.

She shrugs, looking around the area like she's coming out of her daze. "It doesn't matter."

"What were you going to say?" I prod.

"I didn't want to like her. She looked so much like my mum. I didn't even trust her. I mean, who offers someone money to go live with them until they get an education?"

I shrug. "She loves you." And she does. Ivy has just made it hard for Nova to show her.

"There are times when I think she does, but then something happens and it makes me wonder if I can trust her or not. Life back home was crap. Mum owed drug dealers money, which is what she was doing the day she died. I guess she thought she had a way to get herself out of that situation, but she didn't. She ended up dead. Nova was my second chance, a chance at life, and look where I am now, look where Nova is. She's breaking, and I didn't think anything could break her."

"Everyone has their kryptonite."

"I guess," she murmurs.

My phone rings from my pocket and I pull it out, ready to silence the call. When I see it's my brothers, I answer. "Yeah?"

"Bro, you need to come to the roof of the rec room. Grant's drunk and on the ledge."

"On my way," I tell him, ending the call. I close my eyes, wishing I didn't have to leave her. "We need to go. Grant is…" I trail off, not wanting to share his business.

Ivy's eyes narrow into slits. "Grant's what? I swear, if you start this riddle shit up again, I'm done with you for good."

I scrub a hand down my face. I did tell her there would be no more skirting around subjects she wanted answers to. "He's drunk and on the ledge above the rec room."

Her eyes go round. "Go then. I can get back. I want to read Mum's diaries, anyway."

"It will be quicker for you to come with me. I can drop you off as soon as I've sorted it out."

The uncertainty in her gaze nearly makes me change my mind. Grant hasn't always had it together, but he's never gotten like this. Not even when we were teenagers and thought getting drunk made us cooler than the others.

"All right," she says, not sounding so sure.

We leave the building, and I give the guy at the reception desk a chin lift on my way out.

$$\heartsuit$$

WHAT SHOULD HAVE been a forty-minute drive took thirty when Ethan phoned to say he's going to call the police. I told him to hold off on calling them until I got there, worried what Grant would do if he saw authority figures coming at him with everything that is going on.

The tyres skid on gravel when we reach the school, parking outside the rec room.

"Holy crap, is that—"

"Grant? Yeah," I finish for her when she trails off, at a loss for words. Looking through the windshield, I can see him walking along the volley of the roof, above the window of the rec room.

I slam the car door shut and rush through the building. When I reach the rec room, I enter the code and push through the door.

I hear Ivy rushing behind me, and if I had time, I would tell her to stay here, but I don't. The stairs to the sun roof come into view and I rush up them, stepping out onto the flat roof.

"Bro, we can't get him to come off," Ethan says, visibly relaxing when he sees me.

"Oh look, the motherfucking prince is here," Grant growls, pain flashing in his eyes when they land on Ivy. He walks closer to us, swaying as he tries to keep his balance. "What are you doing here?"

There's no venom, just anguish.

"What are you doing, Grant?" I call out, diverting his attention from Ivy.

"You've not heard?" he asks.

"Heard what?"

"My dad's a rapist."

"Grant," I sigh, frustrated. "This isn't the place or the time. Get down so we can talk about this."

"Have a drink with me," he cheers dryly, sadness lurking in the depth of his eyes. He gulps down another swig of vodka, not even flinching at the burn. "One last drink."

My gut churns and I take a step forward. He moves away, back onto the roofing above the boxed window. I pause, my hands shaking.

He can't be serious.

He shakes his head in disgust at me. "I'm just like him."

"No, you aren't," I vow, growing more and more frustrated. Anyone could walk out below and hear him, but more than that, he's going to kill himself being up there in his condition.

His gaze drifts back to Ivy and fills with torment. "I'm just like my father. Just like him. I hurt you and he hurt your mum."

I glance over my shoulder to see how Ivy's handling it. She looks torn, her eyes darting from Grant to me and back to Grant again as she grips the end of her T-shirt. And I don't blame her. We all did messed up shit, but Grant did the worst. If she agrees with his statement, he could jump from the roof. If she doesn't say anything, he could still jump. There is no win-win situation here.

Facing Grant, I take a small step forward, noticing from the corner of my eye that the twins do the same.

"Get down, Grant. You aren't this person."

He laughs without humour, curling his upper lip. "Why? Because I have money? Well, guess what? I don't. It's gone. The only reason I'm at this precious school is because it was already paid for—courtesy of your dad." He staggers a little and I take another step forward, ready to rush at him to stop him from falling, but he manages to right himself.

"What do you mean, because of my dad?"

"He paid my dad to keep quiet. He told me everything."

I hear Ivy's intake of breath as anger surges through my veins. "What the fuck do you mean, he told you everything?" I ask through gritted teeth.

I see a flash of confusion before he clenches his jaw. "He's been arrested. I got the call after I left you and went to meet him where he's being held."

"Royce?" Ivy breathes, and I feel her step closer.

"Nope. Just my dad."

"Get down, Grant. We can talk about this without you being up there," I order, needing him to get down. My stomach is rolling just watching him. I can feel it in my gut; something bad is going to happen.

"Why? What do I have to possibly live for. I'm not a Kingsley. I'm a fucking rapist. A son of a rapist." He takes another sip, and I use the moment to move another step closer, bringing me only a few feet away from him.

"Grant," I warn.

"You aren't a rapist," Ivy whispers behind me.

"What, because I didn't fuck you, it makes what I did okay?" he snaps at her. "I'm just like my dad."

"No, it doesn't. Sexual assault is sexual assault and I won't make excuses for your behaviour. You shouldn't either," she answers, pausing for a moment. "Would you have taken it that far?"

He looks utterly confused for a moment, his brows lowering as he lets her words sink in. "I don't need to rape someone to get a shag," he says, a look of disgust over his face. "I don't know what I was going to do that night in the pool."

She takes another step closer, passing me by a step. "You know what I think?" she asks him, tilting her head. He shakes his head, looking so much younger and vulnerable in this moment that I barely recognise him. "I think you knew someone would stop you. You could have easily cornered me on my own at any given point. You could have bided your time that night or any day after. You guys have been taught that sex is a tool. I was given the same lesson, but instead of following in my mother's footsteps, I went in the other direction, because I'm not her." She pauses, and I'm glad, because I feel like I've been sucker punched in the stomach. She's right, and by the look on the twins' faces, they feel the same too.

"As shallow and judgemental as this might sound, I don't mean it to. But you were given the world. You were spoiled in your upbringing and took everything for granted. You saw sex and money as power and you all use it to your advantage. You wanted to punish me, but how could you punish a girl who was raised with nothing? It wasn't like you could take my car away from me, my home, or bleed me dry. I didn't have anything of importance. I still don't. So, you used the only tool you had left. Sex. It doesn't make what you did right, Grant, it never will. But you need to get down from that wall and stop feeling sorry for yourself. Change the cycle. Change the way of your world. Do it today. If you don't want to be your dad, don't. You said yourself you don't need to rape someone to get sex. You miss your mum, but ask yourself, would she miss you if this is the road you take? No, so make her proud. I believe Sam when he said she was leaving your dad, and she didn't go alone. She didn't want you around a monster. As for money, you'll survive. People survive with a lot less. You have the connections and friends to help you start fresh and make something of yourself."

She's struggling for air when she finishes, and I watch as the life drains out of Grant, his shoulders sagging with defeat. "I don't know how. I don't know how I go on, knowing what he did, who I've become."

"This isn't you," she snaps, and he lifts his head to meet her gaze.

"She's right," I rumble, emotion stuck in my throat. I clear it, taking another step. "You aren't this person. You fight. We fight. Don't take the easy way out, Grant. It's not who you are."

"What if it is?" he asks brokenly, but I can see it's no longer what he wants. He just needs to realise it.

I shake my head vehemently. "It's not. Your dad was weak, so was mine, but you aren't. Ivy's right, we've lived a privileged life and have no clue what real struggle is. We can have our issues, our faults and our losses, but we've never really understood true struggle. Our lives were mapped out for us before we were born. It's time we change that and make our own choices. We acted like spoiled brats the minute she rolled up in her car. We need to stick together."

"Amen," Lucca whispers. "Get down, Grant."

"I thought you wanted me dead?" Grant asks, looking over at Lucca.

Lucca rolls his eyes. "I want my own twin dead sometimes, it doesn't mean I mean it. This isn't you. If that was one of us up there you'd be telling us to pull our shit together and stop acting dramatic."

"Lucca," Ivy snaps, glaring at him. "That isn't helping."

"Not going to sugar-coat it to get him down. If he wants to jump, he can, but it's the coward's way out. We've all gone through shit, Ivy. Every one of us here have in our own way. But we're here for him, here for each other. After all the shit he's pulled lately, he should be able to see that. But he's not seeing past his own pain, which is exactly what Kaiden's problem was when you arrived."

She opens and closes her mouth before throwing her arms in the air. "I give up."

He grins. "But you're here," he declares, pointing to the ground before turning to Grant. "And she has every reason to push you off that ledge, but she's standing there and giving you reasons to get down. So do it. And not just for her but for yourself. You're like a brother to us."

"He told me Mum was leaving him, that he couldn't let that happen, so he cut her breaks and paid people off to leave it out of the police report," Grant whispers.

"Fuck," I whisper, running my fingers through my hair.

"Then make him pay," Ivy tells him, her voice stronger. "Make something of yourself and make him pay. Let him see that hard work pays off, that you didn't need to have things handed to you to get where you are. Let him see you didn't need to impregnate someone for a pay out."

"Why are you here, after what I've done to you?"

She rolls her eyes, crossing her arms over her chest. "Because I'm not an arsehole like you lot. And honestly, I have no fucking clue, because I've been imagining killing every single one of you since I woke up in hospital."

"*Me?*" Ethan calls out, pointing to his chest. He looks dejected, hurt that she would say it, and I inwardly laugh.

"You were first," she mutters, but I can tell she's lying when her gaze flicks to me. I sigh, knowing I've got my work cut out for me.

I turn back to Grant and reach my hand out for him. "Come on. You can stay with us for as long as you like."

His empty hand reaches out, but he stumbles, and I watch as everything moves in slow motion around me. One foot twists towards this side of the wall and the other twists off the ledge of the roof, his arms flailing in the air.

All of us move at the same time, grabbing anything within our grasp.

The fabric of his shirt tears when I curl my fist around it and pull. The twins each grab a sleeve of his blazer next, and somehow, we manage to secure him, half his body dangling off the roof, the other half on. I breathe a sigh of relief, pulling him over the small wall and falling back on my arse. I breath heavily, looking up at him as he leans against the small portion of brickwork.

"Fucking hell," I gasp out, staring at him. He looks green, and when it dawns on him how serious that could have been, he retches, vomit spewing out of his mouth.

"Are you fucking serious? These shoes cost me four-thousand quid," Ethan barks, crawling back. He gags at the smell, kicking his shoes off as he continues to retch.

The sound of laughter fills my ears, and I look over my shoulder to see Ivy's hand covering her mouth, laughter spilling from those perfect lips.

"This isn't funny," Ethan growls.

"He's safe, isn't he?" she says, her expression sombre now.

He rolls his eyes. "Don't, I'm still tempted to throw him over. These aren't even out in the shops yet."

"Shouldn't have worn them if you didn't want them getting ruined."

"Because I knew dickhead was going to get drunk and vomit on them," Ethan snaps back.

I look up at Grant, who's wiping his mouth, still looking out of it. "You going to be okay?"

He shrugs, not speaking for a moment. "She's right. We can't keep thinking we're gods. We need to earn what we have." He breathes through his nose, massaging his temples. "I don't want to be him, Kai. You met my grandfather. He was as abusive as my dad. What if this is who I am?"

Having heard him, Ivy kneels down next to him, avoiding the vomit. "Every cycle can be broken, Grant. You just have to want it badly enough."

"Let's get you back to mine and get you cleaned up. You need to sober up, and then you can fill us in on everything else that has happened today. Yeah?"

He nods before trying—and failing—to get up off the floor. With Lucca's help, we get him standing, tucking our shoulders under his armpits to support him.

"I'll call Annette, see if she can get someone to pick me up," Ivy comments, digging into her bag.

"Call Nick. I'll meet you back at the house," I tell Ethan before turning to Ivy. "Stay with Ethan and get a lift back with him. I'll call you after."

She looks like she's about to argue, but thinks better of it, shaking her head. I leave her with Ethan, knowing she'll be safe, and head downstairs to my car with Grant and Lucca.

"Has she forgiven you then?" Lucca asks and I sigh, looking back up to the rec room after closing the door behind Grant.

"Not by a long shot," I admit.

chapter twelve

IVY

THE HOUSE IS QUIET WHEN I LET MYSELF in and it's eerie. It still takes me aback to think my mum was raised here. I just can't imagine her in this home. Everything is clean and tidy for starters, and not very kid friendly. I've never thought of having kids, but I know there's no way I'd trust one to play in this house. If they didn't break some antique, then they'd smash their head open on the marble floor.

"Ivy?" Annette calls, and I scream, twisting towards the staircase, my hand over my chest.

"Jesus fucking Christ, Annette, you scared the shit out of me."

She frowns, shaking her head at me. "Do not use that language, Ivy. You're a lady."

Thoroughly scolded, I nod, even though I'd like to laugh at her 'lady' comment. "Is Nova awake?"

"She is. Go on up to her room. The tablets have made her drowsy, but she's resting."

I nod, taking the stairs two at a time before following the halls to her room. I knock lightly.

"Annette, I told you I'm not hungry," she growls, making me smile. I push open the door, stepping inside, and her eyes widen at the sight of me. "Ivy."

Her eyes are red-rimmed and swollen. I want to put this crap behind us and start moving forward. Seeing Grant up on that roof put a lot in perspective. I realised I'd been acting like an ungrateful cow since the minute she showed up.

"I acted like a bitch from the moment you showed up," I blurt out, and her eyebrows pull together. I shake my head, stepping further into the room. "I was acting out. I'm not a bully. I'm not a bitch. Yes, I've hardened myself so I can't get hurt, but I've never purposely been mean to someone. From the minute you found me, all you wanted to do was help, and I kept pushing you away. I didn't trust it or want to."

She smiles, her expression softening. "Sweetheart, I knew you didn't agree to move here for the money. You would have figured it out eventually, but you have your own. You'll get it when you turn twenty-one. That's not saying I still won't pay for your school and other needs. I will. I'd do anything for you. But you needed a reason to come with me. You didn't like that you were hurting over your mum, and about my intentions, so you wanted to lash out. When you refused to come, it wasn't because you didn't want to, it was because you were protecting yourself. Being forced into coming and making out you were only here for the money, you did just that. But it was a lie."

On shaky legs, I move towards her bed, sitting down on the edge. I suck in a breath, the pain hitting my chest.

She's right.

She summed up everything I had been feeling when I couldn't. Maybe I'm forgiving her too easily, maybe I was too hard to begin with, I don't know. I just know I can't keep living like this. I want to start enjoying life.

"No one has ever wanted me, Nova. Not my mum, and all my life, my dad was on that list. I put my trust in you without even realising I had done it, and you lied to me," I explain, holding my hand up when she goes to speak. "And I understand why you lied, but I don't have to like it. I'm tired of trying to figure out your motives, tired of not feeling safe or wanted. I need you to be straight with me, to tell me if me being here is what you wanted or if it was out of obligation."

She sits up straighter, rolling the blanket off her chest and into her lap. "I swear to you, with everything I am, that I've never had a hidden agenda for you being here. There are no more secrets. This isn't a game to me. You aren't a pawn. You are my niece and I love you."

I nod, feeling a lump in my throat. Shaking it off, I look at Nova and sigh. "No more mushy shit because this isn't me, either."

She laughs, sounding lighter than she has in a while. "All right, but before we stop with the heart to heart, I need you to know that I'm sorry for how I've handled things. It will change."

"Did you get the email?" I ask, and her face pales.

"I did. I've forwarded the email to the officer in charge of the case. They're looking into it. But there's something you should know about Neil Tucker."

"He was arrested earlier this morning, I know."

"You know?" she asks. "How?"

I explain everything that has happened from the moment I left earlier until the moment I got back. She stares at me in shock, her eyes wide and her mouth agape.

"I'm going to tan their hides. How dare they treat my niece with such disrespect! Their mother is going to kill them," she shrills. She tries to get out of bed but gets tangled in the blanket.

I can't help the laugh that slips free as I push her back down. "It's okay. I'm not made of glass."

She stops trying to leave and looks up at me. "I'm getting that, sweetheart, but they can't get away with behaviour like that. Why didn't you come to me?" she asks. As soon as the question slips past her lips, though, her eyes widen at the realisation. "You didn't trust me to protect you."

I shrug, not bothering to lie. "I didn't know you. You might be my aunt, but they were more of a family to you than I was."

"I'm going to prove to you that I'm always on your side. But you need to trust me. Just let yourself trust me."

"I'll try," I concede.

"Nova!" Selina yells from the distance. "Nova, Ivy's gone. I couldn't find her anywhere at school."

"Shit!" I curse, mad at myself for not texting her.

She comes barging into the room, her face as pale as a sheet of paper. "We need to call the police," she bursts out. Her gaze lands on me and she trips over her own feet. "You're here."

"I'm sorry. Some stuff happened this morning and I had to leave. I forgot to text you."

She rushes at me full force, knocking me back onto the bed. "You're here," she cries. I'm stumped at her behaviour. I try to wriggle free but pause when I realise she's crying. "You're safe."

"Selina, I say this with love, but you have to stop crying."

She continues to sob, and I glance up at Nova, who has tears brimming in her eyes as she watches on.

"Don't look at me," she says, holding her hands up.

I roll my eyes. "Selina," I call out louder, "stop crying." I can't deal with this kind of emotion. I have no idea what to do. Mum used to cry a lot, but earlier on in my life, anytime I tried to comfort her, she would lash out and scream at me, blaming me for all her problems.

Selina pulls back, yanking out a hanky from inside her blazer and dabbing her eyes. "When I couldn't find you, I asked around. No one else had seen you either. But then Clarissa Whitmore—who, by the way, is scary as hell—said you ran out of first lesson after what sounded like a horror movie played from your laptop, and that Kai followed you. I thought he had hurt you again."

I soften a little at that, also feeling relieved that no one suspected what the sound of the recording was. "It's a long story, but I'm fine. Why are you back so early?"

She wipes the palms of her hands down her skirt, looking away. "I told the sports teacher it was that time of the month and didn't have anything with me. I was worried, okay."

"Why don't we have a movie night later? We can order food for dinner," Nova offers.

"Don't you have work?" Selina asks, looking adorably confused, her lips set in a pout.

Nova laughs lightly. "I've decided to take some time off. It's not like I can't afford not to."

"True!" Selina agrees. "Movie it is. Let me go get changed, and then we can make some popcorn and pig out on junk food."

"Ivy?" Nova calls, gaining my attention.

Seeing hope shining through her eyes, I can only nod. "I'll go get changed into something more comfortable and meet you downstairs."

"No rush," Nova tells me.

♡

STEPPING INTO MY room, I head straight for my wardrobe, wanting to put on some joggers. A scream slips past my lips when I fall to the floor, tripping over the pile of presents I left in here last night.

"Seriously!" I growl.

I sit up on my arse, glancing at the pile. I don't get why they got me presents; for one, I'm too old for them.

I'm not going to lie and say I'm not curious as to what's in them. Sighing, because I know they'll get offended if I don't open them, I reach over and grab the first one, tearing open the pale pink paper that looks like Ethan got a two-year-old to wrap.

I cover my mouth to smother the giggle when a large black vibrator is revealed, a note Sellotaped to the front.

In case my brother doesn't do it for you.

Shaking my head, I grab the next parcel, this one from Selina. I smile at the brand-new Kindle with a hundred-pound gift card attached. I open her card next, a smile still on my face.

We may be cousins, but you are more like a sister to me, so it's my right to tell you what to spend this gift card on. Inside the box is a list of my all-time favourite books. READ THEM!
Happy birthday, Ivy.
Love Selina.

Nova's present is next, and I open the small box, revealing a silver necklace.

"It was your mum's," Nova says, causing me to scream and drop the box to the floor.

I gasp for breath, looking up at her. "You scared me half to death. I'm getting kind of sick of people sneaking up on me."

"Our nan gave it to her for her Holy Communion," she continues, ignoring my outburst.

Picking up the necklace, I take a closer look. Mum's name is engraved into the heart, a silver cross charm next to it.

"It's beautiful," I admit.

Nova takes a seat, leaning against the wardrobe door. "I wanted you to have something of hers from before she broke. She would have wanted that."

"Thank you," I tell her around the lump in my throat.

"I got you these," she says, handing me a gift bag. Inside are art supplies, and something stirs in my chest. Drawing wasn't something I did as a hobby. We never had anything for me to use when I lived with Mum, but I loved taking art when I was in school. It was my favourite lesson.

A sparkly blue box sits at the bottom, and I pull it out, unwrapping the paper. My eyebrows draw together when I see a set of keys.

She smiles. "I know we haven't gotten around to booking your lessons, but you have a car in the garage waiting for when you do."

"Really?" I breathe out, stunned.

"Yes. But you have to be safe. No galivanting around town joyriding."

I arch my eyebrow. "Have you seen your town? It's so small I'd be breaking every two minutes."

She laughs. "There is that. But we are surrounded by a lot of country roads."

"Thank you. I can't believe you all got me something," I tell her, trying to hide how much this has affected me. I'd pretended I didn't care about them, that in putting them aside I could forget they were even there.

"Of course we would, and you're most welcome," she tells me softly. "Who is that one from?"

I blush as I pull the box from Lucca away from my clothes. "I think it might be best if I open this when you aren't here."

She reads my face and laughs. "If I know those boys as well as I think I do, I can only imagine, but you have nothing to worry about."

Curious, I tear open the paper, beaming when a black skateboard is revealed. I pull it out of the box, turning it over, and on the bottom of the board, written in a graffiti style font, it says, 'Monroe', with a small tag on the bottom of the 'e' saying 'Poison Ivy'. Their geek reference makes me laugh, even if it could be taken as an insult. Still, I love the original Batman movies they made me watch once.

I frown when something occurs to me. "I have nowhere to ride this. You have gravel on the drive and the patio out back is surrounding a pool I still haven't learned to swim in."

She beams at me, clapping her hands. "Then it's a bit of a good job that Kaiden's present is a skateboard ramp."

"No way," I breathe out, dropping the board into my lap.

"Yes. I'm surprised you haven't seen it. It's located in the back, near the tree you love to read under."

"How did he even know I loved my skateboard?" I murmur.

She reaches over, patting my hand. "I guess he paid more attention to you than you realised."

"He never let on. We did talk a lot towards the end. It was different between us the night of the fire, but I never realised he cared enough to absorb the things I told him."

"It pains me to say this after I know what they did to you, but he does care. I'm not making excuses for him, but he's had a hard time letting people in. When he was a boy, not knowing or understanding what was transpiring around him, he was so happy and full of energy. But then his mum overdosed the first time and he changed. I've watched him struggle over the years to let people in. He was polite and cordial to me, but to others he was obnoxious and wary. He let you in before he even realised himself. I think he saw a kindred spirit in you."

"Why? Because both our mums used drugs to escape?"

She forces a smile. "No, because you were both neglected by those who were meant to care for you."

I lean back against my shelves, sighing. "What am I supposed to do with this? I'm not ready, if ever, to go back to how things were. I don't know who to trust."

"Oh, Ivy, I'm sorry," she tells me gently. "The only advice I can give you is to follow your heart. What do you have to lose?"

I look up at her, blinking rapidly to stop the tears threatening. "You. I have all of you to lose. And although I know I'll survive on my own, I don't want to. I'm fed up of trying to be tough. I'm tired of fighting."

My admittance brings tears to her eyes. She dabs under them with her sleeve. "I really wish you'd let me hug you."

I carefully slide my arse back a bit, worried she'll hug me anyway. And I can't be hugged right now, it makes me uncomfortable. "Let's not go getting mushy."

"All right. But you aren't going to lose me. We're family. I wish to God every day that things were different. I hate that even though you accept being here, you are still on the fence. All we can do is prove our loyalty to you," she explains, taking a deep breath. "I learn from my mistakes, Ivy. You can push me and push me, but I'm not going anywhere. I'm not going to give up. And it's fine, because it's no hardship showing you."

"Thank you," I tell her, looking to the floor.

"Why don't you go out and try your new skateboard? I'm sure Selina won't mind delaying dinner and a movie. She's on the phone to someone anyway. I think it's the boy I heard her flirting with."

Ah, so there is a boy.

I look down at the board once more and grow excited. "You sure you don't mind?"

"No. Go! Have fun!"

We both lift ourselves up from the floor, and I want to squeal with excitement. I've not been on one in so long. I can't wait. Nova laughs when I rip my shirt off, opting to change into a tight tank.

When I hear her leaving, I remember my manners and yell, "Thank you," over my shoulder.

I squeal, jumping up and down. "This is going to be awesome."

chapter thirteen

KAIDEN

"This is going terribly," I hear Ivy curse.

My lips twitch into a smile as I watch her brush away the dust on her arse. She told me once that she was good at skateboarding, but for the last thirty minutes, I've watched her fall on her arse more times than not.

Sweat glitters over her chest, and I can't help but be drawn to the soft globes of her tits. She's fucking hot; curves in all the right places and an arse I love to dig my fingers into. But watching her on a skateboard has got to be the hottest thing I've ever seen in my life. The way her body bends at the waist as she balances on the board, the twist of her hips when she spins at the top of the ramp, and the way her entire face lights up with happiness… it's captivating. That is, until she falls and starts cursing at the board like it's going to reply.

"Having fun?" I call out, gripping the lowest bar at the top of the ramp and pulling myself up and through them to take a seat on the platform at the top.

She screams, falling down the slope once more, cursing a blue streak as she glares up at me. "That's it! I'm buying fucking bells for you all to wear around your necks."

Laughing, I watch as she gets up, getting a great clear view of her cleavage. I inwardly groan, readjusting my dick as it begins to get hard.

"Sorry?"

"Stop sneaking up on me. I won't be surprised if I go into heart failure soon."

"Sorry," I reply.

Her lips twist and a crease forms between her eyes. "You aren't really sorry, are you?"

"Nope," I tell her through a chuckle.

"Prick!"

"I thought you could skate?"

"I can—well, I could. It's been a long time," she explains. "Thank you for getting me this." She looks up at me and flinches, like she's only just realising who she's talking to. "What are you doing here, Kai?"

"I went to see if Nova was okay and heard you out here."

Exhaling harshly, she runs up the ramp and grabs the edge, before pulling herself up and taking a seat across from me, leaning her back against the bars.

"She's doing better. I've spent so much time disliking her that I didn't stop to think how she was truly feeling. It was always a case of: she betrayed my mum, and she betrayed me by not helping me whilst I was growing up."

"She didn't do it on purpose. I know you don't trust me, but trust that Nova, no matter what went on between her and your mum, would have done right by you. She's a good person. She's been there for me and the twins a lot over the years."

"She said she was best friends with your mum," she murmurs, and I hate that she feels like she can't ask anything personal. I hate that the old Ivy is gone, the one who didn't care what came out of her mouth.

"She was. They all were; your mum, Grant's mum, mine and Nova. My mum called me earlier," I admit. I've not even told the twins she called, not wanting to get their hopes up. Legally, we are old enough to look after ourselves, but maturity in regards to the twins is still debatable. Which is why we need her back. We need her to deal with the fallout Dad has caused before we lose everything.

"She did?" she asks, raising her eyebrow.

I let out a dry chuckle, shaking my head. "She's soft yet strong, so I never know which mum I'll get. She wanted out of the marriage before it ever really began, but Dad wouldn't let her. She was worried about what he would do if she ran. Grant's mum, Flora, tried and died doing it. She planned to follow her that night and leave, but the call about the crash came in and she panicked. That night she started drinking."

"Is it true that she's been sober for a few years?" she asks softly.

I run my fingers through my hair, growing frustrated. "Yeah. She's been in the background, fixing the messes Dad has been making, slowly giving him less control over everything. It doesn't matter though. He has our name and that alone holds power."

"Is she coming back?"

"Honestly?" I ask, and she nods. "Not for a while. She doesn't feel it's safe yet. She wanted me to pass on a message."

"A message? For who?"

"You," I admit.

"Me?" she asks, sitting up straighter and crossing her legs.

"She wanted you to know that when your mum left, she had her followed. After a few months, she went to her, and it was then she found out she was pregnant with you. Mum got her help."

My heart squeezes at the pain in her expression. I can see it as clearly as I can see her. She pales, sitting forward. "Did she get it?" she chokes out.

"Your mum begged her for it. She said she would tell you the rest when she's back."

"But that could take forever," she yells, and I hold my hand up, stopping her from killing the messenger.

"Mum won't make you wait long. She said you've waited long enough to hear the truth."

"Did she tell you?" she asks, her eyes narrowing.

"No. That was all she would tell me."

"This is so fucked up. How did my life get to this? I never cared about anything my mum did or said, nothing. It was all the same. And now, since I've been here, I've wanted to know more, to uncover the truth. She wasn't born the way she was—I get that now—but it doesn't hurt any less to hear it could have been different. I have your dad out for blood, your ex wanting to kill me, and yet this is still the safest I've ever felt."

"That's because you are. I won't let him hurt any of you again," I vow.

"You can't promise that. He's your dad."

"He's nobody to me right now, Ivy. And it's not because of you—even though you are the main reason I got my head out of my arse. But it's been a long time coming. I'm your best chance of finding him."

"You?" she asks dubiously.

My lips twitch into a smirk. "Yeah. I've got someone looking into his whereabouts. And if anyone can find him, it's the team I hired. They're good at what they do."

A solemn look passes over her face when her gaze locks with mine. "I don't think you'll have to look far."

"Why do you say that?"

"Because he's Royce. He won't let me get away with destroying his life. I made an enemy of him the day I was born and I didn't even know it. He's not going to stop until I'm dead."

A sense of foreboding slivers through me. "He won't get the opportunity."

Her phone, which is lying on her jacket, beeps with an incoming message. She picks it up, reading the screen and sighs. "I need to go."

"Stay," I plead, but she gathers up her things before looking over at me.

"I need space. I've had so much thrown at me since the day I arrived, I've not known what's left or right. I might have come across like I had my shit together, may have even told myself I did, but I've been a fucking mess inside. I've been conflicted over everything, so right now, I need to get my head straight. I'm eighteen and need to grow the fuck up, stop playing childish games, and do something with my life," she explains, rubbing at her chest. "When I woke up in that hospital, everything changed once again. It wasn't about being categorised as the rich or the poor anymore. It was life. Our worlds exploded into one and I'm no longer the girl who had nothing. I need to get to know who she is and what she really wants."

I watch her closely, hearing the truth in her words and seeing the determination to get what she wants. I couldn't be fucking prouder, because even with no money, living in a flat, she was made to do big things.

I jump down from the ramp, stepping up to her. Her breath hitches and the swell of her breasts rise and fall with each breath. I tuck a strand of hair behind her ear, gazing into her eyes.

"I'm not going anywhere. Whether you want to believe me or not, what we had was real. It might not have been conventional, but it was raw. I'm not going to give that up. I'm not going to give *you* up. Being with you changed me, changed the path I was leading," I tell her, stepping even closer, so our bodies are flush. She takes in a shaky breath, her eyelids fluttering, and I inwardly smirk.

"Kai," she whispers, briefly squeezing her eyes shut.

"You don't want this to end any more than I do. Deep down, you're just conflicted. You're worried what people will think—" I start, but the feral growl at the back of her throat cuts me off.

"I don't give a fuck what people think of me."

I smirk, seeing the fiery Ivy I know and adore. "But you think society would think you are crazy for being with me."

"I am crazy for wanting you," she blurts out, her eyes round.

I smile, inwardly puffing my chest out with pride. "But you want me," I demand.

"Kaiden, I can't do this," she whines.

"I'll let you go—for now," I tell her, and I watch her shoulders droop with relief. "But I won't stay away for long."

Her entire body tenses as she glares up at me. "I might be putting the bitch façade away for a bit, but that doesn't mean I'll let you or any other person walk all over me. I can't make you stay away, Kaiden. I can't. But don't start crying when your smothering is the reason I stay away completely."

"You wouldn't." I curse.

"Then give me fucking space," she snaps. "If you care, you'd do this for me, for us. I'm telling you I want to change my perspective on life and start living. I need to grow up and make something of myself. You need to respect that or walk away. Our relationship is the definition of complicated and we need to be on the same page before we even think of starting this back up."

"We will start back up," I demand. "I'm not letting you fucking go. I'll give you time, but don't expect me to act like you don't exist."

She snorts, rolling her eyes. "Good of you."

She turns and leaves. I twist around and punch the tree trunk, cursing. My knuckles split and I clench and unclench my fist, already feeling it begin to swell.

She's makes me so fucking mad. Why can't she see how much I want her, need her? I want to be there for her.

"You love her," Grant states, and I spin around, finding him lurking behind the tree.

"What the fuck are you doing out here?" I demand, walking over to him.

He shrugs, pushing his hands in his pocket. I left him in bed, resting, when I got the phone call from Mum.

"I wanted to apologise to her. I always felt this darkness inside of me, but I told myself over and over that it was okay because I'd never truly hurt anyone. I lost my mind when she arrived, Kai, and did some fucked up shit. I don't know how I can move past this. I need her to know I'm sorry."

"Hey," I softly call out. "We all did some pretty messed up shit, Grant. We all have a lot to learn from her."

"Yeah," his whispers, glancing up at the sky and closing his eyes. When he reopens them, his expression is dark. "She's never going to make it at that school with Danielle there."

I lean back against the tree, wincing at the throbbing pain in my knuckles. "She's stronger than we ever gave her credit for."

"Danielle's up to something, and we all know she doesn't have a soul."

"Yeah, but Ivy has us," I remind him.

"It doesn't matter, not if we're too broken to fix ourselves," he snaps.

"Speak for yourself," I snidely reply.

He laughs without humour. "Bro, you are so broken you have missing pieces. We all are. And your love for her will cloud your judgement. You won't be able to do what's necessary to protect her."

"I don't fucking love her," I bark. "And I'll lay my life down for hers. She deserves to be free, Grant. She deserves to have a life, to not have conflict and torment in it. I'll do everything in my power to make sure she gets it, so you don't need to worry about it."

He scoffs, pulling a face. "You can't even admit you're in love with her."

"That's because I'm not."

He shakes his head. "You are. There's been no other chick you've gotten this hard for. You're obsessed with her. And I bet if it turned out she was lying about her mum and the recording, you'd still want her. You wanted her the minute she pulled up. Stop lying to yourself," he says, with a pang of pity in his tone.

"I'm not in fucking love with her," I repeat, but the words turn sour in my mouth. I care deeply for Ivy, but love? I growl, running my hand over my jaw. "I don't."

"When you realise you do, let me know, because you'll need my help with those bitches at school."

I glare up at him. How dare he insinuate I can't protect her. "She's fucking mine," I bark. "And if you've forgotten, you tried to kill yourself a few hours ago."

He grabs me by the scruff of my shirt. "Don't fucking mention it again."

He shoves at my chest and I stagger back two steps. I straighten, glaring him. "So, you're going to act like it didn't happen?"

"No, I'm not. I would have done it without regret. It doesn't mean I'm weak. I just wanted the anger, resentment and pain to stop. Once I realised it was true, I didn't want Ivy seeing my face every day, being a reminder of what he did to her mum or what I did to her. I didn't want to look in the mirror and see the person I've become. I have nothing, Kai. Nothing. It's all gone and there's nothing I can do about it. But you talked me down today, gave me a reason to keep going, to find redemption. It's going to start with Ivy. It might not make what's happened right, but I'll have done more than my dad ever would have. And I'm telling you, she's not safe at that school. Danielle has been recruiting girls in their hall."

"You give Danielle credit where it's not warranted. She might be a bitch, but not all of the girls in the school are like her. And I'll be ready. I've got a few people watching out for Ivy already. I've also hacked into the school security system," I tell him. "I'm sorry for what I said. I didn't mean it to come out that way. I'm here for you, always. We aren't our dads and Ivy doesn't think we are either."

"Yeah, I guess," he murmurs, not sounding convinced. "I'm going to head back to the house. I still feel like I've got more to throw up."

"It's going to be okay," I tell him, needing him to know that. I'm not making excuses for him, but I refuse to turn my back on someone who's been my friend my whole life.

"I hope so," he tells me, walking away. He pauses a few feet away, turning back to me. "Hey, did my lawyer leave a message with you?"

"Lawyer?" I ask, frowning. "I've not spoken to one."

"I'll ask the twins. When I called him back, his receptionist answered and said he left a message with a Mr Kingsley."

"Ask Ethan. He brought your shit into the house."

"You not coming in?"

I glance at Monroe Manor and back at the ramp. "Nah, I'm going stay out here. I need to think."

"Well, don't think too hard. You might cause permanent damage."

"Fuck you!"

He forces a smile. "Just be careful. Your dad is going to have heard mine got caught and he's going to get desperate. He's going to want the evidence destroyed."

"What?" I call out, and he pauses, taking a few steps closer before looking around to make sure no one is listening.

"When I went to see my dad this morning, his lawyer kept questioning the evidence. It's only reliable if it's the original, otherwise they can say it was altered."

I frown, wondering if that claim would work. "I'm sure Nova has already got it in a safe somewhere. She won't give it to the police. She doesn't trust that Dad won't pay someone off to get it."

"Like I said, be careful."

I nod, watching him for a moment before jumping back up the ramp, lying down on my back on the platform.

Life has never been simple—we all have issues—but lately, I feel like we can't catch a break.

Ivy's right. We do need to grow up. I don't want to wake up one day in twenty years and realise I'm just like my dad. I want to be better. *I am* better.

But if anyone comes at what is mine, nothing will stop me from unleashing hell on them.

Ivy might need time, but nothing—not even my dad—will stop me from protecting her. I don't run. I fight for what is mine. And she's mine. She has been since the moment she arrived in Cheshire Grove.

chapter fourteen

IVY

"SOMETHING'S CHANGED WITH YOU," Selina comments, looking up from her phone.

"I'm surprised you've noticed. You've been glued to that phone all morning," I retort when we pull up outside the Academy.

"I'm still listening and paying attention. Something's changed. What is it?"

I grab my belongings off the floor before looking over at her. She's watching me, and it's unnerving.

I shrug, glancing away. "It just hit me that I need to grow up. If I'm going to stay here, I need to embrace the life Nova is gifting me with."

"And Nova? I noticed you seemed more relaxed around her."

"She's my aunt. I'm sick of pretending I don't give a shit about anything."

"You don't?" she teases.

I chuckle. "Okay, I don't really give a shit about anything; some things aren't worth caring about. I'm not one of those girls who has an issue with every little detail of their life or gets crazy about minimal things."

"That's true! I'm glad you are working on things with her. She might not be married to Sam anymore, but she's always been my aunt. She's helped me a lot over the years, and if she was given a chance, she would have done the same with you. It doesn't hurt that she isn't a snob like most of the people in our lives. She's actually pretty down to earth."

I laugh, dropping my hand away from the door handle. "You are kidding, right? When I first met her, she was so formal and stiff. I think it's why I instantly took a dislike to her. I couldn't trust her. She reminded me of a few of the teachers who worked at my old school," I explain, and when she opens her mouth, I hold my hand up. "I know that isn't who she is. I can understand, to a degree, why she kept a lot from me. It doesn't hurt any less, but I'm going to push myself through it. If you had asked me a few weeks ago, I would have told you I hated her and I was leaving."

"Then why did you stay?"

"I guess my subconscious wouldn't let me. It could be because I have selfish reasons for not wanting to go. I've had a lot of time since the accident to think about it, and each time I'll make excuses for my behaviour. But there aren't any. I'm going to give her a chance because whether I like it or not, I need her. I want to have someone I can turn to. For people with money, it's easy to go out into the world and live, but for me and others like me, it's scary. I'd have no family, no friends, nothing. And I'm so goddamn scared I'll end up like my mum, living off benefits and stealing from men who come in and out of my life."

"You aren't selfish for wanting a better life. Everyone in this world wishes for something, Ivy, and I bet most of them wish for the same thing. It's life. It's hard, cruel and scary, but there's also happiness, laughter and love, if you let it in. I don't want you to leave. I'd probably follow you, because I'd miss you like crazy."

I think about it for a moment and nod. "I'd miss your crazy arse too. But I'm warning you now, so you're prepared; if I find out Nova has kept anything else from me, I'm leaving. I can't be around tainted and messed up people anymore. I want to be around people I can trust and who have my back. I'm not saying I trust her—I think it will take a lot of time to build that between us—but I do want to."

"She won't let you down, none of us will," she declares before taking a deep breath. "Let's get today over with. We don't have classes tomorrow and I want to relax and work on my tan before summer leaves us for good."

I chuckle as I push open my door. "You've just jinxed it. This has been the longest, hottest summer I've ever known."

She waves her hand at me, frowning. "I had my fingers crossed when I said it, so we're good."

I roll my eyes because she believes that shit will make a difference.

"What do you have first?" she asks when she finishes reading her message.

"Literacy then Art."

"I won't see you until lunch, then. Just text me when you're done and I'll meet you. I don't have anything after my first class until after lunch."

"All right," I tell her, pulling the map out of my bag. I find where I need to go then tell Selina my goodbyes.

♡

HAVING MADE IT through my first lesson, I can't help but compare the Academy to my old school. I understand one was high school and this is a private university/college, but the differences in teaching and how they are run are so contrast.

It wouldn't hurt the wealthy to donate funds to those in real need instead of to a school that is exceptionally modernised. If my old school could have afforded white boards or even projection boards, I might have done better. Instead, I struggled to make out what was written on the chalk boards.

Still in my own head and thinking how outrageous this school is on technology, I don't feel someone walk up behind me until it's too late.

"Put me down, Lucca," I plead, ignoring the people staring openly at us.

He drops me to the floor, puffing out a breath. "I thought we were friends again."

I sigh, glaring over at him. "Who said we were friends to begin with?"

He smirks, knocking his shoulder into mine playfully. "You did. You said, Lucca, you are the bestest friend a girl could wish for."

"You need friends," I mutter dryly.

"But we're cool, right?" he asks, his voice lower so we can't be overheard.

I stop near a set of double doors and face him. "Did you know any of it?"

He scans the hallway before frowning down at me. "If you're asking if I knew my dad was a monster, yes, but if you're asking if I knew about your mum, then no. We didn't have a clue. Growing up, Kaiden shielded us from a lot," he explains honestly. "I know Ethan and I have explained why we did what we did when we first met you, and had we known the entire situation, there would have been no way we would have taken it that far. It doesn't excuse what we did, I know. We're ashamed."

I run my fingers through my hair, pushing it away from my face. "Don't change, Lucca. I'm not saying to go around groping girls—"

"Unless they're willing, right? We can still grope girls who want it?"

A small giggle slips past my lips and I shake my head at him. "Whatever. The point is, don't change for me. You and Ethan work being dicks. You aren't malicious or cruel unless it's aimed at someone who's hurt you. It's weird that you guys are being nice to me. It doesn't feel real or right."

He feigns hurt, placing the palm of his hand over his chest. "That wounds me. I thought we had something special," he teases before composing himself, his expression turning serious. "You're one of us now. We don't want to lose you. We've never had a girl in our group before, not one we've not wanted to shag anyway. I can't explain it, but since you arrived it feels like we're closer to each other. It's starting to feel more like a family."

The vulnerability in his voice is my undoing. My friendship with the twins has blossomed, and I can't help but have a soft spot for them.

"All right, but this doesn't mean you can sit with me at lunch," I warn him.

He pouts, blinking those eyelashes at me. "One lunch a week?"

"No," I tell him, walking past him so I'm not late to my next class.

"Come on, one lunch. I'm not asking for much," he states, following me. People watch him as he walks by, girls openly undressing him with their eyes and lads looking on with envy in their eyes.

"Will you go away?" I order, pushing him lightly.

"Not until you agree to sit with us for lunch."

"No!" I snap.

When he stops, I don't bother stopping to find out what has diverted his attention. Knowing Lucca, it's probably a girl.

"Ivy Monroe," he yells down the hall, and I pause at another set of doors, groaning. "Have lunch with us. Don't break my heart. Don't ruin this beautiful friendship. I'm sorry I broke your *Michael Myers* doll. I'm sorry I accidently burnt your voodoo dolls."

I groan when he continues to yell out freaky items, knowing I've never owned them.

Just when I'm ready to give in, Clary, the girl I met yesterday, is standing beside me, facing Lucca.

"Kingsley, go hassle someone who cares about your freakish fetishes."

"You love my fetishes. Admit it, Whitmore, you want me to handcuff you to my bed," he calls back, amusement in his voice. When I turn back, he's smirking at Clary.

Her lips twist in disgust. "I'd rather be tied up with wild animals than to your bed. Less chance of catching fleas—you know, with all the dogs you and your brother take to bed."

His smirk spreads into a grin. "But you admit that you want to be tied up?"

She shakes her head, clearly used to his behaviour. "Wouldn't you like to know," she flirts back, winking at him.

I hear him groan, but before I can say anything, she's grabbing my hand and pulling me through the door.

"Art major, right?" she asks.

I shake myself out of it, looking at her in wonder. "I am. How did you know? And, um, what was that back there? You totally handled Lucca."

She laughs, throwing her head back. "No one could ever handle those boys."

"Have you two gotten together?" I ask. I felt a sense of sexual tension between them.

"God no. Have you heard the rumours?"

I nod, wondering if I should say that it isn't true. "Yeah."

"Well, I wouldn't give a fuck if people thought I had them both—they're hot—but they annoy the hell out of me. I'd end up gagging one of them."

"Knew you were into kinky shit," Lucca murmurs, and Clary and I jump back, screaming.

"Bloody hell," she yells, laughing when she catches her breath.

"I hate you," I pant out, pushing his chest. "I'm buying fucking bells."

Through laughter, he manages to say, "I'm going to class. Try not to fantasise about me too much."

"Bells," I mutter, turning and bumping into a hard body. I look up, growing tense when my gaze locks with Kaiden's. I lick my suddenly dry lips and his gaze shoots down, following the movement, and I become aroused.

Shit!

"Bells?" he asks, his eyes twinkling.

"I warned you all to stop sneaking up on me," I tell him, feeling breathless.

"Hmm, so you did," he says, his gaze flicking to the side, to where Clary is waiting. "I'll see you soon, baby."

I give him a sharp nod, watching as he leaves, pushing through the double oak doors. The second he's gone, chatter resumes around me and I come out of my fog.

"Girl, you have it bad," Clary mutters. I open my mouth to deny it, but the words won't come out. "Just be careful with that one."

"I thought you liked the Kingsley's?" I ask, glancing over my shoulder once more.

"I said I liked the twins. Kaiden, on the other hand, can be a big jerk."

My lips twitch. "And yet, that's probably the nicest insult he's ever had."

She laughs. "True. There's no denying he's smoking hot though."

"True," I repeat, making her smile. "So, how did you know I have art?"

"The teacher, Mrs Swansea, had me help go through applications. And I'm guessing no one told you before, but Danielle is in this art class. It's basic draw and design. She's taking fashion and uses this lesson as a way to come up with new designs."

Art just got a lot less interesting for me. "You are kidding?"

"Sorry, I'm not. It's only this one class. It's broken up into three sections, but the teachers combine projects so you aren't overrun with work the first year. I didn't take it last year as I was in and out of school due to personal reasons."

Seeing sadness lurking in her eyes, I don't question her on why. Instead, I bump my shoulder against hers and give her a bright smile. I can see us being friends. She doesn't look or act like the other snobs I've met at this school. She's down to earth and not as nutty as Selina.

"Let's get this over with," I command, inwardly preparing myself for Danielle. It's not that I can't handle her, it's just that I don't want to.

We step into the classroom and I take in the art around me. Tons of paintings, drawings and framed work are hanging on the walls. There are shelves and shelves of supplies scattered around the room.

My eyes bug out at the huge work benches, with two stools at each station. There's four at the front of the room, each having drawers on the side of each station. Towards the back of the spacious room are drawing tables, each one with its own stool and a mini cabinet with what I would guess carry more supplies.

Something knocks into my shoulder, pushing me forward, further into the room. I face the culprit, finding Danielle standing there with a smug look on her face.

"I'm sorry, I didn't see you there," she offers sweetly. I roll my eyes because there was no way she missed me standing in the doorway.

"Whatever," I snap, glancing at Clary for guidance. I'm not sure where I'm meant to be sitting.

"We're at the work stations today," she explains.

"Aww, look at the two of you, already best buddies. Being a loner must have been getting to you, Clary. You'd make friends with anyone."

Clary puts on a full watt smile, and I can't help but be taken aback by her beauty. She's beautiful anyway, but when she smiles, she's something else.

"Careful, you're making me believe you want to be my friend—you know, showing all of this interest and all," Clary replies.

"You wish. The only friend you can get is *her*," Danielle remarks.

Clary's smile gets bigger as she places her hand over her heart. "Isn't she the best. I can sleep at night knowing I've got one friend in this God forsaken school."

"Freak," Danielle sneers, walking over to one of the drawing tables.

Thank fuck she isn't near me.

A woman with ash-blonde hair tied into a bun on the top of her head walks into the room, immediately stepping up to the desk at the front.

She looks up, scanning the room until her eyes land on me. "Ivy Monroe?"

"Yes," I answer, dropping my bag to the floor and taking a seat next to Clary.

"Welcome to Kingsley Academy. I'm looking forward to seeing some of your work," she tells me. "Let me get everyone settled and I'll get you up to speed on what we've been doing."

"Okay."

A young lad steps up to her, whispering something so the rest of us can't hear. She nods then glances at Clary. "Clary, can you get Ivy started? I just need to step out for five minutes."

"Of course, Mrs Swansea."

Once she's gone, Clary leans in closer. "She has a son at the school who likes to get into trouble. Her husband, his dad, is on the schoolboard, so he gets away with a lot of shit."

Before I have chance to reply, a bad smell looms around us. I huff under my breath, peering up at Danielle. "I'm starting to think you are in love with me."

She smiles, resting her palms on the edge of the work station opposite me. "It's a shame about you and Kaiden."

"I bet," I mutter, not commenting further.

"It's okay, he's in good hands. I've been taking really good care of him."

I grip the edge of the table, ready to end this, but Clary rests her hand on my knee, stopping me.

"You know, I've always wondered something, Danielle."

Slowly, Danielle glances at her, her lip curled. "What? How to do your hair?"

Danielle's friends chuckle. Clary doesn't seem fazed, clearly used to their insults, yet I'm gritting my teeth, wanting to put the bitch in her place.

"No, I'm just curious; I thought Barbies couldn't bend their knees, but you clearly spend a lot of time on them. How is Mr Hackett?"

I gag in my mouth as I stare up at Danielle with wide eyes. Her face reddens as she leans across the bench, her hand raised. "You bitch!"

Clary stands quickly, grabbing her hand and shoving it against the hard wood. "Ever raise your hand to me again and you'll regret it. Your sheep might be scared of you, but I'm not."

"You'll regret this!" Danielle spits.

"What, are you going to get the girls here to trash my room, take my clothes and put them all over the courtyard? What are you really going to do? Look around you, Danielle. No one likes you. No one cares for your bullshit. Not every girl will fall in line with you," she snaps, then pointedly looks at the girl standing next to her. "Not all are scared little sheep."

"We will see," Danielle snaps.

"Yes, we fucking will."

Danielle turns her anger on me. "I told you Kaiden would come running back to me. He's mine. Stay away."

"Scared he'll want me still?" I goad, smiling now.

She snorts, shaking her head. "He only fucked you to prove he could to all his friends. I'm the girl he'll marry."

I lose the smile, shaking my head sadly at her. "You have all this wealth to do something with your life, yet you are determined to have a man who will provide for your materialistic things. You don't want Kai. You hardly fucking know him. You just want what his name can give you. And if you think he'll ever fall for that, you are mistaken."

"I know Kai better than you. Trust me, we've come to learn each other very well over the years," she explains suggestively.

"Yes," I retort, "you had great sex, but did he ever talk to you, tell you his likes or dislikes? Did he tell you his secrets, cuddle you while you watched movies or hold your hair while you threw up? No, because you were nothing more than a warm body he fucked."

The corners of her eyes tighten as her lips curl into a sneer. "You think you are special, but you aren't. I'll show you," she snaps, her voice low. "I'll show you all."

I wait for her to leave before turning to Clary. "She won't sing, will she? I mean, I'm all for a musical, but her voice already grates through me. Hearing her sing will kill me."

Clary throws her head back, laughter pouring out of her like music.

"We are going to be great friends," she tells me, leaning into me.

"We are," I agree before turning serious. "Do Barbies really not bend at the knee?"

She laughs louder, and the few students in the room stop to listen. Hearing her laugh helps ease my tension after what just happened.

I'm not bothered by what Danielle has to say. I couldn't care less about her full stop. But what has me worried is her infatuation with Kaiden. It's not healthy. She's delusional and that's dangerous, especially when his rejection isn't registering, not even when he's a wanker about it.

But I can't fix that for him. I've got my own issues with Danielle and fighting over Kaiden isn't one of them.

chapter fifteen

KAIDEN

THE LOCKER ROOM SMELLS OF SWEAT as me and Kyle walk into the changing rooms. We stayed behind to talk to our cricket coach and umpire. Our team have a big game coming up, and although it isn't something I'll pursue after I finish here at the Academy, a few members of the team are counting on being picked up by a manager after. They are pushing themselves to be the best, but some aren't taking it as seriously as others and it's showing on the pitch. I don't want to get involved, but Kyle thinks they'll listen to me.

I walk over to Zac and Neil, two of the best players the Academy has seen in years, to fill them in. Zac is one of the kids who won the funding for his place here. He's a good kid and fits in well. Usually when outsiders come, they find it hard to fit in. Neil's father was once a cricket player and was a legacy here.

"Coach is going to have a word with the rest of them. If they aren't doing their part, they're off the team, but I'll have a word with each of them myself."

"Thanks, man. I'm counting on this game. I need someone to pick me up or all of this will have been for nothing," Zac informs me.

"It will get sorted," Neil tells him.

I give them a chin lift before grabbing my towel off my peg and heading into the showers. It doesn't take me long, and when I come out, a towel wrapped around my hips, the guys are still finishing up, chatting amongst themselves.

"I'm going to fuck her," Jason, a scrawny kid who doesn't know his left from right, comments.

I inwardly snort, wondering if he's ever fucked anyone.

"I bet her cunt is tight," another comments.

"Don't care. Her arse is good enough for me. Have you seen it?" Simon groans, holding his hands out as if emphasising the size of the arse.

"I heard her mum was a slag, went through a lot of men and caused shit between families before she ran away, pregnant. If she's like her mum, we could all have a go," Derren hoots, and the guys cheer.

I stop reaching for my shirt when I register what they said. "Who are you talking about?"

Simon swallows nervously, which is further proof of who they are talking about.

Jason, clearly dense enough not to know when to stop, grins. "The new chick. Eve or Ivy. Who cares. Every hole's a goal, right? Am I right?" He holds his hand up for a high five, and I stare blankly at him. He looks around, still grinning. "You don't think she's hot?"

"Jason," Derren warns.

Jason's gaze flicks to Derren, and he frowns a little. "I'm going to ram her so fucking hard she'll be begging for seconds."

I grip his neck, slamming him against the locker.

"What the fuck?" he croaks, his fingers digging into my wrist.

"If you ever, and I mean *ever*, look in Ivy's direction, I'll fucking end you," I snap, slamming his head back against the locker. He falls to the floor, gasping for breath. "That goes for any of you. She's off limits. She's mine."

"Sorry, mate, we didn't know," Derren affirms.

"Now you do. Spread it around. If anyone tries anything, they'll answer to me," I warn him, and he gives me a sharp nod.

"And me," Grant says, stepping into the changing rooms. He looks around at the guys, glaring. "Go! Don't you have lunch?"

The guys scatter from the locker room as I take in Grant. He looks better than when I left him this morning.

"I thought you were staying at home?" I head over to my locker, pulling out my uniform.

"I was, but I got bored. Idle hands and all that."

"This three-sixty you've done with Ivy—Is it real?" I ask, still wary of his intentions. He's lost a lot, and he blamed her before with less evidence. We all did.

"Yeah," he grits out. "I wish you'd stop questioning me. I've fucked up a lot but it's going to change. I don't want to have to keep repeating myself."

I finish pulling my trousers up then look at him, seeing sincerity. "All right. But one wrong move and we're done. You do know that, right?"

He laughs. "You are so fucking in love with this chick and you can't even see it. You didn't even think on what I said last night, did you?"

"I'm not in love with her!" I bark.

"Yeah, mate, you are. You're willing to ruin a lifelong friendship over her."

I glare at him, gritting my teeth. "We've put her through enough. She deserves to be protected, Grant. You of all people should see that."

Disappointment flickers across his face. "You've done worse to others who didn't deserve it. Hell, you've unintentionally treated Danielle like crap for years. You've never cared what happens with her. You've never stuck up for her."

"Ivy's different. I can't explain it to you. The first time we met, she didn't even react. She didn't swoon. She doesn't lie or manipulate to get what she wants. She's a slap to reality, a taste of the real world, and I like it. I like how she makes me feel."

"Because you love her," he comments.

I take in a deep breath, trying to calm the anger simmering inside of me. I don't know how I feel. I just know she's more, more than someone I fuck, more than a willing body. She's a lot more.

"I don't fucking know how I feel."

"Feel about what?" Ethan asks, stepping into the room.

"Aw, are we having another heart to heart?" Lucca asks, walking in behind him.

"Fucking hell," Grant groans, sitting on the bench. "I've had enough of you two already."

"Aw, did me fucking Morgan last night keep you up?" Ethan asks, and I shake my head. They need to stop sleeping around before they get some chick pregnant.

"Morgan?" Lucca questions.

Ethan grins. "Yep. I might even fuck her again."

"Why are you two here? Shouldn't you be at lunch?" I snap before he goes into detail.

"We were on our way when we received this," Lucca says and walks over to us, holding his phone. He presses play on a video, and I take note of the room before taking a closer look.

"Is that the art room?"

"Yes, just watch."

"You know, I've always wondered something, Danielle."

The video only shows the back of the two girls sitting in front of Danielle, but there's no mistaking Ivy. The other girl is Clary Whitmore, the daughter of a rock star.

"What? How to do your hair?" Danielle snidely remarks, and her friends chuckle beside her.

"No, I'm just curious; I thought Barbies couldn't bend their knees, but you clearly spend a lot of time on them. How is Mr Hackett?"

The twins laugh, pausing the video. "Barbie," Lucca repeats, chuckling. "They didn't record it from the beginning, but Marcus said she insinuated she's been sleeping with you. The remarks go on for a while, but you should hear this bit."

He presses play once more, and I peer down at the phone, listening to Ivy fire back at Danielle at how better she knows me. The video clicks off and I look up at the twins.

"What happened after?" I demand. I'm getting sick of Danielle thinking she owns me. What would normally work to get a girl off your back hasn't worked with Danielle. She's persistent as ever.

"Danielle tucked tail and went back to her workstation, spent the entire lesson glaring daggers at Ivy."

"Even Ivy subconsciously knows you love her," Grant mutters.

The twins give him a dirty look, but it's Ethan who replies. "You're a little late to the party. We figured out he loved her when we found out they were sleeping together. A vendetta as strong as Kai's couldn't be forgotten for anything less. It was obvious."

"Fuck off!" Grant remarks, rolling his eyes.

Lucca grins. "Next time we'll keep you in the loop."

"Shut the fuck up!" I bark, handing him his phone back. "Where is she now?"

They shrug, glancing at each other and rolling their eyes. "We aren't her keeper, but if I were to guess, it would be at lunch."

I grab my bag and leave, hearing them chuckle amongst each other.

"Whipped," Ethan chuckles.

THE DINING HALL is loud when we step inside, the sounds of chatter and cutlery clinking against plates echoing off the walls. We usually eat in the rec room, but since this is where Ivy is eating, it's where we will be until she's back into the fold completely.

I take a seat with Kyle and the rest of the guys we hang out with, scanning the room for Ivy as I do.

"Hey, I heard Clary Whitmore is into some kinky shit," Rome comments, another long-time friend of ours. He'd been on vacation with his family over the holidays, so it's good to have him back.

Lucca leans forward, looking around Ethan to stare at Rome. "Fucking hell. Are the kids here in middle school? It's like Chinese whispers."

"What's up your arse?" Rome comments, giving Lucca a side eye as he shoves a sandwich in his mouth.

"Nothing. I made the joke earlier about Clary, but it's not true," he says, sitting back as he shrugs. "Just think it's pathetic how easily people repeat shit."

"You banging her?"

Lucca arches an eyebrow. "No offence, but you don't have a chance. She doesn't like morons."

Rome smirks. "Touché."

A set of hands stroke over my shoulders and down my chest. Warm breath tingles at my ears and I grow tense at the expression and vibe coming from Ethan as he stares at who's behind me.

"Hey, baby, want to go somewhere quiet for lunch?" Danielle purrs.

I push her hands off me, growling under my breath. I don't give her the attention she wants, instead staring right ahead. "Danielle, the desperation isn't becoming."

"Yeah, I thought I could smell something bad," Ethan chirps.

"You always come back to me. Why put off the inevitable?"

I grit my teeth and refrain from saying something that will truly embarrass her. I'm not bothered about her feelings, just what she'll do to Ivy in retaliation.

"Danielle, unless you want to cause a scene, I suggest you go, 'cause I'm barely holding back on what I truly want to say to you," I caution.

She leans back down; not as close, but close enough that I can smell the stench of her perfume. "Why, because of her?" she asks, then begins to cackle.

The second I look up, my gaze lands on Ivy. She takes a seat with Selina and Clary at a table of Selina's friends. She scans the room, biting her bottom lip, and I know she's trying to hide how overwhelmed she feels right now. The hall is packed with our lunch group.

My gaze narrows as Krysten and Jenny make their way through the tables, a plate of food in hand. Jenny turns back and says something to Krysten before they both start laughing.

The tightness in my gut expands as I read the expressions on their faces. I shove back my chair, almost knocking Danielle over in the process, and get up.

I clench my fists as Ivy shoots up from her seat, wiping hot bolognaise from her shirt and skirt. I might have missed exactly what happened, but it doesn't take a genius to figure it out. Krysten covers her mouth with one hand, pretending to be shocked, but I can see the amusement in her eyes. With her other hand, she holds the empty plate that once held her food.

Danielle cackles, and I slowly turn to face her, feeling a dark, red rage swarm through me. "You think that's funny?"

The laughter dies, and I watch with glee as a spark of fear flashes behind her eyes. She should be scared.

She gulps, straightening her back as a spiteful look fills her expression. "Hopefully someone takes the trash out along with the food. She doesn't belong here, and the quicker you see that, the better. She's making a joke of you," she chides, stepping closer. "How long before your status is revoked? People are already laughing at you."

She eyes me up and down once, shaking her head as if she pities me.

I lean forward, getting in her face, ignoring the commotion behind me. I know the twins will have Ivy's back until I get there. "I warned you. I gave you a chance I don't give others and you didn't heed. You won't see me coming, Danielle. I'm going to take everything precious from you," I promise, taking another step closer. "You ridicule Ivy for her past, but she's stronger than you'll ever be, holds more power than you ever will, because she can survive with nothing. What will you do when you have nothing? Because when I'm finished with you, that is exactly what you will have. Nothing."

I take a step back, enjoying the way her expression falls and her face pales.

I leave her to stew on my words and start my way over to Ivy. As I pass Rome, I pause, turning to him. "Find out everything you can about her, every little secret she holds dear. Start with Mr Hackett and her. Get everything on her friends too. I'm going to make sure she's alone when I take everything from her."

He nods. "You got it. I'll get on it now," he promises, leaving to do what he does best: hack and find hidden things.

I walk towards Ivy, smirking when I find her gripping the back of Krysten's neck, pinning her to the table.

"Teacher," Ethan calls out, and I see Selina whisper something to Ivy.

Ivy lets go, shoving Krysten to the floor. I can see the anger simmering in her eyes, and I know she held back.

I follow them out, giving a chin lift to the twins to let them know I've got it.

"That cow!" Selina curses. "Are you sure you're okay?"

"I'm good. I'm just pissed I have to wear these all fucking day. I don't think Mr Hackett will be pleased if I leave before the day's over to go get changed."

"I have a few spare uniforms in my room. I'm sure I've got your size," Clary offers.

Ivy watches her for a moment. "They've done this to others?"

Clary nods. "Yeah, mostly to the underprivileged kids who probably had to sell all their belongings to buy the damn uniform. It's a requirement here at Kingsley Academy, and you can't be in attendance without one."

"I didn't know," Selina whispers, her lips turning down.

"Why would you? You've only been here a few weeks. And at school, you always had your head in a book. When I noticed it happening last year, I got my dad to buy one of every size of the uniform and kept them in my room. I can't stand bullies and that's all Danielle and her friends are. The others do it because she says so, but she does it for the satisfaction. She gets off on it. I won't be like most of the others in this school who stand by and laugh."

Ivy laughs. "You look so rock chick, but you're a big softie."

"Tell people and I won't give you any more clothes," Clary snaps, making Ivy laugh harder.

Realising where they're going, I keep my head down and make my way to my car. Clary has a room at Kingsley Hall. I want to get Ivy alone, and if Selina sees me, she'll refuse to give us privacy. My best bet is to wait and see if I can catch them off guard.

By the time I reach the building, the girls are already here. I quickly log in to the school system, finding her floor and room number. I rush up the stairs, taking two at a time until I hit their floor. I pull my phone back out, ready to call the twins to come and distract Clary and Selina. But Selina's voice stops me.

I quickly move back into the stairwell, leaning in so I can hear what they're saying.

"We'll give you some privacy and go put these in the wash," Selina calls into the room, giving me the privacy I need.

"Do you remember where the T.V. room is?" Clary asks.

I don't hear Ivy's response, but whatever she says has the girls leaving, walking down the hall towards me. I quickly duck behind the door, knowing they'll take the elevator down to the basement where the washrooms are kept.

The second I hear the elevator ding its departure, I go get my girl.

chapter sixteen

IVY

THE LONG HALLWAY IS LINED WITH DARK oak doors on either side, the carpet wine-coloured, and gold-framed landscape pictures hang on the walls. The only modern decorations are the lights; double drum chandeliers. They fit into the hallways, though, since the tea light candle effect gives the space warmth and that old age feel the rest of the building has. That's not saying the building is old, it's not, but it's decorated with warmth. It has up-to-date features; the living area—or T.V. room, as Clary called it—is a prime example of that with its large T.V. system and added surround sound. The comfy furniture and the knick-knacks that decorate the room give it that modern feel. I only got a small glimpse of the room before we piled into the elevator, but not before I saw the wall-length, stone fireplace. It was beautiful.

"I don't get why you don't like staying here. It's sick," I murmur to Selina when we come to Clary's room.

She gives an undignified snort. "You've never stayed here. Most of these girls have had a strict upbringing, had rules on how to behave, how to sit, how to speak. Here, they are free and free is how they act. It's a mad house."

"I forgot you stayed here when you attended school," Clary comments, pushing open her door.

"Yes. Doing my A-levels with the racket going on was a nightmare. I was lucky I had Nova, but there were times my mum made me stay here to save face. She hated it when it got back to her friends that I was staying with my aunt."

"My dad hates that I stay here surrounded by snobs who think their shit don't stink. But it was the only place I was safe."

"Safe?" I repeat, watching her.

"My dad's a rock star. He's on tour more often than he's home. The second someone finds out who I am, I get attacked by the press and fans who think they can meet him through me. Here, the people don't care. I'm just a girl."

"Holy crap, you have girl stuff," Selina blurts out, spinning to face Clary with wide eyes.

Clary takes it all in good faith, laughing. "Just because I dress mostly in black and have tattoos and piercings, it doesn't mean I don't like girl stuff. Put pink in my face and we won't be friends," she warns Selina.

I head over to one of the shelves that has rows of snow globes on. "These are beautiful," I murmur, picking up the one that has Mickey and Minnie Mouse inside.

She walks over to see which one I have. "That's what I got when I went to Disneyland Florida. I collect them. It was a thing my dad started whenever he went on tour. The ones with a circle on the bottom are the ones my dad bought. The ones without are the places I've visited."

"It's beautiful," I tell her, wishing I had a memory like this I could share about my mum.

Not wanting to bring up those memories right now, I put the snow globe back and turn to the girls. "I can't let her get away with it. I'm pretty sure she's the reason, or the cause, of the tent being set on fire. She's getting away with it, and because of that, she's going to keep doing it. I hate bullies, loathe them, but I won't standby and do nothing. I'm not wired that way."

Selina doesn't seem that upset. "I know. I heard you lot talking in the hospital room and again at home one night. It wouldn't have taken long for me to figure out. Honestly, before they put me to sleep, I thought it was Kaiden, but then you two revealed you were together."

I run my hand down her arm. "She won't get away with it."

Selina smiles before giving me a short nod.

"I heard about the fire," Clary says. She seems to think about it for a moment, before her eyes spark with an idea. "We have the music festival. This place is so dull, with very little to offer, so they rent the field space out for them to have the festival. It brings in tourists and business. We'll think of something for then. She only goes because she doesn't want to be left out. She actually hates the place. God forbid she get her nails dirty."

"We aren't staying there, are we?" I ask, remembering the girl in my old school who mentioned she fell asleep in the wrong tent when she went to one.

"No. People do camp out there and some of the guys stay to hook up with girls, but most of us just head home. It's not like it's far."

"When is it?"

"Saturday through to Sunday morning."

"This week?"

"Yeah, why?"

"I can't go. I'm helping someone Saturday morning, so I won't have time. What about you?" I ask, looking at Selina.

Her gaze flicks over my shoulder. "I'm busy Saturday morning, but I might be able to fit in the night."

"Come the night then. Most of the people don't show until then, anyway. I go on the night; the music is better."

"All right, Saturday night it is."

"Here," Clary calls, placing uniform on the bed. I peek around her, into the large walk-in wardrobe, and my gaze widens. One side has racks of school uniforms. She blushes for a moment before glaring. "Tell anyone and I will kill you. If anyone knew I had these, Danielle would destroy them and I wouldn't be able to help anyone. Hopefully, she'll believe you went home to get a spare set."

"Thank you."

"Go get your stuff off and we'll take them downstairs to be washed," she orders, pointing me to the door on the left.

I peek through the door and smile at all the perfumes and girly bath stuff on the side. I step inside and quickly strip the soiled clothes off me, leaving me standing in my underwear. I cringe at the smell as I pick them up off the floor.

Pulling open the door enough to lean my arm out, I throw Clary the clothes.

"We'll give you some privacy and go put these in the wash," Selina calls, and I push my head out further, seeing her standing in the doorway.

"Do you remember where the T.V. room is?" Clary asks, handing the clothes to Selina.

"Yeah. Thank you for this," I tell her, and she nods. "I'm going to think of ways I can get Danielle back for this. I know this was her doing."

Clary laughs. "We'll get her."

When the door shuts, I breathe in a ragged breath. Danielle and her friends are going to push and push until I snap. And when I snap, they're going to wish they hadn't pushed. I mean, how childish could adults be? This is something high school girls would do.

I groan when I realise I left the fresh clothes on the bed. Heading back into the room, I let out a startled scream at the figure standing by the door. Quickly, I pull the wool blanket off the large oak poster bed and cover myself.

"Kaiden, what are you doing here?" I snap.

His pupils dilate and his irises darken as he takes another step into the room. "I came to check on you."

"Well, you can see I'm fine, so you can go," I tell him, glancing at the door.

"Why? I have you right where I want you."

I shake my head at him. "We can't do this, Kaiden."

He circles me. "Why not? You want me, I want you. Fuck everything that has happened in between."

"Clary and Selina will be back any minute," I warn him.

His deep chuckle sends a shiver through my spine. "No, they won't."

"Kaiden, we can't do this. I'm having a really bad day already."

"Did they burn you?" he asks, stepping closer, standing right before me.

"No. I'm fine," I tell him, my voice shaky as he cups my cheek. I close my eyes, tilting my head into the palm of his hand. His skin is so warm and soft. This… this feeling, only he can evoke. I've missed it, craved it. He wormed his way under my skin the day I arrived and is so deeply embedded inside of me, I can't let him go.

How can something so wrong feel so right?

I slowly open my eyes, blinking up at him. He stares down at me, the intensity of the situation burning through me, igniting the blood running through my veins, and my entire core heats.

"Ivy," he whispers, and the chains keeping him locked out, break—and I throw myself at him.

The kiss is rough, wet, and in seconds, Kaiden is gripping me behind my thighs, lifting me up his body. The sheet falls as I wrap my legs around him, my fingers running through his thick, coarse hair.

I moan, grinding down, needing that friction so badly I could weep.

In the back of my mind, a small voice is screaming at me that this is a bad idea. And the part that is still in the moment, knows that. I just don't care. It's been a crappy few weeks and all I want is a release.

I accidently whack Kaiden with my cast, and he groans, spinning me around and laying me down on the bed, pinning my arms above me.

A guttural noise escapes his throat as he stares down at me, looking at me like he can't quite believe I'm real, that we're doing this, before sliding my thong over my thighs and down my legs. He throws it somewhere behind him.

I pull his blazer over his shoulders and lean up, kissing him once more, needing that contact. Wetness seeps between my legs as I struggle to undo his buttons.

He swats my hands away and undoes them, ripping his tie and shirt off once he's done. His trousers are next, and the hungry look in his eyes has me biting my lip to smother the moan threatening to escape.

His boxers are last, and it's my turn to be hungry, eyeing his fine specimen of a body with a craving so dear, it's almost my undoing.

Lifting up, I trace my tongue over his hard abs, looking up at him through my lashes when I hear him groan. Reaching behind me, he unclips my bra, letting it fall down my arms and onto the floor. The tension in the air thickens as he lightly pushes me back, looming over me with a dark need.

"I've missed you," he croaks, his voice husky and filled with arousal.

I place my finger over his lips. "No talking. Just sex, Kaiden. It can only be sex. For now," I explain.

I grow dizzy with passion when the corners of his lips pull up into a smirk.

"You're mine."

"Then show me," I demand, gripping the back of his neck and pulling him closer. Our lips smash together in a fiery kiss.

His hand reaches down between us, and without warning, he pushes inside of me, my back sliding up the bed.

"Kai," I groan, gripping his shoulders, my fingers digging in.

He pulls back, leaving only the tip in me, before slamming back inside, the force causing a scream to escape.

His thrusts are fast, hard, and with each one, that tightness begins to build stronger, more intense. My breathing comes out in harsh pants, my pulse skyrocketing.

"Kai," I gasp out, clenching my eyes shut.

"So fucking good. So tight. Mine," he vows.

He lifts up, glancing down at me as he grabs a tit in each hand, squeezing them as he pushes them together. I can feel my nipples harden as he rubs his thumbs over them, and a gush of wetness seeps between my legs.

"Fuck," he groans, gritting his teeth.

Without warning, he spins me around, lifting me at the waist until I'm on my knees. He grabs the soft globes of my arse, squeezing to the point of pain. And with pain comes pleasure. I moan, gripping the sheets beneath me. He enters me forcefully, lifting me up off the bed as he powers in and out.

My hair slides across my back as I glance behind me, silently pleading with Kaiden to give me what I want.

The teasing, the torture, it leaves his gaze. He pushes me down on the bed, sliding his hands up my arms, causing my entire body to break out in goose bumps. The air leaves my lungs when he links his fingers through mine, the intimacy too real, too strong. I clench my eyes tightly shut, trying to keep out the onslaught of feelings I have for Kaiden.

It doesn't work, and tears spring to my eyes.

I can't let him in.

Not again, not when I've had a taste of how badly the loss of him hurts. He can't have that power back.

He already has that power.

His fingers tighten at the same time his thrusts become slower, yet harder, our bodies jerking up the bed and back down with each movement.

He drives in deeper, unafraid of hurting me. And he's not. The pleasure overrides the pain, but I know afterwards, I'll be sore.

I duck my head, moaning loudly into the sheets. Skin slapping against skin echoes around the room as he keeps fucking me.

He unlinks one of our hands, reaching between us. "Come for me, Ivy. Come!" he demands.

I lift my head as a powerful orgasm tears through me. A cry escapes as I slam myself against Kaiden, riding out the orgasm and hoping it never ends.

Because the moment this ends is the moment we go back to reality, back to ignoring each other, and a million obstacles keeping us apart.

"I'm going to come," he rasps, his fingers digging into my arse, and I'm pretty sure it's going to leave a bruise.

He pulls out, and I feel him gripping his cock, pumping his orgasm out, blasting cum all over my arse cheeks.

"Fuck!" he groans, his body jerking.

He slumps to the side of me and pulls me into his hard chest. I go willingly, needing another moment with him before it gets torn apart.

"I can never get enough of you," he admits, and I look down, finding him pumping his dick in his hand.

I get up, sliding off the bed and grabbing the sheet and uniform from the floor. "I need to get cleaned up," I tell him, feeling void.

Before he can object, I head into the bathroom. I clean off his arousal from my arse before getting changed and straightening my hair.

I know he's out there. I can hear him moving about. There's no avoiding him, not if I want him to leave before the girls come back, wondering what's taking me so long.

With one deep breath, I wrap my fingers around the door handle and twist, pulling the door open.

Kaiden is dressed, looking sexy as hell with his sex-fussed hair. He scans my expression, reading me, just like he always does. It scares me how well he can do it.

"We're good together, Ivy. This proves it."

I shake my head at him and walk over to straighten the sheets. "It proves we have chemistry. We're toxic, Kaiden. Look at everything that has happened. I'm not saying never, I'm just saying not right now. We need to deal with the things that make all of this complicated. I've done complicated my whole life with my mum. If you really want me, want this, it's something you'll want too."

"I want this more than I care to admit to myself, Ivy. I'm not going to give up. Nothing that has happened with our parents needs to come between us, and I thought you felt the same. You've constantly preached we aren't our parents, but you're using them as an excuse to not be happy. And you can't lie and say you aren't."

He's right, being with him, being a part of the group, it was the happiest I'd ever been.

Maybe I am using them as an excuse, using them as a barrier to protect myself. It doesn't matter.

"It doesn't change the fact that your dad wants me dead and I want him to rot in prison. That is going to come between us; if not now, then eventually. I'm not equipped for that kind of pain, because when it comes down to it, he's your family, Kaiden. You're just angry at him right now."

His laugh is humourless. "You have no idea. If it came down to a choice, it would be you every time. Hell, before I met you, I'd have picked a stranger over the likes of him, and that was before I knew the true monster he is. But it will always be you, Ivy. You need to get that and get it quickly. I like to think myself a patient man, but when it comes to you, I'm not. I want it all. I want all of you."

With those parting words, he leaves. The door slowly clicks shut, the sound causing me to jump as if he slammed it.

I need to get my shit together. I want him. I want him so badly it hurts. But giving in right now… it feels like defeat.

And I'm not one to go down without fighting.

chapter seventeen

IVY

My temples throb as I walk into the kitchen. It's Saturday, which means the twins threw a party last night. Judging by the sound bouncing off the walls in my room during the early hours, they had the entire school in attendance.

"You look rumpled this morning," Nova greets.

"Thanks," I mutter, pouring myself a cup of coffee. "Did it keep you up?"

She lets out a small laugh. "Over the years, I've learned to invest in ear plugs. I didn't hear a thing."

I turn to her, grimacing. "Please tell me you have spares?"

"I'll have some placed in your room before the end of the day," she promises. "You are spending the day with Mrs White today, aren't you?"

"I am. I need to leave soon to go help set up. It's still okay, isn't it?"

She glances away for a moment before looking back at me, taking a deep breath. "You know that I hired someone to find Royce. They aren't as restricted as the police."

"You've found him?" I ask, my heart pounding.

She reaches out for my hand, soothing me. "No. But you need to be careful when you're out today. He doesn't believe Royce has left the area."

"What?" I ask, dropping down on the stool beside me.

"It's fine. I'm going to hire security. I haven't been able to get it on short notice, but hopefully they'll be here Monday."

"Really?" I ask, not sure how I feel about having someone following me. "Is it necessary?"

She arches her eyebrow. "Yes, I really do think so, Ivy. He's dangerous, and until the original copy of the recording is in the right hands, we need to be vigilant. He could say it's been tampered with and altered. We can't let that be an option," she declares. "We will win this. He will pay for what he's done."

"I'll be careful. And you do the same," I tell her. Since our heart to heart, things have been different between us. I don't feel that defence mechanism coming between us. It's kind of refreshing to not have that problem weighing me down.

"I will. Now get going. Ed is grumpy in the morning and I'm afraid your tardiness will set him off."

I laugh, knowing exactly what she's talking about. "I'll be back later, but I'm popping out to some musical festival later. There's a few of us going, so I won't be alone."

Her shoulders sag with relief. "Good. I need to go check on a client's company today, so I won't be back till later. Call me or Annette if there's anything you need. No matter what. And make sure you take your cards."

"Thank you," I tell her, grabbing my jacket before heading out the door.

The air has a chill to it, but I know in a few hours it will be roasting hot. Its due to rain soon and I can't welcome it enough. This must be the hottest summer I've ever known.

I round the corner, stepping into the garage and grabbing my bike. Elle will give me a lift into town and bring me back, but I still need it to get to hers.

Pushing the bike outside, I come to a stop, my heart in my throat when

I see Danielle stepping out of Kaiden's, her expression hard. The second she sees me, she smiles and looks back to the house.

"Thanks for a great night."

The door shuts and I feel it in my soul. The palms of my hands burn as I squeeze the handlebars tightly, closing my eyes briefly at the onslaught of pain. He said I meant something, said I was different, and he'd never choose her. My knees knock together.

A small voice inside of my head is screaming that he wouldn't do this as I watch her walk towards me, her expression filled with smugness.

"It's okay," she coos as she nears. "It was always going to happen. We're meant to be together."

"Why don't you go play on the motorway, Danielle, and leave me the fuck alone."

She laughs, pulling her bag up her shoulder when it begins to slip. "I'm not finished with you. You're hiding a secret, and I'm going to find out what it is. Something tells me it has to do with the disappearance of Royce Kingsley. Rumours are, he left town."

She must see something on my face because a spark lights behind her eyes before her smile turns into a smug grin.

"Were you sleeping with him?" she taunts.

I mask my expression, looking bored. "If this is what you want to do with your time, go for it. Rest assured, you'll be wasting time, it just won't be mine. But you're good at wasting time on people who don't care about you."

Her expression hardens. "I'm going to make sure he sees you for who you really are. Mark my words."

"No, watch yours. I don't do well with threats, Danielle. You keep pushing and pushing, but the minute I snap, you'll go run to Daddy. You're weak. You're nothing. The only thing you have going for you is your looks and even those will fade over time. Your time will come. You'll get what is coming to you. Everyone does eventually."

She huffs before trotting off in her high heels. She's near her car when her ankle twists and she collapses to the floor.

I let out a laugh, ignoring the angry glare she sends me as she lifts herself up and gets into her car.

The front door to the Kingsley house opens and out steps the twins, their eyes narrowed on the car speeding away from the house.

"We can only guess what she said to you. We were waiting to come out to find out what she said. She's up to something. She tried saying she left her phone here last night at the party."

"She implied she slept over with Kai," I tell Ethan.

His face scrunches up with disgust. "No, she fucking didn't. Kai locked himself away in his room all night. He's been in a bad mood since Tuesday."

I shamefully look away, knowing the reason. "She knows there's something to know about your dad. She's determined to find out."

The twin's glance at each other, silently communicating. "We can't guarantee she won't find out, but we can distract her enough that she doesn't have time."

"All right. I need to get going, but you two should fill your brother in," I warn them.

Lucca grins. "Tell him yourself later," he tells me before walking away with his brother.

"Later? I'm not seeing him later."

"Have a good day, Ivy."

"Lucca, answer me, dammit," I yell, only to be ignored. "Arseholes," I call out, even if they can't hear me since they've shut the door behind them.

I grab my bike, already wishing the day was over and it's barely even begun.

♥

THE JOKE NOVA made before I left the house comes to mind and I begin to laugh at the sulking expression on his face.

Elle found he had whiskey in his flask of tea and confiscated it immediately. He's been a sourpuss ever since.

It's lunch time and the crowd has thickened immensely since we first opened this morning. I didn't even realise this many people lived in Cheshire Grove, but Elle assured me there were hidden villages and a load more private communities like the one the Kingsley's and Monroe's built many years ago.

"I'm starving, Elle. Could we retire for an hour and go to the food venders up the lane?" Ed complains.

Elle finishes serving the lady in front of her before turning to her husband. "I made sandwiches. They're in the cool box."

He rolls his eyes at me. "I ate those after I worked up a hunger putting the stool together."

"Then eat mine," she scolds, placing her hands on her hips.

He has the brains to at least look shamefaced when he admits, "I ate those in the car. We missed breakfast."

"Because you insisted that we sleep for another hour." She lets out a harsh breath, shaking her head like she doesn't know what to do with him. "And let me guess, you ate Ivy's."

He throws his hands up in the air. "You made her pasta. I had a midnight snack. It's not like there isn't food here."

She turns to me, exasperated. "Could you mind the stall for a little while? We'll go grab some food and bring it back for us all to eat."

I nod, smiling, before winking at Ed over her shoulder. "Go, feed the beast."

"Beast," he mutters under his breath. "I'm a growing man."

I roll my eyes as I pat him on the chest. "You're fully grown," I tell him. "Now, weren't you hungry?"

He smiles, kissing my forehead before linking Elle's arm through his. It shocks me how far we've come since we first met. One, he was so unapproachable to begin with, he kind of intimidated me. Secondly, if he had tried kissing my forehead when we first met, I would have busted his nose. "Be back soon, little one."

I wave them off, still smiling to myself as I rearrange the brown paper bags under the table. When a shadow looms over me, blocking out the beaming sun, I stand, lifting my head to greet them. My smile falls when I see Kaiden standing there, repeatedly tossing an apple up in the air and catching it.

He stops, smirking at me. "I'd like to buy this, please."

"That will be thirty-five pence," I tell him.

"Keep the change," he tells me, handing me a tenner.

I shrug, shoving it into the money tin. "What are you doing here?"

"Came to see how you were. Annette mentioned you being here," he explains. "The twins said Danielle stirred up some trouble this morning."

"Doesn't she always?"

"I'm sorry. I'm sorting it," he explains, taking a chunk out of the apple.

"I can fight my own battles."

"But she's not yours. She's only a problem because of me," he remarks.

"Possibly. But it could be that it's not even really about you," I tell him, lying through my teeth. "Not everyone is obsessed with you."

He smirks, walking around the table until he's in front of me. "Are you saying you aren't obsessed with me?"

I inwardly groan as my arousal spikes at his proximity and the feel of his finger running over my cheek.

"Yes, because there's no way in hell I am."

"Liar," he whispers, pressing his lips against mine. I sigh, gripping his T-shirt as I kiss him back.

Once I realise where we are and what we're doing, I push him back a step, looking around to make sure no one saw. "Kaiden," I hiss.

He doesn't seem fazed that I pushed him away. If anything, I think it's turned him on. "I'll be seeing you."

"Yeah, yeah," I mumble.

He walks back around the table, chewing on another bite of his apple. "And I'll sort Danielle. I'll make sure she doesn't bother you again."

"She'll get what's coming to her later," I declare.

"What?" he asks, his jaw dropping, surprised by my revelation.

"Goodbye, Kaiden," I mutter dryly.

He leaves me stewing over the kiss. I can still feel him, taste him. It's only when another customer stands in front of me that I realise I forgot to tell him about the news Nova shared with me this morning.

My phone beeps with a message alert. I pull it out of my pocket, seeing Kaiden's name.

KAIDEN: Don't let Clary pull you into shit. I just remembered she's the chick that brought a tarantula into school and set it free in Danielle's locker. And I'm pretty sure it was her who let a bunch of goats into the auditorium when Danielle had a fashion show.

I burst out laughing. That is definitely something Clary would do. I might not know what we have planned, but I do know it won't involve animals.

I think.

I quickly pull up her name and send her a message.

IVY: There's not going to be animals involved, right?

CLARY: No. My dad's being a spoilsport and won't get me anything. I was going to get some stray rats and put them in the car. Apparently, that stuff takes time to get and he's worried one will bite me and give me rabies.

IVY: LOL!!! So glad you had the mind to ask him first. I think seeing a rat would have scared me more than her, anyway.

CLARY: Yeah, the stick insects I put in her school bag gave me nightmares for weeks. I kept finding ones that got loose and it freaked me out.

IVY: Stop, you're killing me. LOL!

CLARY: Got to go. Just had the best idea. Talk later!

IVY: No animals!

chapter eighteen

KAIDEN

THE SMELL OF FRESHLY CUT GRASS permeates the air as I speed through the narrow, zig-zagging roads after having left Ivy to her day.

She was strong, but then, I always knew that. I just wish she'd stop fighting against us being together. I get her reservations, I do, but we're two jagged souls meant to be together. The quicker she realises that, the sooner we can just be.

But first, I need to get rid of the obstacles determined to get in our way. And as much as I'd love for my father to be the first, there isn't much I can do until we've found out his whereabouts, so Danielle got pushed up the list.

I'm meeting her father away from prying eyes and cameras. Because what use is blackmail if someone manages to use the same ammo.

The shrill of my phone ringing blares through the speakers. I glance down at the screen, seeing Rome's name. I pull off into a layby, pressing the button to connect the call.

"Rome," I greet.

"Wish I was calling for something else, but one of the guys took Jenny

Fields home last night. Apparently, she likes to talk after being fucked and let slip that Danielle has something planned for Ivy."

"What, pray tell, do they have planned?"

"I've got no idea. He was drunk so didn't even think twice about it until this morning."

"Did you get anything else?"

"Well, after watching the video that's trending around the school, I looked into the comment Whitmore made about Hackett. I spoke to Miss Crapper and she had a lot to say."

"Go on," I encourage.

"She said Danielle is the most frequent student to visit Mr Hackett. She's in there for hours and Miss C is often sent out for lunch when she's there."

"She's fucking him?" I ask, my lip curling in disgust.

I grit my teeth at the news. The only reason I ever dipped my dick inside of her was because of the fact she didn't sleep around. And all along she was sleeping with him.

"I've got no proof, but yes, I'd say it's pretty clear she is. She's manipulative. You know that. We just need to get something on Hackett, to see why she needed to keep him happy."

"Find out," I order, clenching my hands around the steering wheel. "I owe you."

"Nah, call this a freebie. It's about time someone put her in her place."

"Later," I tell him, ending the call.

I take a moment to compose myself. Because of me, Ivy is in danger once again.

Maybe she is right. Maybe this won't work because of who I am.

But I'm selfish and I never give in, not when it involves someone I care about.

I put the car in gear and drive off, wanting to get this meeting out of the way. The secrets I have uncovered, the lies that have been told, it will all come to an end one way or another.

It's a crowd of lies that have infested everyone around them.

The burnt down church is barely standing, the stone crumbling from weather damage. It's a place we've used for the races since the field isn't owned by government or any living person. But because of the landmark, it's protected, which means it can't be bought or built on, which gives the police grounds to show up and break up the fighting, racing and gambling.

It's the perfect location to meet Malcom Holden.

I pull the car to a stop opposite Mal, who looks annoyed to have been summoned to such a dire place. He leans against the bonnet of his car, hands tucked into the pockets of his trousers, and his eyes narrowed on my car. His lips press together as he widens his stance.

I grab the envelope off the passenger seat, taking my time before sliding out of the car.

"Holden," I greet.

"Why have you dragged me out into the middle of nowhere, Kingsley? Does your father know about this?" he demands.

"If he does, I wouldn't know, and I doubt it's on his list of priorities right now. I brought you here because of Danielle."

He frowns. "Don't tell me you've broken up again. I thought you got rid of *that* girl."

I force a chuckle as I try to hold back from the urge to wrap my fingers around his neck. "Is that what she's telling you, that we're back together?"

"You aren't?"

"No, it seems your daughter has become quite delusional as of late. You need to reign her in, Mal, or I will. I'm giving you a chance to do it before I take matters into my own hands."

His jaw hardens as he takes a step forward. "How dare you threaten me, boy! You go near my daughter and I'll have you arrested so quick you won't know what's hit you. And as, going by rumours, you don't have anyone to bail you out, I would be careful if I were you."

I smirk, ducking my head a little as I pull out the blown-up photos my investigator got when I hired him after the tent incident. I knew this time would come.

"I wouldn't say anything else to the *boy* who holds your way of life in his hands," I warn him, passing over the photos. "I guess Mrs Holden won't like that her husband has gotten a sixteen-year-old pregnant, now, would she? I'm guessing the prenup states that she's only entitled to a settlement if you are unfaithful or pass away. And your political seat will be gone within the hour of the newspaper articles being published."

He glares up at me. "These don't prove anything," he snaps, sliding them back in the envelope.

"You should have looked through the rest; there are photos of you together, proof of your betrayal, and statements showing you've been paying her weekly to keep her mouth shut. Money talks, and she's willing to give a DNA test. I mean, she just wants to be with the man she's in love with. What quicker way to have that than to get your wife and children out of the picture?"

"You bastard! You won't get away with doing this. You aren't the only one who can get blackmail material. I know things about your father," he yells, his face red with anger.

I tilt my head, my lips pulled into a firm line. "You seem to have a preconceived notion that I care about my father or what you have on him."

"You do this, and it will ruin my life—my wife's."

"Then get your daughter in line," I bark. "I'm sick of her trying to strong-arm those around her. She's hurting people I care about and it ends, otherwise these, *and* the copies, will get sent to every newspaper—but not until I've personally delivered them to your wife."

The veins in his neck pulse as he charges towards me, his fist raised. I dodge the punch, gripping his neck and driving him backwards until we hit his car. I smash him down on it, looming over him, anger coursing through me. "That wasn't a smart move," I grit out, squeezing his neck tighter.

He wheezes, words unable to form, which makes me smile.

"Now, we're going to start again. Are you going to reign in that brat of a daughter of yours? Because it won't be just leaking those photos that I'll do to you. I'll take everything from you, including taking over Holden Limited.

I hear you've hit a bad patch, and the board will only be all too welcoming of another investor, even if it means casting you out. And your parliament seat... Your image will be ruined."

Hatred burns behind his gaze as he looks away.

"Three, two—" I chant.

He jerks his head and I let go of his neck, giving him room to breathe. "Yes!"

I let him go and he slides off the car, onto the ground, gasping for air. "I'm glad we have this settled," I tell him, bending down in front of him. "Don't make me come after you, and never, and I mean never, try to touch me again."

Lifting myself up, I chuck the envelope at his feet before walking off to my car. I don't look back as I drive off. I want to find Ivy. She's the only one who seems to settle the storms threatening to brew inside of me.

I'm just angry, angry that again there's another person who knows something about my dad.

It's always him.

I glance in the rear-view mirror, noticing a black hybrid Camry following me. It's the same car I saw earlier on the way to the market. I wouldn't have thought much of it, but it's a new car that was only released a few days ago, and it was one I saw yesterday on the way to school.

There's only one way to find out if the person is really following me. I take a left turn down a road I know leads to a farmhouse on sale. It's land my mum was going to buy to build another large estate on, but this one affordable for middle-class families. It fell through when she was refused planning permission.

When the car follows behind me, I grit my teeth, speeding up a little. They've picked the wrong day to fuck with me.

The car tries to be conspicuous but clearly fails as it tries to keep up, not realising this road leads nowhere. I jerk the wheel when I come to the drive of the old home, coming to a sudden stop facing the car following me.

I peel out quickly, standing at the front of the car, waiting. Ready.

The guy steps out, and I tilt my head, trying to figure out where I recognise him from. He's clearly got money; his watch and clothes are verification of that. That or someone is giving him a hefty paycheque.

He has a stocky build made for security, but the gleam of the sun reflecting off his sunglasses covers his identity.

"Why are you following me?" I demand. He steps forward into the shade, sliding his sunglasses up onto his head. "Kieran."

Kieran is my dad's head of security—a better word for lacky. He deals with things my father can't be seen meddling with, such as forcing people to sell companies to him. Kieran is the one dad sends to persuade them.

"I didn't realise Father was paying you so well," I tell him, eyeing him cautiously.

He chuckles, stepping forward. "Your dad can't afford not to. He's got himself into quite the mess, one not even I can get him out of."

"Where is dear Dad?" I ask, slowly side-stepping him when he moves forward.

"Royce asked me to deliver a message," he admits, moving closer. Hearing he's been in touch with my father has adrenaline pumping through me. This is the break we've been waiting for. Kieran is the key to finding my father.

"Go on," I order, still side-stepping him, trying to look for a weakness. The only one I've seen so far is that he favours his left leg, meaning he has an old injury causing him pain on the right.

"He wants you to retrieve something for him."

"And why can't you?"

He sighs, like it pains him. "Because my price was far too great, and it seems your father is running low on money. He needs it, wants it."

"And that's what he wants, money? He has it stashed in oversea accounts."

"Ah, but he can't access them until he's out of the country, which has become troublesome. He said you have access to a vital piece of evidence with which the police could convict him. He wants it. Without it, they have nothing to charge him with."

"And why on earth would I give it to him?" I snap.

Kieran grins. "Because Mr Kingsley… he will make sure the ones you love suffer if you don't."

"Are you threatening me?" I ask, walking up to him.

"No, it's a promise. He's given me permission to get what he wants by any means necessary. We can do this the easy way or the hard way, but mark my words, I'll always win. Your father always wins."

I stare at him dead in the eye as I tuck my hands under my armpits. "Is that so?"

"I'm going to enjoy beating the superior out of you, something your father should have done many years ago."

I smirk at him for a moment, not saying anything, not blinking, and before he can counter my move, I snap my hand forward, whacking him in the nose. He staggers backwards, holding a hand to the blood pouring from it.

There's a hardness in his eyes as his head snaps up to meet my gaze. With one large stride, he comes at me. I duck, weaving in and out to miss his punches, but one hard blow to the ribs and the air is knocked out of me. It was a heck of a shot, but not enough to stop me. Pain ripples through my chest, and yet, the pain is welcome. I've fought most of my life, so I'm used to the discomfort. With adrenaline coursing through my system, I manage to get my bearings and hit him back, pleased when I see blood dripping from his lip.

He's bigger than me but not quicker. Fighting is like a dance; you have to know where to stand, what move to make next. You have to be in the moment.

Pain radiates through my jaw when his fist connects with it. I take a step back before kicking out hard, hitting him on the side of his knee, knocking him to the floor, where he howls in pain.

His movements are sluggish when he stands, trying to hit out me, but the knee injury is too much for him and he falls back down. A sickening crunch fills the air and I smile in satisfaction.

Gripping his shirt, I drag him over to his car, pulling him up and over the bonnet until he's lying down on his back, his expression scrunched up in pain.

I slam my hand down on the bonnet, next to his head. "Where is my father?"

"Why the fuck would I tell you?" he pants out, trying and failing to shove me off.

I slam my fist down in his gut and he doubles over, coughing madly. Bending forward, I get in his face. "Don't test me. I can do this all day, and I'll enjoy it."

"Your father will hear of this," he rasps, still trying to catch his breath. "I'm not telling you a thing."

"And yet, I don't care," I bite back. "Now tell me, where can I find my father?"

When he doesn't answer, I pull out my pocketknife. I flip it open and stab him in the leg, missing any vital arteries.

He wails, writhing in pain as I let him go. Dust from the dirt-laden ground flies up around him.

I lean down, pulling the knife out, grimacing at the scream that tears from his throat.

"Shall we try this again? You've got plenty other places I can shove this blade into. It won't cut you deep enough to cause major damage, but it'll be enough to cause excruciating pain."

"I don't know," he groans, dirt sticking to the blood on his face.

Numbing myself, I grip his thigh, pressing my thumb into the wound. "Are you sure?" I yell over his cries.

"I'm telling the truth. Your father messaged me with orders. I was to let him know it was done and then he'd take care of the rest," he rushes out.

I dig my thumb in one last time, cringing at the feel of flesh and blood over my hand. But it needs to be done. To protect her, to protect my brothers, my mum, it has to be done.

I search his body for his phone. When I find it, I grab his finger and press it onto the screen, unlocking his phone. There's no record of a message from Dad, but I take the lock off, pocketing the phone before leaving him and heading to his car.

Inside the glove compartment, there's another phone, this one old without any features.

As I pass Kieran on the floor, still writhing in pain, I pause, bending down and grabbing a chunk of his hair, lifting him to face me.

"If I ever see you again, I will dump your body in the river. From here on out, you no longer work for my father, and if I hear any differently, all of this..." I say, gesturing to his body, "will seem like child's play. Nod if you understand me."

He nods, making the right choice.

I dust off my jeans and head back to the car. I have places to be, people to see, and I've already wasted enough time.

It's time to make Ivy mine.

chapter nineteen

IVY

THIS PLACE IS CRAZY. We're only in the carpark and I can hear the bands playing in the background. People are going wild, screaming and dancing before they even get inside. They're weaving in and out of cars, plastic cups of beer in their hand.

I don't want to show it, and I try hard not to come across like a little girl, but I'm looking forward to getting inside and listening to those bands play.

"Your cousin is on my shit list," Clary grumbles as she sorts whatever she has inside the boot of her car.

I laugh, lightly running my fingers over the glitter on my face that Clary is still groaning about. Selina was all for going and made sure we knew it by forcing us to have glitter sprinkled above our eyebrows and around our eyes. She even put some on our cleavage. And then she left, saying she would meet us here.

I decided to wear a white tank top, silver necklaces and a pair of ripped jeans and trainers.

Clary wore the same, except her tank is black with slashes across the back, showing more skin.

Together, I thought we looked pretty hot, especially when Selina did my makeup. The only thing I wish I didn't have on is my cast. It's pissing me off, my skin itching to the point I want the damn thing off.

"Where is the terrorist, anyway? I thought she was meeting us here?"

"I don't know," I murmur, pulling my phone out to ring her. She's been acting weird for weeks, ever since the accident.

Ringing blares in my ear, but I also hear a ringtone at the same time. I spin in a circle, searching the nearby cars, when I see Selina up ahead, pressed against a car and frowning at her phone.

"Holy fuck!" I yell, then squeak, ducking down behind the car, pulling Clary with me.

"What the fuck?" she yells, and I place a hand over her mouth.

"Selina," I tell her, pointing in the direction she's at. "She's with… she's with—" I cut myself off, too shocked to say it.

When Clary goes to stand, I pull her back down, glaring at her. "What are you doing?"

"Seeing what has your knickers in a twist. Don't worry, she won't see me."

I nod, following her as we look through the car door windows, seeing Carter Remington look down at her, his expression soft—before he kisses her!

"Holy fucking shit, that's Carter Remington," Clary declares, her eyes wide. "Way to go, Selina."

"The twins are going to kill her."

Clary laughs. "It will be worth it. I heard he's phenomenal in bed."

I narrow my eyes at her. "That's not the point."

She grins at me, winking. "Let her get some."

"What are we going to do? She's going to see us and it's clear she's not ready for anyone to know."

Clary's eyebrows bunch together as she seems to gather her thoughts. "You aren't annoyed she hasn't divulged to you?"

I shrug, not really seeing it that way. "If it had something to do with me, she'd tell me. She's the one person who has been honest with me from the start. If she's not telling me, it's not because she thinks I won't be supportive but because she's trying to figure out if there's anything *to* tell me. When she's ready, I won't get her to shut up about him."

"You really aren't like most people," Clary murmurs.

I wink, teasing her, "If you're going to hit on me, at least buy me food first."

She laughs, shaking her head. "If I was into girls, trust me, I'd take you up on that."

Laughing, we're both interrupted by the shrill of my ringtone. We squeal, jumping apart when we see Selina's name on the screen.

"Hello?" I answer.

"Where are you? I'm in the carpark."

I clear my throat, standing and pulling Clary with me. "We just arrived," I answer, then remember the section we drove into. "We're in Row D."

"Row D?" she squeaks. "Um, where? I'm here."

"Woah, that's quick." I look around, pretending to look for her. "Selina," I yell, ending the call and waving.

Clary laughs, shoving her head back into the boot, her arse sticking in the air as she reaches for something. "You suck at acting."

I smack her arse, shushing her as Selina nears. "Hey, you been here long?"

Her face reddens. "Not long. How long have you been here?"

"Few minutes," I lie, and she relaxes, beaming over at me before frowning at Clary.

"What is she doing?"

"No idea," I mutter, crossing my arms over my chest.

"Ah ha," Clary mutters, beckoning us over. "I found that damn spray. It got loose."

"Um, why do you have a pair of knickers with Danielle's name and face on them?" I ask sheepishly, eyeing Clary warily.

Arching her eyebrow, she gives us both a dry look. "Because I like her kissing my arse, that's why," she answers sarcastically. "For the revenge plan of course."

"And that includes posters of her too?" Selina asks, picking up a leaflet before laughing.

"I knew Ivy didn't want me to bring animals, and I'm guessing you won't reach her level and her hurt her physically. It was last minute, but I managed to get them done."

"And what is that exactly?" I ask, my lips twitching when I read the poster.

For every drink thrown on me, I will donate £100 to charity. If you are caught, then it's you who must pay. Let the fun begin.

Clary grins, rubbing her hands together before picking up the small spray bottle. "This is a toxic spray. It's rare to get now. It was originally made for practical jokes, but when people started getting reactions to it and the complaints were made, it was banned."

"What is it?" I ask, going to take it, but she pulls it back, away from me.

"You don't want to do that. One spray of this and you'll stink for hours. And the best thing about it is that water or any liquid magnifies the smell, making it stronger. When Danielle goes to wash it off, she'll just make it worse. Only soap mixed with hot water can remove the smell. Add in people throwing drinks at her, she'll reek by the end of it and no one will want to stand near her."

Impressive. "But what's stopping her from leaving?"

Her answering grin is evil. "Then the first part of the plan will stop that. We're going to sabotage her car. I kind of let myself into her house earlier after getting off the phone to you and took the spare set of keys. What does Danielle pride herself in more than being popular?"

"Fashion," Selina answers, looking as intrigued as I.

"Exactly! So, when someone finds those hideous pants, she'll be embarrassed. She won't live that down, and someone is bound to get her downfall on camera and use it against her." She takes a deep breath before continuing. "The only way to get a group of people to come and look is to make it look like her car was broken into. She leaves half her shit in the boot, so she'll want to see it's okay. We just have to make sure the person hosting will announce the car."

"Ah, leave that to me," Selina adds, blushing. "I know someone who's friends with the guy hosting on stage."

Clary nods. "Let's get this car done first. She usually has V.I.P parking but I swapped the ticket when I was around her house earlier and put her in A." She hands us each a pile of posters. "Hand these out to anyone and everyone."

"Is it wrong that I'm excited?" Selina muses.

"Nope. It's our time. Is everyone ready?"

"Hell yeah," I cheer, waiting until she locks her boot before leaving.

♡

TRASHING DANIELLE'S CAR was harder than we all thought. People kept walking by so Clary, ever the actress, acted like a spoiled brat who couldn't find her Jimmy Choo shoes. It worked, more than once. And it was dark enough that no one could see the slashed tyres, making it impossible for Danielle to escape from her upcoming misery so easily.

Now it's time for the spray, and if it weren't for Facebook, where Danielle has posted constant selfies, we would never have found her in such a huge crowd.

It's larger than I imagined and has more than one stage. It has a fair few, spread out amongst beer tents, food vendors and a fair. There's something to do at every turn.

Danielle and her friends are hanging out in the main stage area near the beer tent, where a group of lads have their shirts off, trying to stay on the mechanical bull.

We had handed out the posters not long after entering the main area and made sure to tell people to pass the posters on.

"That girl is going to throw that drink at her," Selina hisses, pulling on our arms.

"What?" I yell over the music, then look in her line of sight, seeing a girl around our age holding the poster up, staring in Danielle's direction.

"Here's my chance," Clary declares, rounding her shoulders. We watch her leave, following behind the girl holding a beer.

She pretends to trip, the cup flying out of her hand and splashing all over Danielle's bare legs. I laugh at Danielle's thunderous expression, but I soon lose sight of her as a crowd of people drunkenly stumble into the beer tent. A flicker of movement catches my attention and I watch as Clary blends into the crowd, spraying the toxin all over Danielle.

"No," Selina painfully whispers, her expression filled with anguish and heartache.

I gawp at Carter, who has a girl rubbing herself over him, before turning back to Selina. Clary comes back, grinning. I quickly snatch the bottle from her hand and make my way through the crowd, ignoring them when they call my name.

As I get closer, I notice Carter subtly trying to elbow the girl out of the way, looking annoyed.

It doesn't matter. Selina doesn't deserve to see shit like that.

I pretend to bump into the girl humping Carter's leg, spraying her without anyone noticing before stepping back. I force a glare, snatching the beer out of Carter's hand and throwing it all over her bare skin, since she's only wearing a bikini type top. Hopefully the liquid will cause the smell to increase on bare skin.

"Watch where you're fucking going," I snap at her. She stares at me, dumbfounded, wiping the droplets of water off her skin.

An arm grips my bicep, stopping me from leaving. "Ivy?"

I glare at Carter. "You're lucky it was her I got and not you, because you wouldn't like where I got you."

"Huh?" he mumbles, but then glances over my shoulder, his eyes widening before staring at the girl still standing there. "Shit!"

"Exactly!"

Before he can say anything else, I storm towards the girls. When I reach them, Selina ducks her head. "You know?"

"Not until earlier. I guessed you would tell me when you were ready. I'm

LISA HELEN GRAY   180

not making excuses for him, but it looked like he was trying to shove her off without using force."

She nods, lifting her head. Her mouth opens, a squeak escaping as she looks over my shoulder. I turn, rolling my eyes at Carter walking towards us.

"Can I catch up with you all later?" Selina asks. "I'm not ready for the twins to find out and they're walking towards us."

"Go," I rush out, pushing her towards Carter. He stops short, seeing the twins also, and makes a beeline between the tents, hiding from view.

"I'm kind of jealous. He's so fucking hot. It's that cocky attitude that always put me off him."

I laugh, shaking my head, and spin to face the oncoming twins, pretending to be surprised to see them.

When I look down at the paper in their hands, the blood rushes from my face. They laugh. "I guess we don't need to ask if this was your doing. Your expression says it all."

"Actually, it was all Clary's idea."

Lucca takes a step back, his lips curled. "Please don't tell me you sacrificed an animal."

Clary glares at him. "I didn't know the locker had no air holes, Lucca. If I did, I wouldn't have put a frog in her locker. I didn't bloody sacrifice it."

He chuckles, wrapping his arm around her shoulders. "Good, because the kinky shit needs to be tamed if we're ever going to be together."

"We're never going to be together," she snaps, trying to shrug his arm off.

He sniffs, not slighted in the least. "Of course we are."

My phone alerts me of a message, distracting me, so I miss her reply. I pull it out, reading the message from Selina.

SELINA: Carter has sorted the announcement. He's not on stage for another forty minutes, so hopefully she doesn't leave before then.

SELINA: This is great! I just watched someone spill a drink all over her shoes. I think she's crying.

IVY: Are you okay?

SELINA: Yes, I'll talk to you after.

Meeting Clary's gaze, I wave my phone at her. "Selina has the other part of the plan ready. It will be in forty minutes."

"What plan?" Ethan asks.

"I'd tell you, but then I'd have to kill you," I tease.

"Does it have anything to do with Danielle getting drinks thrown on her?" Lucca asks, his lips twitching as he stares at something over my shoulder.

"Maybe," Clary muses.

"Well, if we have forty minutes until whatever you've got planned goes ahead, let's go have some fun," Ethan announces.

"Yeah, I've always wanted to get you alone on the ghost train," Lucca flirts, fluttering his lashes at her.

She rolls her eyes as she shrugs, letting me decide what to do. I'm not sure how I feel about going on a ride. I've never been on one. But it beats standing around waiting to get payback on Danielle. She's not worth it.

"Why not," I announce, turning to leave.

Arms reach out to steady me when I bump into a wall of solid muscle. Lifting my head, I lock gazes with dark green eyes.

chapter twenty

KAIDEN

THE MUSIC FESTIVAL ISN'T SOMETHING I normally attended. It's not my scene at all. But when I found out Ivy was coming, I knew I had to be here, if for nothing else but to make sure she was safe.

Grant hands me a beer as I follow Ivy's movements. "Cheers."

Seeing who I'm staring at, Grant questions, "Does she know you're here?"

"No, not yet. I've got a feeling she'll be here soon," I tell him as I keep Danielle in my peripheral vision.

"Have you seen who else is here?" Grant bites out.

I sigh, knowing he's referring to Carter Remington. "Yes."

"And you're okay with that?"

"He saved her life," I remind him. "And we're not part of our ancestors' feud."

"Does he know that?"

"He will when I get around to talking to him. Right now, he has his own problems going on, starting with the girl dry humping him."

"Isn't that his best friend's sister?"

"Yep. Which is why he hasn't shoved her off. She's got her brother so far wrapped around her finger he does anything she asks. Carter's trying to keep the peace."

Ivy, Clary and Selina come into view and I step to attention, scanning the area.

"Before you go off to her, there's something I need to tell you," Grant declares.

"What's that?" I ask, briefly glancing at him.

"My lawyer called. It seems Mum hid money from my father. It was to be released to me the second I was out from under his thumb. Sam's parents were the beneficiaries."

"That's good news, right?" I ask, giving him my full attention for a minute.

"Yes, it is. But I'm not ready to go back," he admits, looking away.

"Then don't. Stay with us."

He nods, not saying anything further on the subject. "Are you going to go over?"

"I want to see what they're up to," I admit, my lips twitching into a smirk. Clary walked off a moment ago with a black canister in her hand, leaving Ivy and Selina behind, standing close to each other.

There's a commotion near the entry of the tent, but something in Selina's expression has me on alert. Sorrow and devastation fill her expression.

Ivy notices, following Selina's line of sight to where Carter is, and I grin as I watch her get angry.

I lean back against the post, watching it all play out.

"Are you not going to intervene? Why is she going to Carter?" Grant asks, looking ready to start a fight.

I place my hand on his chest, stopping him. "He's fucking Selina. She's getting payback, watch. Look at her expression," I demand. Her lips move, her expression hard as she gives Carter shit.

"Carter and Selina?" Grant asks, gaping.

I chuckle. "Selina thought she was being sly, but she forgot that I have spies on the gates who keep me informed of who comes and goes. I also have a friend whose brother is friends with Carter's group, and he mentioned seeing her."

"No offence, because she's hot as hell, but I thought she was a frigid virgin."

I laugh, shrugging. "She isn't now."

I spot the twins walking up behind them and know it's time to reveal myself, otherwise they'll have them doing all kinds of shit and I'll never find her again.

Grant eyes my hand. "Are you going to tell her?"

I filled him in earlier about Kieran and what message my father sent. Since the roof incident, there's been a change in Grant. There's still a weight he carries with him, but the darkness that was plaguing him no longer exists. His attitude has also changed, not only with life itself but with school. Ivy's speech helped him more than I believe he even realises.

Which was why I trusted him with earlier events, knowing he'd have my back. He's another set of eyes that can watch out for Ivy.

"Yes, as soon as I get her alone. She deserves to know he isn't far, that she's in danger by keeping that recording."

He glances over my shoulder. "I'd hurry before you lose your chance, because the twins look ready to party."

Smirking, I give him a chin lift as I pass him my beer.

Her back is to me, and with people weaving in and out, no one else notices me, not until she turns and bumps into me.

Reaching out, I steady her. "You really need to stop falling all over me."

"Kaiden," she breathes, licking her bottom lip.

Looking over her shoulder, I address the twins. "I need to speak to Ivy. Alone."

"We'll take Clary on some rides," Ethan offers, his gaze flicking to Ivy.

"Or ride her," Lucca flirts, winking at Clary.

"I don't think so, Kingsley. We've got plans," Clary argues.

I grit my teeth. "And she'll be back. I wouldn't pull her away if it wasn't important."

"Fucking her isn't important. What we are doing, is," she snaps back, crossing her arms over her chest.

Ivy ducks her head before facing Clary. "It's fine. I'll meet you at the car in thirty minutes."

Clary doesn't seem convinced and looks from Ivy to me, then back to Ivy. "Are you sure?"

Ivy nods. "Yes. Don't forget to be there."

They say their goodbyes before I take Ivy's hand, pulling her away from the crowd and towards the carpark.

On our way, I look to her. "Do you want to tell Selina to meet you after she's finished tearing Carter apart?"

The flash of fear has me feeling like a jerk. She's worried I'll go after Selina for being with Carter. Even before Ivy, I wouldn't have done that; maybe just isolated her at school so she had no one. The Remington's were the enemy, had been before I was born, but things have changed.

"How did you know?"

"I've known for a while. It started during your recovery," I admit.

"Please leave her alone. She likes him, probably even loves him. She deserves to be happy."

I hold my hands up in surrender. "If I was going to do something, it would have already happened."

I take her hand again, heading down the line of parked cars to where mine is parked in the corner.

"Whose car is this?" she asks, eyeing the black sleek exterior with its black tinted windows.

"It's my mum's."

She twirls to face me, grinning. "You didn't want to ruin your car, did you?"

I give her a sheepish smile, shrugging. "We tried racing here once, but it has so many potholes it caused damage to the car. Mum's is better equipped to handle it."

Pulling open the back door, I gesture her inside.

"I know what happens if I get in that car, Kai. I'm not stupid."

My lips twitch, despite the topic we need to talk about. "It's about my father, but I prefer what you have in mind." I reach out, pulling her into my arms when her face pales and she begins to tremble. "Get inside. There's much I need to tell you."

Her grip on my T-shirt tightens as she blinks up at me, guilt written over her face. "There's something I need to tell you before we get in that car. I forgot to mention it earlier at the market. You kept distracting me," she rushes out. Taking a deep breath, she looks me square in the eye before continuing. "Your father hasn't left."

"I know," I tell her softly. "Get in the car."

Lifting herself up into the car, she elegantly slides across the seat, giving me room to enter.

I scan the area, checking for anyone out of place or possible threats. It's only when I deem it safe, do I enter the car, closing the door behind me.

"You can tell me," she whispers.

She says that, but I can hear the indecision in her tone. She's afraid of what I need to say.

Taking a deep breath, I start, beginning with Kieran and who he is. "Kieran, my father's head of security, paid me a visit today. He had a message from my father."

With a trembling hand, she reaches for mine, comforting me, soothing the anger rising from the reminder of what I had to do.

"Is that why you've got a bruise along your jaw and your knuckles are raw?"

"Yes."

"What did he say?"

"He wants the recording. He believes the charges will be dropped if it's gone, and then he can leave. He wants access to the money he stored in oversea accounts. He can't reach it until he's free to leave the country."

"Kaiden," she whispers painfully. "I can't give you that recording."

I pull her into my lap. "I'd never let you, even if you offered. I meant what I said when I told you I was on your side."

"This is such a mess," she groans, resting her forehead against mine.

My fingers tighten around her hips. "He'll be caught," I promise her.

"I need to go. I need to tell Nova," she explains, but I tighten my grip, stopping her.

"She knows. I was at her house before coming here. She wanted to call you home, but I told her I had you covered."

"Is she okay?"

I hear the sincerity in her question. "You two okay now?"

She shrugs as she ducks her head, watching as her fingers play with the hem of my T-shirt. "We've had a lot to talk about. I've had a lot of time to actually still my mind. Since my mum died, I didn't stop. I didn't stop to let myself acknowledge what I was feeling, to pick apart those emotions and find out what they meant to me. I just lied to myself and those around me. I'm not saying I've been fake. The closed off, not give a fuck girl you all met, it was amplified. It rooted inside of me and I let it. It gave me the numbness I needed to cope with everything that had happened." She pauses, blinking up at me. "But I do care. After the accident I got so angry it scared me. I wanted you all to pay. I turned into the very person I never wanted to become. When I returned after my recovery, I went back to lying to myself, pretending I needed Nova to escape from my old life. But the truth is, I know I can survive without her. I just don't want to. I want to have family. The love that comes from that kind of bond. To taste normalcy. And I realised I pushed her away because a part of me was scared she'd reject me eventually. I didn't trust her motives to want me for me."

I nod in understanding. "But you're certain now that she's not out to get you, to use you. She loves you."

"The fear is still there, but I'm giving her a chance—a real chance this time. No more acting, no more keeping her at arm's length."

"Good," I murmur softly. "She loves you."

A moment passes between us, neither one of us looking away. A flash of acceptance crosses her expression, before she masks it. Or tries to. It makes me inwardly smile. She forgets how easy it is for me to read her.

My thumbs dig into her hip bones and she inhales, her eyes dilating with heat.

She takes me by surprise when she slides forward in my lap, her fingers running over my scalp as she leans in and kisses me.

I groan into her mouth, cupping the back of her head, and kiss her back, deep, hard.

"I need you," she moans against my lips.

Not giving her time to change her mind, I rip her top up her body and over her head. Pushing the silk covering her breasts down, I take her nipple into my mouth, sucking it deep.

"More," she moans.

Leaning back against the seat, I let her pull my T-shirt off before pressing my lips to hers. Her movements speed up as she rocks her hips, grinding down on my rock-hard cock.

She breaks off the kiss, and when I go to protest, her eyes widen, looking around outside. "Oh my God, someone might see."

"It's tinted," I tell her, moving forward, but she leans back.

"No! Not here. Someone will see or hear."

I smirk, twisting her nipple between my finger and thumb, causing her to close her eyes and moan. "Like you've been bothered about being heard before. You love the excitement," I tell her, my tone hoarse.

"No," she moans, but it's a pathetic attempt, because she continues to rock.

I grip her hips, lying her down next to me and sliding her jeans, along with her knickers, over her thighs and down her legs, leaving them bunched at her ankles. With one hand I play with her clit, pressing harder every time a word forms in her mouth. With my free hand, I undo my jeans, lifting up a bit to pull them down enough to free myself.

She squeals as I lift her back up until she's straddling my lap.

"Oh god," she moans, still looking out the window.

"Eyes on me, baby," I order, gripping her chin to tilt her head until she's looking at me. I reach between us, lining up my cock at her entrance.

Her eyes glaze over in a haze of lust as she seductively runs her hands up my chest, over my shoulders.

My cock is like iron, pointing to her entrance. I grip it tightly, feeling pre-cum bead the tip. I want her. I want her so damn bad.

And as she nears, her lips a breath away as she blinks up at me, it takes all my strength to hold back. If I take over, I'll hurt her. And she doesn't need that from me right now.

She flicks her tongue against my top lip and a shiver races up my spine. She releases her grip on my shoulders, leaning back a touch before pressing down over my cock. My cock slides between the slippery wetness, my full length entering her.

"Fuck!" I grip her hips, stopping her from moving. I've never been one to hold back, ever, no matter how much of a release I need. But with Ivy, it's different. I never know how much I can take before I blow my load.

Easing up on my grip, I let her move. Her hair falls around her face, blanketing us as she cups my jaw. Her breathing is erratic as she drives up and down my hard length, using her knees for support.

"Kai," she breathes, leaning back. Voices from a crowd of people sound close by, blinking Ivy out of her haze, and her eyes dart around the car.

There's no way I'm letting her leave this car, even if those fuckers are standing right next to the window.

I'm close.

She's close.

chapter twenty one

IVY

I'M CLOSE. IT'S A MIXTURE OF KAIDEN and the chance of being caught. It's heightened everything I'm already feeling and everything I'm not.

But hearing voices close by is a wake-up call. A part of me doesn't care, the other is scared they will see, hear. I feel vulnerable in this moment.

"We need to stop," I breathe out, but the second he massages my breasts, I arch into him, my body pleading for more even if I don't say the words.

Traitor.

I want to savour the sensation, the feeling of being the one in power, the one in charge.

The voices sound closer and a small squeak escapes past my lips. I try to reach for my shirt, but Kaiden stops me, his heat and desire sucking all the air out of the car.

"Finish it, Ivy. Fuck me. Fuck me like there is no tomorrow, like a part of you doesn't hate me."

His words hit me in the chest, and I shake my head at him. "I like you more than I could ever hate you."

My words have an effect on him. I can see it in his expression, in the way his fingers dig into my hips.

"Then fuck me. Fuck me before they get close, fuck me before they see your pretty little tits bouncing for me, before they hear how you sound when you come."

I moan at his dirty words. My arse cheeks slap against his thighs as those words propel me to drive myself harder on his dick.

My tits bounce with my movements, and for a moment, Kaiden is transfixed, licking his lips as he watches.

I can feel my orgasm approaching as I continue to ram myself down on him, my movements frantic.

"I'm going to come," he growls out, flicking his tongue against my nipple.

The voices get closer and tingles shoot up my spine.

"Oh my God," I cry out. I drop my forehead against his.

I knew I was close, knew it would happen, but the power of it sneaks up on me. I cry out, my internal muscles squeezing his cock in a vice grip. It's powerful, consuming, and as Kaiden groans out his orgasm, I slump against him, feeling exhaustion creeping in.

It makes me wonder if it will always be like this between us; euphoric, passionate, fiery.

Then it clicks. I unintentionally just admitted this would happen again. We would happen again.

I pull back, ready to tell him I'll give this a try. There might have only been one guy before him, but I know without the experience that what we have is rare. People have great sex every day, but what we have is a connection beyond the passion, beyond the sex.

He watches me, his eyebrows scrunched up in a frown.

"Kaiden," I start, but the blaring of my alarm interrupts us. I cringe, rolling away, onto the other seat.

"Don't go," Kaiden groans, pulling up his jeans, but he pauses on his button. "Fuck!"

I finish pulling my knickers and jeans up and reach into my pocket for my phone before switching off the alarm.

I glance up from putting my bra on, seeing him still frozen on his button. "You okay?"

The fear staring back at me stops me from reaching for my shirt. All I can think is that someone has seen us, but scanning the area, I don't see anyone. I don't even hear the group from before.

He's starting to worry me.

"I didn't use a condom."

I sag with relief, reaching for my shirt. "It's okay. I'm on the pill again. I have been since the incident. While we were there, they sorted me out a prescription." What can only be described as relief runs through him, and I watch him take his first breath since he admitted he didn't use a condom. I smother my giggle and turn to give him a stern look, ready to tease him. "You don't want to be my baby daddy?"

He finishes pulling his T-shirt over his head and looks at with me wide eyes. I can see the flicker of panic, not knowing how to answer me. "Kids?"

"I think we'd make a cute baby. We could get married, buy a house."

"What?" he squeaks, and hearing him so undone, I burst out laughing, slapping his chest.

"If there's anyone not ready for kids more than you, it's me. I'm not ready for that kind of commitment. I don't think I've really thought about it, but seeing your face is priceless."

"You bitch!" he grouches.

I giggle, tying my hair up in a bun. "Get over it, because we really do need to go."

"Can't we go back to mine?" he asks. "I wouldn't mind stripping you down for a shower. Tossing myself off while you play with yourself, suds of soap running over your tits."

My breathing escalates, and for a moment, I consider saying fuck it, but I've been waiting for this moment since I first met Danielle.

"No, you'll want to see this too," I warn him and open the door nearest me before sliding out. The breeze has a small chill to it as I hold the door open, arching my eyebrow at him. "I'll leave without you."

"Fucking hell," he groans, sliding out of the car and standing in front of me. He cups my cheek, leaning down and kissing me briefly. "You're lucky you're hot."

I wink at him and look around for the sign near where Danielle is parked. We weave in and out of cars, making our way over to where Clary, Selina and the twins are waiting.

"Just in time," Clary hoots, and I turn to see what she means. Danielle is standing beside her car, screaming at those around her that they aren't her knickers.

People are taking photos or videoing the scene, which is making it worse. She gets in her car, starting the engine, but then Jasmine leans through the window, whispering something.

"What the fuck is going on?" Kaiden asks, stepping up behind me. I close my eyes at the touch, savouring it, but open them when Danielle's scream echoes through the air.

She looks out the window, down at the wheels, to see them deflated.

Seeing her more clearly, she's covered in drink of all colours. I even get a whiff of the foul spray we used. Clary was right, it got worse. It reminds me of the mouldy eggs my mum boiled once. The flat stunk for weeks afterwards.

"Keep watching," Clary demands, snapping photos of her own.

"Who did this?" Danielle screams, her hands slapping against her sides in frustration.

Jasmine steps back, cringing as she covers her nose.

The minute Danielle's gaze locks on mine and hardens, I lose all amusement, glaring back at her.

"You!" she yells, pointing in my direction.

I grin, giving her a little finger wave. She storms over to me, but halfway, trips over something, landing on the ground.

She screams, dirt on her chin and clothes when she gets back up. She's barely holding it together. I wouldn't put it past her to start smashing stuff up around her. I'm thinking this is the first time someone has ever gone against her and won.

Her friends run to her aid, but the minute they get close, they take a step back. "I think you have poop on your face," Krysten points out, squeaking when Danielle slaps her hand away, her face thunderous.

She keeps coming my way, her hands balled into fists. "I'm going to kill you!"

Kaiden steps a little in front of me, pushing her back when she gets close. It annoys me, because I can handle myself, but having him willing to protect me sends my heart racing.

"Don't touch her," he warns, his low, menacing voice sending shivers down my spine.

"She did this," she screeches.

"Did I?" I ask, standing by Kaiden's side.

Her narrowed eyes harden. "You know you did."

"Seems to me you had what was coming to you."

Noticing Clary, she turns to her, sneering. "I bet you had something to do with this, you freak."

"Better a freak than to be you or one of your minions."

"You'll regret this too. You both better watch your backs," she threatens before turning to Kaiden. "And you. You let them do this to me. I was your girlfriend."

He snorts. "No, you really weren't."

"Yes, I was," she yells, and those around her begin to laugh. Her face tightens as redness spreads up her neck and over her face.

"You really are delusional. You need medical help," he sneers.

She looks around at everyone, frowning when it clicks that no one is taking her seriously. They aren't following her. Even her friends have stood back a little, looking unsure of what to do. They bought into her lies, into her fantasy of what kind of relationship she shared with Kaiden.

"Go home, Danielle. Let this be a lesson to you," I tell her, crossing my arms over my chest.

"You're just a slut like your mum," she snaps, and my gut twists at her bringing Mum up. She laughs, clearly reading me before her twisted mind attacks Kaiden. "Do you know she slept with your dad and that's why he's left?"

I throw my head back, laughing. She couldn't be further from the truth, and as long as she stays that way, anything she says won't get to me.

"You don't know what you're talking about, Danielle, but whatever helps you deal with not getting fucked by Kaiden. Because that's all it was. A warm hole he could shoot his load into. I mean, he could have used his hand, but why bother when you are clearly so willing."

She steps forward, but Kaiden pushes her back.

"Don't," he snaps.

"What will you do?" she yells, pushing at his chest.

He shakes his head, looking down at her with pity. "You really have no idea."

"This doesn't have anything to do with you. This is between me and Ivy," she warns, trying a new tactic.

"You'll have to get through me," he growls, low.

"And me." I feel Grant step up on my other side, also showing a pact of loyalty, along with the twins, Selina and Clary, all of us standing side by side.

"And me."

"And me."

"And me."

"And me," Clary finishes, glaring at Danielle and her group of friends. They try to pull her back, but she shrugs them off, standing against us.

Looking down the line of people on either side of me warms my heart. I swallow the ball of emotion, not wanting them to see how overwhelmed it's made me. I've never had this before. Never even craved it. But they are there. For me.

I smile, feeling a true sense of belonging for the first time since arriving.

It washes over me, giving me a sense of purpose, of safety. And although a part of me is scared to lose it, I'm not going to fight it anymore. I'm going to let each of them redeem themselves, start all over again, and not let the past define our future. I'm going to hold on tight to this feeling, this belonging.

Danielle pulls me from my thoughts when she begins to laugh maniacally. "You really have no idea, do you?" she asks, a sly smile twisting her lips.

"What?" I try to act unaffected but my gut twists at the look she's giving me, like she's been keeping something back until this very moment.

"They're playing you. They used to laugh about the poor girl coming to live next door. Hell, Grant and Kaiden planned this. They wanted to get you to let your guard down so they could break you. And you're so utterly ridiculous, you've let them. Once Kaiden has finished with you, it's Grant's turn. By the time you've wished you never met them, every lad will have fucked you. Just like your mum. We would lie in bed laughing at how pathetic you were, thinking you were welcome."

She really has no idea.

Her words would have cut me, but I know the truth. Even if I hadn't, I'm hoping I wouldn't have been naïve enough to have believed her.

I step away from the others, getting in her face and smiling sadly. "Danielle, you really are a sad, lonely girl. You have all these people around you and yet, you are still alone. You bully them into liking you. But you can't bully me. You saw what I had, and you wanted it. You were witness to the moment I truly became one of them. I accepted them back and you didn't like it."

"That's not true," she snaps, glancing at her friends and frowning.

"But it is. If it wasn't, you wouldn't be telling me this. If I was being played, you wouldn't have announced it to all these people around us. You would have let them continue and made sure you had a front row seat to my downfall. You said it in the hopes I would believe it." I chuckle, flicking my top lip with my tongue. "You'd use anything in the hopes to tear us apart."

"It's true," she says, glaring at Kaiden, then Grant. "I heard them."

Grant steps forward, a noise escaping the back of his throat. He looks lethal as he glares at her. "No, what you heard was a revenge plan that was redundant the moment she walked into our lives, and you knew that the moment you saw them together. Get over this vendetta, Danielle, because what I said back then about her, I meant it, but people grow up, evolve.

We were wrong, and if you touch one hair on her head, I'll make you hurt tenfold." He looks up at those around us and notices a few people from school. "It goes to all of you. She's one of us, protected by us, and if anyone fucking touches her, speaks to her in a way we don't deem respectful, we'll put you down."

Even though his words are strong, cemented in stone, I notice a few of the guys look to Kaiden for validation. He nods, glaring down at Danielle. "You had your warning, Danielle. You are done at Kingsley Academy. Your place in the hierarchy is over. And whoever shares in your malicious stunts, you'll be held accountable."

"You can't do this," Danielle whispers in fury.

He smirks down at her. "I can do whatever the fuck I want. I'm Kaiden Kingsley."

Her fury is aimed at me next, her lips in a hard line. "Don't forget what I threatened you with this morning. I'm going to find out, and when I do, no one will accept you here."

"And my reply from then still stands. Go ahead."

"This isn't over," she threatens.

"I'd take you seriously if you didn't have shit all over your face and smell like a rotting corpse."

The sound of her screeching has me wincing, wanting desperately to cover my ears. I laugh as she trips again when heading to her car. Her friends go to help, but she shoves them all away, screaming at them. She throws her shoes into the crowd and we laugh at her outburst, watching as her friend steers her into her car that's parked next to Danielle's.

Once she's gone, I turn to Kaiden, gripping his T-shirt. I pull him down until his face is close and grin at him. "You promised me a shower," I flirt, fluttering my lashes.

He smirks, pulling me close. "Then I won't disappoint." He scans my expression, a spark in his eyes that he didn't have before. "You've accepted this?"

I shrug, still smiling up at him. "I guess I needed the wakeup call. I guess Danielle has her uses."

His deep chuckle vibrates down my chest, causing a small moan to slip free. His pupils dilate and his fingers tighten on my hips.

"I don't care who or what changed your mind. I'm over the fucking moon."

I sense a *but*.

"But?"

"But… I wish you could have done this somewhere I could strip you naked and fuck you raw."

"And they say romance isn't dead," Clary mutters, interrupting us. "Are you two finished being mushy?"

I laugh, resting my cheek against his chest as I face her. She smiles, and I can see she's happy for me. "Sorry," I lie.

Rolling her eyes, she shakes her head at me. "No, you aren't. I'm going to get a lift back with the twins. They said they're going to finish the party at theirs."

Kaiden groans, making me chuckle. I hadn't even realised they'd left. "I'll meet you there."

She nods before running to catch up with the twins, Grant and Selina. I look up at Kaiden, feeling nervous.

"Before we go, can we do something?" The heat in his eyes express the dirty thoughts he's having. I giggle, shaking him a little. "Get your mind out the gutter."

Grinning, he asks, "What do you have in mind?"

Feeling my cheeks heat, I duck my head briefly before looking back up. "Can we go on a ride?"

I love the way his face gentles as he runs his fingers over the curve of my neck and shoulders. "Yeah, baby, we can do whatever you want to do."

And I know in this moment, he really would do anything for me. Even risk his bad boy image by going on a ride. All because he knows I've never been on one.

I don't know what the feeling is that's swarming through my system, threatening to burst my heart wide open, but it's strong, powerful, and I never want it to leave.

chapter twenty two

KAIDEN

*I*T HAS BEEN TWO WEEKS OF PURE BLISS. There's still a black cloud over us where it concerns my dad, but we haven't let it get to us. The twins are getting frustrated, wanting Mum back. They don't say it, but I can read it in their expressions every time she calls to check in on us, something she hasn't been able to do in a while. It's different. She sounds different.

Everything is quiet again in Cheshire Grove. Even Danielle has stayed out of our way. After the pranks Ivy and her friends pulled, she'd taken the week off and had come back at the beginning of the week.

I've been watching her. She hasn't been bothering Ivy or her friends, but I know her. She's planning something, and I don't feel good about it. I want to hope her dad had talked some sense into her, but whenever she thinks no one is watching her, I can see the rage boiling behind the façade. It's not something I've brought up with Ivy. I don't want to stress her out. She has been herself for the past two weeks and I don't want to ruin that for her.

I couldn't see it before, didn't care to, because to me, she'd been perfect. But for the past two weeks, I've seen another side to her, one that has also crawled under my skin. There are no sides of her that I don't want, don't crave.

People at school were shocked at seeing us together, mostly because I don't do public affection and because of the rumours Danielle had spread about Ivy.

A slap to my chest brings me to the present and I smile up at Ivy, who's leaning across the bed. "Are you even listening to me?"

"Sorry, I must have spaced out," I admit, grinning at her when she frowns.

"You said you wanted to watch this."

I pull her into my chest, kissing the top of her head. "I know. I'm sorry."

"I guess you're lucky I like you," she grumbles. "That clown thing is scary."

My chest vibrates with laughter. "Why don't we—Let me get that," I groan, grabbing my phone from the bedside cabinet. "Hello?"

"Mate, I'm next door. Get your arse over here. Got the crap you needed. But there's something else… You should get over here."

"Give me five," I tell him, then end the call.

"The twins?" Ivy asks, resting her chin on my chest.

I hate to ruin our night, but I've been waiting for this information. Ivy might be with me again, but there are times when I see her indecision on whether to trust me. It kills me, but I'm willing to fight for her trust. It's all I can do.

I run my fingers through her hair. "No. It was Rome. You remember me telling you about the information I asked him to dig up?"

"About Danielle?"

"Yeah."

"But she's been quiet," she murmurs. She's unable to meet my gaze when she says it, so I know she doesn't believe it's over.

"Let's go see what he found out. I don't know why, but I've had this sinking feeling in my gut for a week now, and with all the crazy going on, I just want to be a step ahead at all times."

"You've been busy a lot this week. You need a break," she tells me.

I smile at the care in her tone, and shift down the bed until we're facing each other. "I love that you care, but I had to do some stuff for my mum. She has a beneficiary, but with Dad out of the picture, she wants me to keep an eye on things."

"All right, let's go and see what Rome wants, but then you owe me."

I pull her back down on the bed when she sits up, ready to leave, and lie between her legs. "Oh, I plan to make it up to you."

"Oh yeah?" She grins, her hands locking behind my neck.

"Definitely. I plan to do naughty things to you, Ivy Monroe," I rasp, leaning down to kiss the corner of her lips.

She moans, pressing hers to mine and deepening the kiss. I groan into her mouth, wondering if Rome will care if I'm another thirty minutes.

She pulls back, and satisfaction runs through my veins at the sight of her swollen lips.

"Let's go then, Kingsley."

Laughing, I roll over to the side and let her get up. I pull on my shoes before grabbing my shit off the side cabinet and putting them back into my jacket.

Nova is walking through the foyer when we hit the bottom of the stairs. "Ivy, just the girl I wanted to see."

"Everything okay?"

She waves her off her concern. "It's fine. I just wanted to run something by you. I'm not sure if you're aware, but Kingsley Academy is throwing a charity event in two weeks and I'm hosting. There will be music, silent auctions and a two-week getaway competition for anyone who bids on an item. This year we are using the event as a platform for young, talented minds to show off their talents. There's going to be a fashion show for designers, food from the cooks and a few other things. Me and Mrs Swansea will also be adding in artwork to be auctioned off."

Ivy's face pales and she glances at me briefly. "If you're mentioning this because you plan on using my artwork, no. It's terrible."

Nova shakes her head. "Sweet girl, you have raw talent. I've been surrounded by art my whole life, but nothing has ever come close to yours."

Ivy shifts on her feet, looking uncomfortable with the praise. Personally, I've not seen her work, but now that Nova has mentioned it, I'm intrigued.

"Mrs Swansea said it was dark," Ivy mumbles.

"Which makes it more captivating. She's pleased with the work. Would you please consider putting it up?"

"Okay."

"Good. Now, I've bought you and Selina tickets. Are you okay with Sam being there?"

Sam, in all his failures, has been here a lot since the hospital. I'm not sure what their relationship is like since he's been away for three weeks on business. Or so he says. Something tells me he's looking for my dad, and I don't blame him.

"Yes. He messaged me last night to say he was coming back this week and asked if I wanted to meet his parents."

Nova's face softens. "What did you say?"

Ivy shrugs, shoving her hands in her pockets. "I'm not ready to meet anyone else. I'm still getting used to having *you*. I'm not sure how I feel about Sam. I'm worried it will turn to shit if I add more people in."

Nova steps forward, tucking a strand of hair behind Ivy's ear. "I have faith you'll both get there. I know he's not been around lately, and he feels bad about it, but he'll be back soon and will make it up to you." She steps back, taking a deep breath. "As for everyone else, I understand it can be overwhelming, but you won't meet nicer people than Sam's parents. You'll be shocked by how much they'll remind you of Elle and Ed. And they're chomping at the bit to meet you. They just won't force you."

I watch a smile light up Ivy's face at the mention of the old couple she's become close to. "I'll think about it. Right now, I just need a little more time."

"Then time is what you'll get," she declares. "As for the charity ball, I'll have someone come in to fit a dress for you. I'm hosting this year so we're going all out."

Ivy glares at her. "You didn't mention anything about dresses, Nova."

Laughing, Nova waves her off. "It will be to your style, don't worry."

Ivy continues to glare, standing with her hands on her hips. "It had better not be frilly, short, or have any pink on it," she rants, before taking a breath. "Just pick black to be safe."

Nova's lips twist. "What about blue? Or dark green, like Romeo's eyes over there?"

For a moment, I think she considers it, making me smile until she says, "No. Just no. I'm not doing girly crap. My uniform is ridiculous enough."

"Language! And as long as you come, I don't mind," she explains sweetly.

"All right. We're just popping next door. Is that okay?"

Tears brim the edges of Nova's eyes and the calculating look from before disappears as sorrow fills her expression.

"You okay?" I ask, nervous about the way she's watching Ivy.

She wipes under her eyes, chuckling, but then a sob tears through her throat. She stares at Ivy, shaking her head in disbelief. "It amazes me how far you've come since you first arrived. You were so angry at the world, at me, that I never thought we'd get to this place."

I can see how uncomfortable Ivy's becoming and I want to laugh at her horrified expression as her gaze shifts from side to side. Some things never change, even if a person progresses.

"Nova, we really need to get next door," I tell her softly.

She nods, wiping her tears away. "Go! Go! I'm being a silly old fool." She laughs at her own dramatics. "God, I'm so sentimental lately."

"It's okay," Ivy murmurs.

"I'll see you later. Remember, don't be late back. You're helping Elle tomorrow."

"I won't," Ivy promises before saying her goodbye.

The second we get outside, Ivy spins to face me. "She's going to get me a girly dress, isn't she?"

I laugh as I wrap my arm around her shoulders. "Yeah, but if it makes you feel better, I can be at the dress fitting and scare them into giving you what you want."

She slaps my pec, smiling widely up at me. "For a second there, you made me believe you were doing something sweet, but you really just want to see me naked, don't you?"

Grinning, I shrug. "I'm a bloke."

"Will you two hurry the fuck up!" Ethan yells, grouchy as ever. He's been a nightmare the past week and it's getting on my last nerve.

I'd tell him to get laid, but it's nice to see him not fucking every girl in sight.

"Ethan, do you have balls?" Ivy asks sweetly, stopping outside of our door.

I growl, my arm tensing around her shoulders. Ethan, eyebrows drawn together, nods as he stares down at her.

"Then don't yell at me again, because that can change. You forget, I have access to your bedroom."

He licks his bottom lip, eyeing her up and down. "I knew you'd want me eventually."

Groaning, Ivy pushes him out of the way. I don't want to have to punch my brother, but I will if he keeps flirting with my girl.

Rome is lazing in the front room, his ankle resting on his knee as he watches Grant and Lucca going at it on the Xbox. Noticing me, he gives me a chin lift and straightens in his seat.

I take the sofa, pulling Ivy down next to me, keeping her between me and Grant.

"What you got?"

He runs his hand over his face, apprehensive about something. "You aren't going to like what I've got to tell you."

"Just say it, man. I need her gone, but I need to know everything."

"First, I couldn't locate her whereabouts after the festival. She made a large withdrawal the day after so I'm guessing she didn't want Daddy dearest to know either. There's nothing for me to go on."

"Go on," I encourage.

"Most of it is petty stuff with her friends. Danielle is the one who broke up more than one of her friends and their boyfriends. She posted the pictures of Jasmine before she started high school."

"The liposuction one? It still baffles me that Jasmine was ever huge," Lucca comments, still half engrossed in the game.

"Yeah, and the picture of Krysten's breast implants, she leaked the photos and made it look like Krysten's guy did it. There's a bunch of shit like that. She even has a folder on her computer with secrets her friends have told her. My guess is she's waiting until they step out of line to use them."

"Most of them are bitches, but not all are cruel," Grant adds.

"I know, so I deleted most of them," Rome admits, smirking.

"What about Hackett?" I ask, not caring who's a bitch or not. They go against me or mine, they're all as bad as each other and deserve what's coming to them.

Rome grimaces, looking a little green. "She's sleeping with Hackett. According to her teachers, she's not doing so well in her other classes, but excelling in Design. Hackett's computer shows he's been doctoring her results. She keeps him happy, so he keeps her in Design."

With a weary expression, his gaze flicks to Ethan, then to Lucca. It has me on the edge of the seat because whatever it is, it affects the twins, and I'm not good with that. The twins look from Rome to me, and whatever they see has them glaring.

"We aren't fucking going anywhere. Whatever he has to say, Kai, we deserve to know."

Groaning, I sit back, running a hand across my jaw. With a chin lift, I gesture for Rome to continue.

"Jasmine was drunk at the festival. Danielle was her ride home but left her there, stranded. I took her home and she was ranting about Danielle and you." Rome gulps, gripping the edge of the cushion he's sitting on.

"And?"

"She was drunk. However, I don't think this is something she made up. It wasn't rehearsed." Taking a deep breath, he continues. "That said, I can't prove if it is or it isn't. I'm still going through her files. She kept a lot of shit."

"What did she say?" I ask through gritted teeth.

"There's no easy way to say it so I'm just going to give it to you. According to Jasmine, Danielle slept with your father."

"What the fuck?" I roar, getting up from the sofa. A cloud of anger storms through me as I take a step towards Rome.

"Don't hit the messenger," he warns in a deadly tone. "This one hits back."

I take a step back, clenching my fists. My dad. Her. She had me fooled, made me believe she was someone else. How didn't I see how repulsive she was, that she'd do anything to get higher in the chain?

I'm embarrassed, ashamed she got one over on me, probably laughing the whole time we were together.

I don't care if she's left Ivy alone, she isn't getting away with this.

And my dad… I can't act surprised. He constantly pushed me towards Danielle, informing me she would be good for my future. I never wanted a relationship with her, but from the moment those words left his mouth, it was cemented in stone.

The fog blocking my hearing clears and I look up to see the twins yelling about going to Danielle. I step forward, pulling Ethan back while Grant keeps a lock on Lucca.

"Stop!"

"No. I'm going to go around there to see if it's true," Lucca snaps. "How could we not know who our father was? Not only did he rape someone, probably more girls than Cara, but he's sleeping with women his kids' age."

"Just stop!" I demand, shoving him down on the sofa.

Ivy, who I hadn't noticed standing, speaks up. "It doesn't make sense. She's obsessed with Kai."

Walking over to her, I pull her into my arms, holding her close. "Who the fuck knows why that bitch does what she does."

Rome clears his throat, looking around the room before his gaze lands on me. "I can answer that too. According to Jasmine, Danielle wanted Kai, and to make sure that happened, she wanted his father on her side."

"Ah, so what better way than use her body. It got her what she wanted when she used it before," Ivy comments, cringing.

"But that would mean…" I start but trail off when the truth hits me.

"She would have been fifteen," Grant finishes, looking as defeated as I do.

Lucca gets up, throwing his controller across the room. "I'm going to get drunk."

Ethan, quiet, looks around the room. "My blood fucking crawls over the fact we share his DNA."

"Ethan," I call out when he heads for the front door.

He looks back, sadness filling his features. He forces out a laugh, his gaze going to Ivy still in my arms. "You opened our eyes to a lot of shit, so I'm going to return the favour. Get out. Get out while you can, because this life, this world, it will swallow you whole."

He leaves with those parting words. I inhale deeply, trying to calm myself so I won't go after him. I'm not in control of what I'll do.

Soothing hands rub along my chest. "He didn't mean it," she whispers.

I step away from her, shaking my head. "He's fucking right though."

"Maybe, maybe not."

I turn, and seeing the uncertainty, the vulnerability, is my undoing. I shoot forward, pulling her into my arms. "I'm sorry."

"It's okay. Things are just heated right now."

"I'm not sorry about that."

Pulling back to tilt her head up at me, she says, "What then?"

"For being a selfish bastard. I know what this life can do to a person and yet I'll do anything to keep you with me, here."

She smirks up at me, surprising me. "It's funny how you think you hold that much power over me. If I wanted to leave, I would. Not you, not Nova, not anyone could stop me. But it's a moot point. I don't want to leave. We'll see this shit storm through together." She looks around at Grant. "All of us."

Rome clears his throat, holding his hand up. "I'm gone for the summer and I'm forgotten about. But I'll let it slide this once. If you guys cheer the fuck up and get me a drink."

A deep chuckle vibrates through my chest as I give a chin lift to my friend. "Whatever you want."

chapter twenty three

IVY

THERE IS A CHILL IN THE AIR THIS MORNING, blowing through my bedroom window. It feels good whispering along my bare back. I'm still not used to sharing a bed with Kaiden. He's like a furnace through the night, even though he sleeps naked.

"We need to get ready, otherwise we're going to be late. Again," I whine.

Groaning into his pillow, he rolls away from me. After the news last week, the boys have done nothing but drink. They feel stunned by all the things they were blind to for years. It's one thing thinking and knowing someone is bad, and another to find out how sick and depraved someone is. And their father at that. From the get-go, my mum never hid her true colours, so I can understand why they are so angry.

But it is a new day and they can't let him win. Or Danielle.

"Can't we skive today? I just want to spend the day with you," he moans.

I smile because as sweet as those words are, I know I'm not the reason he doesn't want to go today. "I thought you were okay with the Remington swim team coming today?"

I'm still shocked Kaiden let them compete at the school. When we first met, it seemed they couldn't be in the same proximity.

Rolling over, he glares up at me. "No, but today of all days is not the day to deal with Carter and his fucking friends."

I kiss his cheek and jump out of bed. "Well, you said you'd take me today. I've got to help Mrs Swansea, so I can't miss. Clary signed me up."

"Remind me why we like Clary?"

My chest vibrates with silent laughter as I button up my shirt. "Because she's awesome and has my back."

"Fucking hell," he growls.

Arms slide around my waist and I smile when he pulls me back against his chest. "Are you sure you'll be okay at school? You can't get into any fights."

He nips at my neck, groaning. "I make no promises. I'll go get ready. Meet me outside in thirty minutes."

Turning, I kiss him on the lips. "And go easy on the twins. You were hard on them last night."

Narrowed eyes stare back at me. "Lucca put my laptop in the pool. It had all my assignments on it."

"He thought it was your dad's," I explain.

"And Ethan smashing my office?"

"He was drunk?" I offer, biting my lip, because I know Ethan was mad that Kaiden didn't inform them of what transpired between him and Malcom Holden, or their dad's security guy. He was lashing out and it could have been worse. I heard them talking about his car.

Chuckling, he leans down, pressing his lips against mine. "I'll be thirty minutes."

I nod, watching him leave for a moment before shaking myself out of it and getting ready for the day.

♡

THE ONLY THING that kept me going through track was knowing that lunch was next. I thought once you left school, your choices were yours, but it seems physical activity is a requirement here at Kingsley Academy. It sucks, because if they knew how long Kaiden kept me up last night, they'd let me pass today's lesson.

Walking into the changing room, I'm surrounded by endless chatter about Carter and his teammates being here. Some are talking about how hot they are, yet most are curious as to what Kaiden and his mates have planned this year. As far as I'm aware, Kaiden has no intention of messing with Carter.

I've just finished changing when a hard hand shoves me into the locker in front of me and I smack my face against the door.

I whip around, glaring at the culprit. However, I end up rolling my eyes when I see it's Danielle, surrounded by a group of followers. The only one from her normal clique is Krysten. Sometimes I wonder if she's there as Danielle's guard. Danielle is cruel, yet I think if someone were to fight back, she'd run off and hide behind Daddy. Krysten, however, is another story. She loves being cruel and could probably back herself up if she ever crossed the wrong person.

"Sorry, didn't see you there, Monroe," she calls loudly, making sure the girls around us stop to listen.

"I bet," I snark.

"I'm sorry I've been so hard on you," she shoots back, her voice sickeningly sweet.

I arch my eyebrow, wary as I scan the room to make sure this isn't being recorded. Because this must be a joke. I'm not going to drop my guard around her, and if that's what she thinks I'll do, then she's got another thing coming. I wasn't born yesterday.

"What do you want?" I ask, tired of the crap.

"Just to apologise. I didn't realise how bad you had it. I wanted to help you settle into the school, but you are so standoffish, you make it hard. So, me and Krysten went to your old town, asked around about you."

I freeze, knowing the blood has drained from my face as a chill forms its way through me.

"You did what?" I ask in a deadly voice, scrunching my hands into fists.

All week I had known she was up to something. Not once did I let Kaiden or the rest know it was worrying me, but it did, because I wasn't sure when she'd come at me.

But this… I never expected this.

"Snake had a lot to say," she mentions, her lips twisting into a smug smile.

I shove the coldness away. Nova paid Snake off. She doesn't know that I know, but I heard her talking to him outside the flat when she asked me to grab a few of my belongings.

In a way, I knew then that part of my life was over. Snake wouldn't have sought me out. He wouldn't waste his time. However, if I had stayed, he would have made sure I ended up like my mum, reliant on him. She was all too willing to do him favours, never getting paid for it.

"Ah, I see you remember Snake."

I look around the changing room, noticing everyone's attention is on us, transfixed on what Danielle is about to reveal.

I step forward, getting in her face. "If you don't want another nose job, I suggest you shut it," I snap.

She places her hand on my arm and I roughly grab her wrist, shoving it away. "Calm down. I'm sure everyone here at one point in their life wet the bed. Maybe not at the age of fourteen though."

The laughter rings through my ears and I try to simmer down the anger boiling within me. Her lips move, but no words register.

Knowing someone like her has personal details about my life doesn't sit right. I want to lash out, hurt her, but violence isn't something she responds to. In fact, I'm sure she'll use it as a way to tell herself she's won.

Shaking myself out of the fog, I shove her back forcefully, knocking her into a couple of girls.

"I swear on my life, I will put you down if you keep sprouting shit about me, Danielle."

She giggles, looking around the room. I can see her chest puff out, proud of what she's achieved, and it hits me just how vile the girl is.

This is a joke to her.

"No, you won't. He said you owed him money. I was all too happy to pay him as a gesture of good will, but I can always bring him here to get it off you personally."

I snort to myself. She doesn't even realise she gave him money for fuck all. Or maybe she knew I didn't owe it, but knew she'd get more out of him if she flashed her cash. And money talks, no matter what class you're in.

"You're a playing a dangerous game, Danielle. I'm not the only one with secrets."

She grins, stupid enough to believe I don't know anything. The way she scans the group of girls, I know she has more, and she wants to make sure they're all listening.

"And your mum… He mentioned that even selling her body wasn't enough to buy you food or clothes. No wonder Kaiden feels sorry for you. He always was one to donate to charity," she snidely remarks, yet somehow, to the others, she'll come across as concerned and worried. She's a good actress, I'll give her that. "Tell me, how much did your mum charge?"

I roll my eyes. It isn't the first time I've been asked, and it surely won't be the last. It's one thing that's never truly gotten to me. Mum may have been a lot of things, but I'm not sure if there was a word to describe what she did. The closest one I can think of is a hustler. She never outright sold her body. She didn't say, for a blow job, it will cost you so and so. It was more the fact she'd see a bloke she thought had money, or one she could manipulate, and she'd sleep with them, using her body as a tool to get what she wanted. Sometimes they'd be all too willing to buy her what she wanted; drugs, alcohol, fags or money. Other times, she'd steal or blackmail them into giving her what she wanted.

What Danielle fails to understand, is that my mum was too fucking lazy to work, let alone stand in all weather conditions on a street corner, hoping someone would fancy a go.

Too much effort, even for Mum.

"Why don't you ask your dad? He was a regular," I tell her.

Some of the girls laugh, others keep quiet because they're scared of her. But not me.

Danielle shrugs it off, but I can see my comment got to her. It makes me wonder if she knows about her dad and if I hit a sore spot by bringing him up.

She steps forward, veins bulging across her forehead and along her neck. It's the second time I've seen her wearing the ugly inside of her on the outside.

"Your time is up here, Ivy, so I'd make the most of today. I mean, going back to a flat where there's no heating, no actual bed and having clothes handed to you by people you've never even met, must be scary. But that's where you belong. Where you'll always belong. No one is going to accept a low-life scrounger who sells her body for food. And if you think that is the only piece of information he gave me, you're wrong. By the end of today, everyone in this school will have you running back to the gutter you came from. But you never know, the guys here might be willing to pay for sex—at least, some might," she sneers, raking her gaze over my body in disgust.

A darkness overcomes me, and before I realise what I'm doing, Danielle is staggering backwards, hitting the wall behind her. I get in her face, sneering. "Careful, Danielle, because out of the two of us, I'm not the one who sells her body," I growl low, hoping the others haven't heard my words. Kaiden has plans and I'm not going to be the one to get in the way of them, not when he's promised I get front row seats to her downfall.

Her face pales as she shakily looks around the room, also praying no one heard me.

A small smirk lifts at the corner of my lips as I arch my eyebrow at her. "And let's get one thing clear here, Danielle. I'm not the one with things to lose. Take away the school, the money, the nice house and food given to me, I'm still me. I'll still survive. I'll still be somebody. But what will you be, Danielle, when all of this is ripped away from you, when you are no longer relevant? Nothing. Because without your fancy clothes, fancy house and your wealth, you are fucking nothing. You are no one," I bite out. I take a step back, speaking a little louder when I say, "These girls around you? They don't like you. I'm fairly certain they can't stand you and have your picture on a dartboard. When they leave here, you'll cease to exist. You'll just be some girl who bullied her way through life and those around her."

"Fuck you, Monroe. You don't speak for me," Krysten snaps, and I grin, glancing to the side where she's standing, arms crossed over her chest.

"No, I don't," I murmur, looking from her to Danielle, then back again, something clicking. "But if you weren't in love with her, you wouldn't give her the time of day either."

A gasp slips through her lips as she stares wide-eyed at Danielle.

"You'll regret this!" Danielle screeches.

I barely spare her a glance as I leave. It isn't until I'm at the door that I turn back around, giving her one last word of advice. "When you threaten someone, make sure they have more to lose than you do. You can't beat me. You can't hurt me. So get over yourself, Danielle, and grow the fuck up."

I hear her high heels clicking behind me when I turn to leave.

"Not even the secret between Kaiden, his father, and you?" she asks, her words stopping me from shutting the door behind me. When I don't move, I can imagine her grinning, thinking she's back on top. "Oh yeah, it's amazing what you can find out these days. I wonder how Kaiden will react when he finds out what you've spread about his father."

Gritting my teeth, I glance back at her. "I wasn't the one to spread for him," I snap, ignoring her cry of outrage as I slam the changing room door. I didn't miss the horror on her face. I hope she drowns on her panic over what Kaiden will do to her.

I'm not even a few steps away from the changing room door when Jasmine and Jenny come storming down the corridor, each yelling to be heard over the other.

"I knew it!" Jasmine screeches. "She was the only one who knew about my weight problems. I told her in confidence, and she spread that rumour like it was butter on toast."

I laugh at her description, tightening my lips when they pause to glare at me.

"That bitch. She told everyone about my third nipple. She made me believe William was the one who posted the picture of it online."

"I know things about her," Jasmine declares as she pushes through the changing room doors, nearly falling into Danielle's arms.

"You backstabbing whore," she screams in Danielle's face, and I grimace, walking off so it can play out.

Part one of Kaiden's plan has begun and it won't be long until this is all over and we can finally be normal.

chapter twenty four

IVY

MY MOOD HAS WORSENED BY THE TIME I get to the dinner hall. Danielle's words keep playing on a loop in my head and it's driving me crazy. Crazy enough to forget my knife and fork. With a sigh, I slam my plate and drink on the table Selina has deemed ours, drop my bag to the floor and head back to cafeteria line to grab my cutlery. I'm still steaming by the time I get back to the table, not noticing Selina, her friends, Si and Bee, or Clary at the table. The group have eaten with us a few times, but the majority of the time, they stay away, not wanting to get involved in the clique that comes with being friends with a Kingsley. I can't blame them. I guess the attention is a required taste, and I'd rather be the girl no one noticed.

"Well, I guess someone didn't get laid ten times today," Clary mutters before digging into her food.

I sag back in defeat, wincing at the group staring at me. "I'm sorry. It's been a long fucking day and it's not even halfway through."

I grab my drink, gulping half the contents down before putting it back down on the table.

"What happened?" Selina asks, biting her lip worriedly. I'm surprised she's even here. Carter and his teammates must be here somewhere at the school, and I would have thought she'd jump at the chance to go see him.

"If you were with me, you wouldn't be in a foul mood. I know how to get a girl off," Bee flirts, winking.

Clary snorts. "Girl, don't make me fall for you."

"Did something happen?" Selina asks, blushing, and I grin at her changing the subject.

A headache begins to form, blurring my vision slightly, and I grip the table to steady myself. "Yeah, Danielle and her cronies."

"Yeah, they tried sitting here before Clary shoved them away," Selina comments.

"Although, Jasmine was glaring at Danielle like she was about to murder her," Clary adds.

I chuckle, but the sound is weird, like I've got water blocking my ears. I use my fingers to try and unblock them, but it only makes it worse.

"Guys, I'm just going to head to the loo. I think I'm coming down with something," I tell them, my tongue feeling heavy in my mouth.

Reaching out, Selina places a hand on my arm. "Want me to come with you? You're looking a little green."

I shake my head, groaning when the movement causes the room to spin. I want to vomit. "No, I'm good. I just need to splash some water on my face. It might wake me up a bit."

"All right, just call if you need me."

It takes a few attempts for me to get a grip around the strap on my bag, which seems to have doubled in size, and when I do, I nearly topple over, missing the bag completely.

"Woah, maybe I should come with you," Selina calls out, sounding distant.

I wave her off, not even sure if it's in her direction as my vision splits in two, dots of bright pinks, greens and oranges scattering through my vision. "I'll be back in a minute. Eat your lunch. I'll be fine. Promise."

I head towards the exit, taking in a deep breath. Nova said she was feeling iffy last night so maybe I'm coming down with something too.

"Ivy," is whispered close to my ear as I walk into the toilets. I spin around, swearing it was my mum's voice calling me.

"You are losing it," I mutter to myself, heading to the sink on wobbly legs. Laughter rumbles through me when the sink twists, blurring with a luminous colour. It kind of reminds me of a picture of a moving object.

The sink snaps back with a pop. Wary, I scan the bathroom, hoping no one will take my magical sink.

I need it.

The cold water cools me down somewhat, yet the heavy feeling is still there, and everything around me is unfocused, yet bright with colours.

"Ivy," is called again, and this time, it's a male voice, one that has haunted me since I found that recording in Royce's office.

"Who's there?" I call out, clutching my head when a wave of dizziness hits me.

"You're next," Royce taunts, and I spin again, looking for him.

This moment was bound to happen. I knew he was gunning for me. I'd prepared myself for that very moment, but not like this, not when something is seriously wrong with me.

Cold hands touch my breasts, the feel of them freezing the blood within me, and I scream, the sound so loud I cover my ears with the palm of my hands.

The scream swirls in front of me and I end up on my arse on the stone-cold floor.

I scrabble back on my arse in a bid to flee, kicking out in terror at the black blob in front of me.

"You want it, just like your mum," he growls, the black blob slowly turning into a solid form, sparks of yellow and orange splashing out around him. "Kaiden said you like it hard."

There's nothing there, nothing but darkness with orange and red splashes surrounding it, giving it a glow.

I blink, clutching my head to shake away the nightmare. It's not real. It can't be. There's a squeak, and I dart my gaze in all directions, laughing when I realise it was me.

The floor is cold, and the florescent light doesn't help with my headache. It's almost blinding.

Wetness slips down my cheeks as the colour around me dims a little.

Deep down, I know I need to get help, I know something is wrong with me, but the fog clouding my mind has me unmoving, unwilling to register the danger.

Gripping the sides of the counter, I pull myself up, leaning heavily against the sink. My pulse races the more paranoid I get.

"Did you think you could get away with ruining my life?" Royce asks.

I squeeze my eyes tight, whispering, "It's not real. It's not real."

Kaiden.

Kaiden will know what to do.

I move to leave but stop short at the sight of the dark blob transforming into a solid form once again, this time the black tar-like liquid changing colour. Before I know it, Royce is standing in the doorway.

I blink, and he's still there, watching, taunting, his face twisted into the monster I've always seen him as. His malicious smirk taunting me.

"You aren't real," I whisper, gripping the counter when my knees begin to wobble.

"I'm not? Are you sure?"

"I'll scream," I warn him, hating this vulnerability inside of me.

"Your mum screamed. She screamed so loud I thought my ears would burst."

He comes at me and I run, slamming into a solid wall of muscle. I scream when I see him smiling down at me, that coldness lurking in the back of his eyes.

"Get away from me," I scream.

He tears the blazer from my body, my shirt ripping in the process, and I punch and kick out at him.

"Shush," he whispers in my ear, licking his way up to my earlobe. "You want it."

"No!" I scream, clawing at his face as he gropes me, trying to shove his hand up my skirt.

My vision clears, and it's no longer Royce in front of me, gripping my shoulders, but the guy I met on my first day. Leeroy, I think, and his lips are moving, but I can't hear the words.

A bright flash of pink brings me back to the moment, and Royce tries to shove my skirt down.

"No," I yell, clawing my nails down his face. I can feel the skin under my nails, the blood on the tips of my fingers.

Somehow, I manage to push him away from me, and I head for the door, nearly falling through when the steel door that used to be wood, flies open.

I press my hands over my ears, blocking out the sound of my mum screaming for help. Disorientated, I twirl in a circle, watching as the crowd of people point and laugh. It's deafening, and then they suddenly stop, smiling so wide they look sinister.

The ear-splitting screams are all I can hear. It's unbearable.

"Mum," I whisper, my voice cracking.

The smell of sweat fills the hallway, the tension and fear so thick that I find it hard to breathe. She's twisting and turning, struggling to get away from the men looming over her. The tall, lanky form pins her down on the bed while Royce, a sinister smile on his face, spreads her legs.

They laugh, and the sound knocks me back. I bump into another hard form.

I turn, crying out, only to come face to face with Royce again. "You're next," he promises, reaching for me.

"Ivy?" I hear roared, and shivers run down my spine at the chilling voice.

It's like I don't have control over my body, sound and movement slowing around me as I turn to the voice.

I blink, searching through the crowd until my eyes land on Kaiden, pushing his way through to get to me.

"He won't save you," Royce whispers in my ear.

"Help me!" Mum screams.

"Ivy!" Kaiden roars.

"I'm going to make you scream," Royce whispers.

"No, no, no," I cry out, taking a step back.

"You were never who I wanted," Mum screams. "You selfish bitch!"

"I'll ruin you like I ruined your mum," Royce taunts.

"You were always good for nothing," Mum screams, suddenly in front of me.

"Mum," I beg through a sob. "Why didn't you love me? Why didn't you protect me?"

"I never wanted you!" she confesses.

"Come here," Royce snarls, grabbing for my arm. "Take your clothes off."

I cover my ears to block them out, but it doesn't work.

Nothing works.

It could be seconds, minutes, but it feels like forever before I finally find feeling in my legs. I run, not looking at those still watching my mum being raped.

I don't stop when I hear her call my name.

I dodge Royce when he goes to grab me, the smell of his cologne and cigar smoke choking me.

My knees smack onto the floor, my palms scraping along the dark wooden flooring, but I get back up. I get back up and run away from the taunts, the screams for help, the laughter.

The double set of doors call to me like a beacon, a white light illuminating the frame. I push through, glancing over my shoulder when rough hands rip my skirt from my body, causing me to trip.

My lids tightly shut as I freefall, knowing this is the moment that I plummet to my death.

Coldness blankets me, soaking me until it pulls me down. My lungs burn, water closing in on me.

And the last thought I have before everything goes blank, is that I never got to live.

There are moments in time where you want love, you want money, a home. But life is hard. Love can be painful, heart-breaking, and at times, life ending. You work years making sure you have money to pay the bills, to buy luxuries and just stay above water to make a home.

But there comes a point in your life when you need to stop and enjoy the time you have left in the world with your loved ones.

I'm never going to get that moment.

If this is my death, all I've ever known is struggle and suffering.

But at least I finally got to experience love.

I got it when Selina became my friend, my cousin, my sister.

I felt it the moment I truly let Nova in.

And I got it in the moments I shared with Kaiden.

And now, I'll never be able to show them that love back.

chapter twenty five

KAIDEN

"I've put the proof into their lockers," Rome comments as we head to the dinner hall.

I clap hands with him, my way of a handshake. "Thanks, man."

"There's also something else," he murmurs, stopping me before the double set of doors in the hallway that lead to the dinner hall.

"What now?" I groan, just wanting to get to my girl.

Things between us have been so fucking good. The sex has been off the charts, explosive, and I'm hoping I can get her to sneak off with me to our room for a quickie.

"I managed to hack into the live feed in Hackett's office."

"You got into his private feed?"

"Yeah, it's good you noticed that camera."

I shrug. He refused to have a security camera, saying it breached his privacy. When I went to see him at the beginning of the week, I saw a red light flickering on his bookshelf. On closer inspection, I noticed it was a camera and got Rome right onto it.

"What did you get?"

"A recording of Danielle seducing him into changing her grade and a lot more of him blackmailing other girls into sexual favours. He left them no choice, man," he grits out, clenching his hands.

I pat his shoulder. "He's done here at Kingsley Academy."

He scrubs the back of his neck, looking over my shoulder. "I've not gone through them all, but there's one with your dad sitting in a chair, watching Hackett bend a girl over his desk. She was crying."

"Fuck," I roar, slamming my palm against the wall. "I'm going to fucking kill him."

"Look, I know you wanted to handle this your way, but I'm going to send this to the police. He can't get away with that."

I nod, trying to calm my breathing. "Get it done. And, Rome," I call when he goes to leave. "Give it to an Officer Sullivan at the local police station. He can be trusted and doesn't mess around."

"Can he be bought?"

I shake my head. "He's a good one."

"All right. You going to be okay?"

"It was going on under my nose. How do you think I feel?"

"True. I'll get this done."

"Rome, can you make a list of the girls for me? I want to make sure they get the best help. I'll have Nova Monroe help me set up a funding for them too."

He leaves after giving me a chin lift. I sigh, feeling older than my nineteen years. It takes me a few moments to get my anger in check, but when I feel I'm calm enough to hide the newest Royce revelation, I move forward.

It's never ending.

I never knew him, not really, and I'm struggling on whether that's a good thing or not. Did I want to live my life blind to the monster he was? No. But finding out new pieces of information, more crimes he's committed… sometimes I wish I could erase it from memory.

The wood is rough under my palm as I go to push through the door. However, hearing my name yelled from the other end of the hall, stops me.

It's Rome, his gaze wild and concerned. "Dude, your girl is going mental outside the men's room. She's clawed the fuck out of Leeroy's face."

"What the fuck did he do to her?" I ask, running into action as I meet him down the hall.

"I don't think he's done anything. Something's wrong. She's going fucking crazy."

I hit the hallway and my heart stops when I see the pure, unadulterated fear across her face. I've seen her angry, I've seen her hurt and upset, but never in the small amount of time I've known her, has she ever looked like this. Not even when we fucked her around or when Grant pushed her into the pool.

People shove and push to get a closer look, and I curl my lip in disgust.

"Ivy?" I roar, pushing people out of the way to get to her. I pause when her gaze locks on mine, the breath getting stuck in my throat when I get a clear image of the fear she's going through. She looks terrified, pure and simple. It's difficult seeing her so tortured. It's a big pill to swallow.

She ducks her head, like she's trying to block something or get away from someone. A whimper escapes her lips as she ducks the other way, like someone is there.

"Ivy?" I roar again, needing her to see me, hear me, to know that whatever is going on, she is safe.

"No, no, no," she cries, and I struggle to get through.

"Fucking move," I growl, pushing a guy into a group of students, all the while keeping my eyes on Ivy, worried when she places her hands over her ears, crying out.

Frustration consumes me as I fight to get to her.

"Fucking move out of his way, you fucking tossers," Ethan yells from somewhere behind me.

"Ivy?" I yell, finally reaching the circle. But she's gone, running down the hallway before falling to her knees.

I move to go to her, but then notice Leeroy stepping out of the toilets, holding tissue to his face.

I see red and shove him against the wall, squeezing his neck in a vice-like grip. "What the fuck did you do to her?"

His eyes bulge. "Nothing, man, I swear. She was in the bathroom, talking to herself, screaming out. When I went to see if she wanted help, she attacked me. I fucking swear it."

Letting him go, I run in the direction Ivy went. I don't see her, but it's not hard to find which way she went, people are still looking in the direction, whispering to their friends.

"Fuck," I curse, seeing the pool entrance up ahead. I pick up speed. The second I push through the doors, there's commotion around me—and I find Carter mid-dive, before he goes under.

"No," I whisper, jumping in after him.

By the time the water surrounds me, Carter is lifting her to the surface. She's still, lifeless in his arms.

When he looks up at me, I can read what I don't want to tell myself.

She's not breathing.

I watch her chest, praying for it to rise, but there's nothing, not even a slight movement to give me an ounce of hope. I pull her from his arms, moving to the edge of the pool where Ethan is waiting to help pull her out.

Her lips are blue when we lay her flat on the side, water pooling around us.

"Call an ambulance!" I scream to anyone who will listen as I reach for her. Carter pushes me away and I growl, ready to lay into him.

"I can help," he says, his tone serious.

"No!" Selina screams, running towards us, and the moment Carter hears her, sadness lurks in the depths of his eyes.

"She's not breathing," I snap, running my hand through her hair.

He grunts, and before I know it, he's pressing down on her chest, giving her CPR.

Ethan tries to pull me away to give him room, but I shrug him off, leaning down close to her ear. "Please don't leave me," I whisper.

Her body jerks with each compress. I sit up, watching her chest, waiting and pleading for it to start rising and falling.

I can't lose her.

I can't.

This can't be happening. Not now, not when she was so close to accepting me, to accepting the new life she's been given.

There has never been a more beautiful sound than hearing Ivy choking. A noise rises through my chest as I watch water spill from her lips.

Carter rolls her towards me, onto her side, and I bend down, kissing her head and thanking God for not taking her.

"She's going to be okay," I whisper. "She's going to be okay."

Feeling hands on my back, I startle and look up to find Grant, watching in concern. My vision blurs through the tears, and I'm shocked as they roll down my cheeks.

♡

THE HOSPITAL IS a hive of activity. Not only is Carter and a few of his swim team here, but Selina, Rome, the twins, Grant and a few other friends are all outside the room they've placed Ivy in, waiting to be informed on her recovery.

I can't leave her side though. The doctors couldn't understand why she wasn't waking up so had bloods done an hour ago.

Nova is sitting opposite me, on the other side of the bed, silently crying. "I keep failing her at every turn."

"You've not failed her," I reply, my voice rough.

Sam walks back through the door before she can speak, his expression tired and weary as he sighs, running a hand through his ink black hair. "The doctors are coming in. They have her results."

We stand when the doctor walks in, anxious to hear the results. He looks up from the file in his hand, scanning the three of us.

"Am I okay to speak freely?"

Nova steps forward, curling her arms across her chest, and nods. "Yes. We're family," she tells him, her gaze briefly reaching mine.

"Ivy is going to make a full recovery. She had a bad reaction to acid, a drug known as LSD. Do you know if Ivy has been involved in any substance abuse before?"

"What? No!" Nova and I proclaim.

"So, she was tripping?" I question.

"Yes. The drug will still be in her system for five days, but the effects from the dosage will clear in the next twenty-four hours. The high can last up to fifteen hours."

"So, she's going to be okay?" I ask for confirmation, needing to get out of here.

Ivy has only just started drinking, and apart from the two times she's gotten paralytic, she's not had more than a beer. There is no way she'd ever go near drugs, not after what her mum put her through with her addictions.

"Her blood pressure is still increased, even in her comatose state, and her heartrate is still high, so we'd like to get them down. She might feel a little nausea and suffer with mild insomnia for a while too."

"And her drowning?" Nova asks, her voice cracking. "Her skin is slightly blue still."

"We're going to keep her in for monitoring, but so far, there are no signs of pneumonia or respiratory distress, but please expect her to have chest pains and shortness of breath for a while. She's been through a lot. She's a very lucky girl. One incident in itself is life threatening, but the two at the same time… She got really lucky."

"Thank you, doctor," she sniffles, leaning into Sam when he wraps his arms around her.

The doctor gives her a gentle smile, patting her arm. "A nurse will be in soon to check her vitals."

As the doctor leaves, I turn to Nova. "I need to go somewhere. Can you call me if she wakes up?"

"Where are you going?"

"There's something I need to do," I tell her, evading the reason. I can't tell her I'm going to hunt down the bitch who did this.

"Okay," she replies, her attention back on Ivy. She runs a hand over her head, the sweetness of the touch something a mother would do.

"Thank you," Sam calls out, stopping me at the door.

"What for?" I ask, still not convinced of his motives towards Ivy.

"For getting her here. For saving her," he tells me, his pupils dilating as they fill with tears. "I'm going to be the dad she was robbed of having. And it kills me that now it's twice she's nearly died. I should have protected her. I'm glad you were there."

I wouldn't call it lucky. I promised her I'd protect her, make sure nothing else happened. I'm worried this will push her over the edge and she'll leave.

And the scary part is, I'll fucking follow.

Because you love her.

The blood drains from my face and I nearly stagger backwards.

But the feeling I got when she was run off the road was the same feeling I got at the pool. It wasn't just fear, it was a loss so deep it weighed me down, suffocating me to the point there wasn't a way of recovering.

I've never believed in love, in romance. I never exactly had role models to show me that love did exist.

And that was fine with me.

But there is one person in the world that fits you. Some call it true love, some prefer soul mate, some their other half. But Ivy... she's more than that, more than words can describe.

The feeling I get when I'm with her can't be measured. It can't be bought, and it can't be faked.

And maybe if I hadn't met her, I would have met someone who made me feel like that, but it wouldn't have been anywhere close to how I feel about Ivy. It wouldn't have been this deeply rooted inside of me.

chapter twenty six

KAIDEN

I'M STILL REELING OVER ADMITTING MY feelings for Ivy when I leave the room, the door quietly clicking shut behind me.

Everyone stands away from the wall, waiting for me to fill them in. But I can't. I need to hit something, someone.

Grant follows me, stopping me at the end of the hall. I'm unable to meet his gaze.

"Move!"

"No. Where are you going?" he asks, side-stepping me.

"To go fuck someone up. I'm sure they can pull together a fight last minute."

"No!" he growls.

I glance up at him, narrowing my eyes. "Since when do you tell me no, Grant? Huh?"

"You want to hit someone, hit me," he throws out, pushing me back.

It's enough to give me pause, but not enough to calm down my anger. "Move! I'm not fucking hitting you."

"Why? I sexually assaulted your girlfriend. I hurt her. Nearly drowned her," he taunts, pushing me to the brink.

I punch him, and footsteps come running down the hall from behind. "Shut the fuck up, Grant," I roar, kicking him in the stomach.

He coughs, looking at me from the floor where he's doubled over. "Again!"

"Woah, man, calm down before they kick you out," Carter says, holding me back with Ethan on the other side of me.

Grant gets up, narrowing his gaze on me. "She needs you right now, man. You can't leave."

"I can't sit around and do fucking nothing."

"Yeah, and fighting is going to help this situation? You'll end up killing someone, Kai."

I sigh, shoving Carter and Ethan away before taking a step back, needing the room to breathe.

"What happened, Kai? What's wrong with her?" Lucca asks.

"People are saying she had a psychotic break," Selina adds, sniffing. Carter walks over to her, openly pulling her into his arms, surprising me. I look to the twins, and they each shrug.

"He's got a pass for the day. He saved Ivy," Lucca explains, not looking happy.

"Again," Carter boasts, yet somehow it doesn't sound like he's gloating, more like trying to lighten the mood.

"But there's always tomorrow," Ethan snaps.

Carter just grins, pulling Selina closer.

"She didn't have a fucking psychotic break. She had LSD in her system, a lot of it. She was having a bad trip."

Ethan and Lucca share a look. "But she doesn't take drugs."

"I know."

Selina sniffles, and I'm shocked to see her openly hugging Carter and finding the twins are okay with it.

"It's all over Facebook. Someone recorded the whole thing, even in the bathroom," Selina informs us.

I grit my teeth and look to the ceiling. "So, the person was watching out for her reaction the whole time." I turn to Grant, finding it hard to keep my anger in check. "There's only one person who would do this."

He nods, wiping blood from his lip. "What do you want to do?"

"Give her a taste of her own medicine," I grit out. I might not physically hurt her, but she went too far. That drug alone could have killed Ivy in so many ways. It's time she felt a sliver of what she's put others through.

"I'm in," Carter calls out, surprising everyone. He looks to his teammates and they all nod, standing straighter.

"Us too," Ethan and Lucca vow.

I turn away from the crowd, slamming my palm against the wall and taking deep, heavy breaths. Once I'm composed, I face them again, ready to come up with a plan.

High heels click on the marble floor and we all turn towards the sound, seeing Jasmine and Jenny heading towards us.

"They've really got a death wish," I grit out, moving to meet them halfway. "What the fuck are you doing here?"

"We need to tell you something," Jasmine explains, twisting her hands together.

I cross my arms over my chest, glaring down at them both. "Talk!"

"It was Danielle," Jenny blurts out, looking like she's seconds from peeing herself. "I didn't know until it happened. And by then, Ivy was already on her way to the hospital. We came to tell the doctors what she gave her, so she doesn't die. Are we too late?"

"Are you fucking serious?" I snap, stepping closer. "It's been nearly three hours."

"We were scared," Jasmine squeaks, her voice high-pitched.

"Tell me what you know."

They share a look and a low, guttural growl rumbles through my throat, making them jump. "We don't know much. Danielle didn't tell us. She and Krysten have been besties for a few weeks now," she explains bitterly.

"I don't give a fuck. Tell me about Ivy."

233 Crowd of Lies

"Oh," Jenny mutters. "She spiked her drink in track. She didn't think she gave her enough when nothing happened, so she spiked her drink in the lunch hall. That's when we found out. We didn't know what to do. We thought it would be like doing coke, you know?"

My lip curls in disgust. "Not everyone has a tolerance for drugs, you bitch. They could have killed her."

Her face falls. "We didn't know."

"Have you gone to the police?" Grant asks, and I'm relieved he's thought ahead.

"Not yet. The police were at the school, asking what happened, but we wanted to come here first."

"Yeah, then spent most of the time panicking in the carpark," Jasmine explains, looking nervously at the crowd forming behind me.

"Don't tell the police anything. In fact, don't tell Danielle you told us," I warn them.

They clearly aren't understanding, both sharing a look of confusion. "I'm so confused. I thought Danielle was lying when she said you were secretly together. I mean, you seemed pretty hot and heavy with Ivy," Jenny rambles.

I roll my eyes, wishing I could shake some brains into them both. "I'd never go near fucking Danielle. Just do as you're told, and if I find out you've spoken about any of this, I'll kill you in your sleep."

Jenny whimpers, clinging to her friend who rolls her eyes. "We won't," Jasmine vows, then flicks her gaze to Selina. "It was Danielle who set the tent on fire. I'm sorry you got hurt."

Selina gasps, holding tightly to Carter, who tenses, looking ready to commit murder. "How the fuck do you know?" he growls.

Twisting her hands, Jasmine looks away, unable to meet anyone's gaze. "She was wearing her Dior costume and her Prada sandals all day. But on the night, she was wearing Hermes and Chanel."

"What does that have to do with the fire?" I ask, wondering if this bitch is crazy.

She rolls her eyes, cocking her hip. "Because, that Dior Costume wasn't even released yet and she threw it in the bin. I got it out, thinking she'd accidently dropped it, and she went mad, saying Dior was so last season. But… she wore Dior the following day."

"That still doesn't prove anything," Ethan mutters, his lips twitching, and I can see he's struggling to hold back laughter.

"Of course it doesn't. But they smelled of smoke and she wasn't wearing that near the fire. Duh," she mutters sarcastically.

"Seriously!" Carter growls. "Give me fucking strength."

Ignoring Jenny and Jasmine, I turn to Grant. "I've got the perfect idea," I tell him, and his answering grin is sinister.

"Just make sure I'm involved," Carter adds, and I turn to glare at him.

"Why the fuck are you still here? Ivy is fuck all to you."

He shrugs, looking down at Selina. "But she is. And it hasn't been you who has listened to her screaming out in her sleep."

"You've slept with him?" Ethan screeches, stepping forward, but Grant places a hand on his chest, pushing him back.

"Not now."

With two fingers in a V, Ethan points them at his own eyes, and then at Carter, mouthing, "I'm watching you."

Carter blows him a kiss before turning back to me, waiting to hear the plan. I look at the others around us and shake my head. "Meet at mine tomorrow night. Ivy will be released then."

He nods and I sag with relief, finally having an end near. I didn't want it to end this way, but if there's one thing Danielle needs to learn it's that all actions have consequences. And she's about to be hit with a boat load of them.

IT'S THE EARLY hours of the morning and Ivy still hasn't woken up. Nova and Sam are sleeping on the love seat in the corner, both cuddled up together. Seeing them yesterday and last night made me wonder if there's more going on between them. No longer is Nova defensive around him, tense. In fact, she seems to be drawn to him, seeking him out for comfort.

I'm not sure how Ivy will take the news that they're getting closer, maybe even fucking. It's something they need to hide until she's strong enough to deal with it, but it isn't my place to say something.

Taking in Ivy's appearance, I notice she's got colour back to her skin, yet she's still a little pale.

A small groan slips past her lips and I sit straighter, the chair creaking under me. With only the machines quietly beeping, it echoes around the room, rousing her from sleep.

"Hey," I whisper, running my hand over her knotted hair.

She blinks, disorientated, before focusing on me, her breathing escalating. "What happened to me?" Her voice is hoarse, raspy, and the torment I hear in her words have me gripping the edge of the bed.

"It's okay. You're okay," I tell her.

She shakes her head, the movement causing her to whimper and close her eyes for a moment. "It's not. Your dad. My mum," she says shakily, looking around the room.

"It wasn't real, baby. You were spiked and hallucinating."

"But it felt so real," she croaks out, her bottom lip trembling. "Who did this to me?"

I tighten my lips for a moment, not wanting to tell her. "We'll talk about that when you're at home. You fell into the pool at school, and that, combined with the drugs, meant it wasn't safe to take you home."

She seems to be mulling something over, taking her time. I might not be able to read her mind, but there's no mistaking she's thinking back on yesterday's events, trying to put pieces of the puzzle back together. It's in the change of her expressions, different emotions flashing through her mind.

"It was Danielle, wasn't it?" she asks, rolling until she's lying on her side, facing me.

I give her a sharp nod. "The bitch is going to pay."

"No!" she calls out sharply, but her voice breaks at the end. I hand her a glass of water, letting her suck some from the straw. She leans back, taking deep breaths before composing herself. "I want to deal with it."

I take her hand in mine, leaning in closer. "I can't let you do that. And I'm not saying you can't handle Danielle, Ivy, but the plan is already in place. She fucked with the wrong people, and hurting you was her gravest mistake."

"You don't get to decide for me. You have no idea what I went through," she tells me, closing her eyes, shutting out the fear and pain lurking in them. It's too late though. I saw it.

"I'm not dropping this, Ivy. I know you are strong and that you can take care of yourself. You proved that every time you went up against us, not taking our shit. But, baby, you don't have the means to do what needs to be done."

"What do you mean?" she whispers, scanning my face.

I shake my head, looking down at the bed. "No one is going to physically hurt her, even though I'd love to see the bitch be put in her place. What we have planned is far worse for her. Bruises can heal. Pranks can be forgotten, moved past. By the end of the week, she'll never come back to Cheshire Grove. And by the end of it, I hope you can still be with me."

"I've met cruel people, Kai. You might be a wanker, but you aren't a monster." She pauses, licking her bottom lip. "As long as no one does anything sexual to her, I'm good with whatever you have planned."

"I hope you mean that, because there's no going back now."

She nods, quiet for a moment. "Danielle went to my old home, asking around about me, and ran into Snake, my mum's drug dealer."

"I guess that answers the question as to where she got it. I had Rome ask the local dealers, and none of them admitted to giving it to her," I explain, running my hand through my hair. I push back in my chair, needing to move, but she reaches out and grabs my hand.

"Kai," she calls, a plea in her tone.

"Yeah?" I push the chair back up against the bed, gently lifting her chin so she's looking at me. Tears pool in her eyes, and I know she's trying her hardest not to cry.

"It felt so real. In the back of my mind, I knew it wasn't. It was like being locked in a cage in my own mind, the part that made sense anyway. Everything else was bright, loud, and felt more real than you sitting in front of me right now."

"It was because you were hyper aware of everything around you. Your senses were heightened."

"I was so scared. Even now I'm still trying to put together what was real and what wasn't."

"It's okay. You will in time. The drug is still in your system so it will mess with your head."

She wipes at her eyes before gripping my hand. "I want to live, Kai."

Not understanding, I ask, "What do you mean?"

She looks up, blinking. "I can't go another day living in the past. Once they've caught your dad, I want to enjoy life. I don't want to be afraid of letting people in or losing them."

I smile, running my hand over her hair. "When all our shit is behind us, you can do just that. Nova was talking about taking you to meet your grandparents. I could come with you to America, show you my favourite places."

She shakes her head and I swallow, wondering if this conversation isn't just about living, but living without me.

And who could blame her? I put her through so much, things no other person would forgive me for, let alone be in the same room as me. She was bound to wake up and realise she's better off without me.

"Kai, I'm not talking about materialistic things, I'm talking about getting the most out of life. Yes, I want to go places, but I want to enjoy the rest of my school years. I want to experience the things I missed out on. I want to love and be loved," she declares, her voice strong yet hoarse.

"You are loved," I whisper, hoping she can read the truth in my eyes.

Her pupils dilate, pooling with tears. "Yeah?"

"Deeply and irrevocably. I'm never letting you go."

Sniffling, she wipes her nose with the back of her hand. "I get it now."

"Get what?" I ask gently.

"Love. It isn't what you can do for one another. It isn't what you can buy or what you look like. It's in moments, actions and words. It's something that can never be measured or described." I hold my breath when she pauses, blinking up at me through her lashes. "I think I love you too."

The tension rolls off my body and I grin, tilting my head at her. "You think?"

"I've never loved or been loved. I have nothing to compare it to. But if this isn't love, then I don't know what is. I mean, who would want you after the shit you pulled if it wasn't more than sexual chemistry?"

I laugh, leaning down to kiss her forehead. "I love you too, but if you ever make me admit it in front of people, we're going to have problems," I tease. Kind of.

"Don't worry, your man card is safe with me," she tells me playfully before taking a deep breath. "I don't think we're that couple anyway. You don't need to tell me, just keep showing me."

"Anything," I vow.

She groans, hiding her face in her pillow. When she glances at me, her face is pale. "People saw me lose it, didn't they?"

I bite my lip, not knowing how to answer. She growls, looking away. "Great. I don't even remember half of it, so I'm not going to know what's true or not. They're going to think I'm crazy, proving Danielle's rumours about me."

"No, they won't. Jenny and Jasmine came by earlier to check on you. They told us it was Danielle who spiked your drink. Not everyone is standing by her. She's finished at Kingsley Academy. As for anyone else, I'll rip their fucking head off."

"You can't do that to everyone."

"I can," I snap.

She rolls her eyes before covering up a yawn. "Is there anything else I need to know?"

I don't want to tell her yet, but if she finds out from someone else, she'll think I'm hiding shit on purpose and going behind her back. And although it's partly true, it's not for the reasons she'll cook in her head.

"There's no easy way of saying this, so I'm going to go ahead and tell you. It was recorded. From the moment you walked into the men's toilets to the time you hit the pool. I don't know who she had record it. We're still trying to find that out."

"Great, just fucking great."

"Rome's working on getting it taken down," I tell her, not wanting her to stress over it.

"What's the fucking point? It's been seen by everyone already, I bet."

"It will be okay," I promise.

She sighs, not looking convinced. "I'm tired."

"All right. Get some rest." I lean over, kissing her forehead.

She looks up, biting her bottom lip. "Can you stay?"

I grin, resting my feet on the edge of her bed as I lean back in my chair. "I'm not leaving until you do."

She studies me for a few moments before she tiredly blinks, struggling to keep her lids open. It's not long before she's in a deep sleep, her chest rising and falling.

And I stay.

I watch.

Because for a few moments yesterday, I didn't, and I never want to feel that loss again.

chapter
twenty seven

KAIDEN

*I*VY IS ANGRY, WITHDRAWN, AND ALTHOUGH she did well to hide it at the beginning of the week when they discharged her, she's now done pretending.

She spent the week at home, recuperating, but Nova was starting to worry and ordered us to get her out tonight for the charity event she's hosting.

We're hanging out in the rec room while we wait for the event to start. The large space is more modern looking than the rest of the school. With its wide bay windows, the room has a great view of the landscape surrounding the school and a majority of the carpark.

What I love most is the light that shines brightly into the room during the day, even though it doesn't need it since the white furnishings give the room a bright and open-spaced look. The view we get when it's dark isn't something to sneeze at either, especially when the night sky is clear and all you can see is stars. It's one of my favourite places to be, and if it wasn't for the twins being at home alone with Dad last year, I would have lived here permanently. It doesn't feel like a prison, unlike how Kingsley Manor had become with all its strict rules and bad memories. Kingsley Manor didn't feel like a home, even if it was the closest to one. It hasn't been the same since Mum kept taking her 'extended spa trips'.

Here it was different. The walls are dark grey and black, along with some of the furnishings, blending nicely with the white. It screams guys. With three rooms, two with an adjoining bathroom, the rest is an open space; a living room and open kitchen, with a pool table in the corner. And then there's the pull-down ladder that leads up to the rooftop.

The girls haven't long finished getting ready in my room. Ivy had walked out first, her shimmery silver dress with dropped back that fell to the top of her arse looked flawless. She took my breath away. She's stunning without all the makeup and fancy clothes; my cock that has been rock hard will attest to that.

Her head isn't here. She's lounging on the sofa, gazing out the window, lost in her own head.

I don't know how to fix this. She wants to confront Danielle, to confront the people spreading rumours that she's crazy around school. And I can't blame her. I'd have knocked everyone out and burnt the school down by now if that had happened to me.

Ivy isn't like me. She doesn't get mad, she gets even, and I'm pulling her back from that.

I walk over to her, taking a seat on the footrest, my hands pressed together between my legs.

She jumps a little before turning her attention to me, forcing a smile. "Is it time to go?"

I shake my head. "Look, I know I told you to come tonight, but if you want to leave, we can leave. I can't stand you being angry with me."

"I'm not angry with you, Kai. I'm livid at the situation. I've never hated anyone as much as I hate her. I didn't even feel this contempt towards my mother, and she put me through hell. Danielle brings out the worst in me. I want to kill her, Kaiden."

Tears of frustration pool in her eyes. I learned early on to never mistake those tears for sadness. She's on a warpath of destruction, and until Danielle gets what is coming to her, she won't be okay.

My phone alerts me of a message. I pull it out of my blazer, reading the message from Rome saying that it's on and to get downstairs.

I grin, ready for this to be done.

We have people coming in from all over for tonight's event. But the most significant and prominent attending is New York's top fashion designers, arriving to see Danielle's work. She has a lot riding on tonight, hoping to team up with one to build her own line.

Only, I have plans to ruin any kind of future she thought she'd get once she left Kingsley Academy.

"Come with me," I order, taking Ivy's hand.

She looks up, puffing out a breath. "I'm really not in the mood. And I'll only embarrass Nova if I see Danielle."

I roll my eyes, because Nova would stand on the side-lines and cheer her on. It's taken me awhile, but all I see is a mother's love when Nova looks at Ivy. Her reaction to the drugs and to what happened cemented that. She was ready to kill Danielle, Sam not far behind. They really do want her to be happy.

"You really don't want to miss this," I tell her, amusement in my voice.

"This had better be good, Kai," she snaps.

"Aww, lovers spat," Grant calls out by the door.

"Fuck off, you tosser," Ivy snaps before pausing by the door, looking around the room. "Where's Selina?"

Clary laughs, linking her arm through Ivy's. "Seriously, you need to wake up, girl. Selina said she'd meet us here, that she was going to dinner before, with Carter."

"Oh yeah," Ivy mumbles, shaking out of her fog.

Grant and I share a look at her behaviour, worried she won't snap out of it. The only cure is Danielle getting put down, so hopefully, what I have planned, works.

♡

THERE'S A CHILL in the air tonight and the promise of rain. When goose bumps begin to rise over Ivy's delicate skin, I pull off my jacket, wrapping it around her shoulders.

She smiles gratefully up at me, pushing her arms through. "Thank you."

"Don't even think about it," Clary snaps, pushing Ethan away when he tries to be a gentleman, handing her his own jacket.

Looking like a wounded animal, he backs away. "Was only trying to be nice."

She rolls her eyes as she pulls the sleeves of her dress down, covering her hands.

Danielle's white convertible pulls into the school parking lot, police sirens following not far behind.

"What?" Ivy's astonishment brings a smile to my face.

I pull her back so she's leaning against my front. Leaning down, I run my lips over her earlobe, feeling smug when she shivers. "Let the games begin."

"What did you do?" she whispers, watching as Danielle gets out of her car, completely unaware of the police parking up behind her. I snort, disgusted that I ever fucked her. I've never known anyone to be so self-centred that they aren't even aware of the predicament they're about to be in.

"You'll see," I answer Ivy, kissing the crease in her neck.

"Miss, put the bag down and step away from the car," Sullivan calls out, yet Danielle ignores them, walking to the back of the car.

The curvy female cop with Sullivan runs up behind her and pins her arms behind her back, cuffing her.

Danielle screams, her eyes widening when she finally takes notice of her surroundings.

"What are you doing?" she screeches, struggling to get free. "My father will have your jobs."

"We've been tipped anonymously that you are in possession of drugs with intent to sell. We have bank statements faxed, informing us you took out a large sum of money. We also had a young lady come in to file a statement this evening, informing us that you purposely drugged an unwilling victim, who nearly died."

Danielle is ashen as he lists off the crimes she's committed, before that scathing expression twists upon her face. And I know she's about to try and worm her way out of it.

"I paid a man called Snake for information," she fires back. "And I've never touched or bought drugs in my life."

Sullivan takes out his pad, reading his notes. "Do you mean a Johnathon Walker, a drug dealer who goes by the name of Snake?"

"Yes, but I didn't buy drugs off him," she screeches, struggling. "Let me go!"

He holds up his phone, showing her a picture that has her turning green. "Is this the man?"

"Yes," she whispers.

The picture is one my PI got, who's still in the area looking for evidence that my dad had Cara Monroe killed. It was by chance that he saw Danielle, all too happy to take pictures, along with witness statements stating they saw my dad a few weeks before Cara was killed.

"Yes, a Mr Walker who has recently turned his life around. He was helpful in our enquiry when he went to his local police station, informing them of a girl, who fits your description, who offered him money to buy a lot of drugs."

"What?" she yells, shoving forward. "I paid for information."

"That's not what Mr Walker says. He had a feeling you were going to hurt the daughter of his ex-girlfriend and would get the drugs another way. He found the courage to speak up this morning, having heard of the near death an Ivy Monroe experienced last week."

Ivy tenses at the mention of her mum. I didn't like not warning her, but I wasn't sure Snake would fulfil his end of the bargain when Grant and Rome offered him a lot of money to go to the police and make up a statement.

We listen to them read Danielle her rights, the corner of her eyes turning into slits when they mention Ivy's name. She scans the parking lot, her gaze landing on us.

"I'm going to fucking kill you," she screams at Ivy. "You did this!"

"Miss, calm down before we add to your charges," the female cop warns her, feeding Danielle's anger.

Her gaze meets mine, softening a little. "Tell them they've got it wrong. Tell them she did this to get me away from you."

I stay silent, yet I'm unable to look away as Sullivan opens her boot, pulling out bags of LSD and other substances, all over the amount to be classed as personal use. It cost us a lot, but watching this moment, it was fucking worth it. And what better way to enact our revenge than to use her own dirty tricks against her.

A crowd forms around the vehicle, all watching as Danielle struggles to get free. Sullivan steps back from the car, reading out the estimates and guesses of which drugs are in the car and how much they weigh, over the radio.

"What? That's not mine," she screams, paling when he unzips another garment bag; sealed bags of cocaine piling to the floor.

"Does anyone else have access to your vehicle?"

"Just my parents," she tells him, glancing around at those watching on. Rome walks up with the fashion designers, shaking his head like he's disgusted with what Danielle has been up to. Even from here I can see him lay on the charm. Hopefully all his talk works and he can still get them to keep funding the fashion design programme. If he doesn't play the drugs as an isolated incident, we're fucked. But it was something I was more than willing to gamble.

Danielle notices them and moves towards them in a blind panic, but the cop jerks her back, quietly giving her a warning.

Danielle glares behind her before turning back to the designers. "It's not what you think. I've been set up. I've never seen this before in my life," she cries out, but they snub their noses at her. I watch in relief as they smile up at Rome, patting his arm before walking away. He gives me a chin lift, letting me know we're good. "Wait! Don't go! This is all a mistake. My dad will be here to clear this up."

"Are you the only one who had access to these garment bags, Miss Holden?"

"Of course. My designs are worth a fortune, which is why you should put them down," she snaps, looking a little green when he throws a dress back into the car.

"Did you put these dress bags into your car today?"

Danielle glares at Sullivan. "Yes."

"And you live in a home that is gated and has security?"

"Yes," she growls, blowing hair out of her face.

"So, no one can enter your property without being seen?"

"Yes. What does that have to do with anything?" she snaps, glaring at the female cop when she pulls on her arms.

"Did you leave your vehicle unattended at any moment since leaving the house? Maybe to get a drink or fill your tank?"

"For God sakes, no!"

"That is all we need until we can interview you later. I suggest you get a lawyer, Miss Holden."

"What? No! I didn't do this. It isn't mine," she screams, when the cop begins to drag her towards the police car. I pull out my phone, ready to snap a photo so Ivy can look back and feel nothing but satisfaction.

She gently places her hand over the phone, twisting until she's staring up at me. "I know what you're doing, but seeing this, seeing her downfall… It's enough. She's finally getting what she deserves."

"You!" Danielle roars, her face turning an ugly shade of red as she directs her anger towards us. "This is all your fault. You did this."

"Me?" Ivy asks sweetly, pointing to her chest.

It only angers Danielle more, and she takes the cop by surprise, pushing her out of the way. She charges at us, her hands cuffed behind her.

I pull Ivy beside me, knowing Danielle can't hurt her yet not willing to take the chance.

"You just couldn't live with the fact that he loves me," Danielle screeches. "I should have set you alight, not that fucking tent when I had the—" The cop tackles her to the ground and Danielle screeches, kicking out, forcefully knocking the cop back.

The skies open and drops of rain begin to sprinkle from the sky, but nothing could make me move right now, not even a comet falling from the sky.

It's too good of a moment to pass up.

"My dad will have you fired. He won't let you get away with this," she screeches at the cop, kicking Sullivan in the face with her high heels. I wince, feeling sorry for the guy.

The female cop pulls something from her belt, holding it up in front of Danielle, and the scream that tears from her mouth opens up the sky.

"Was that CS gas?" Clary asks, grimacing when they roll Danielle onto her stomach, the cop shoving her knee into her back to keep her still.

"Yeah, it stings like a bitch," Ivy comments, surprising me. She shrugs when we all stare at her. "What? I accidently got sprayed once when they arrested one of my mum's boyfriends."

I chuckle, shaking my head. I tuck her against me, grateful when Ethan passes us an umbrella to shield us from the rain.

"It burns!" Danielle screams. "And I can't see. Why can't I see? I'm going to sue you for everything you own."

Sullivan recovers, helping the cop lift Danielle to her feet. He glares as he wipes blood from his cheek. "Go ahead. What we earn must be pennies to you."

When we get a glimpse of her, she's covered head to toe in mud, a sight Danielle would never be seen dead looking like.

"Now you can take a picture," Ivy muses.

"Kai," Rome calls, gesturing for me to follow him. I hold up my finger, letting him know I'll be a minute.

Turning Ivy around, I lean down and kiss her, flicking my tongue against hers. She moans, clinging to my waist.

Her eyes dilate when she pulls back, scanning my chest. My shirt clings to my stomach, outlining my six pack. Her gaze turns hungry as she licks her lips. I smirk, winking when she sees I've caught her checking me out.

She shrugs. "You're hot, and I'm horny."

I laugh, pulling her closer for another kiss. If I didn't know Rome had information for me about our next part of the plan, I would drag her back to our room and fuck her until she couldn't see straight.

"I need to go see what Rome wants. It might be important," I tell her, not wanting to fill her in on the other part just yet. I want to get through tonight first.

She pushes on my chest, groaning. "Hurry up and I'll show you what underwear I'm wearing."

I groan, wondering if Rome will wait an hour or so.

"Kai, man," Rome yells, and I turn to see him covering the mouthpiece on his phone.

I turn to Ivy with regret. "I promise I won't be long."

She smiles, looking better than she did earlier. "Go, I'll be fine."

I leave, my stomach twisting at the first step I take, and it has nothing to do with not getting laid.

It's something else, something I can't explain. I shake it off, feeling ridiculous. Rome watches me with concern, mouthing, "You okay?" but I nod, waving him off.

And yet, it feels like something is pulling me back, away from Rome and to Ivy.

chapter twenty eight

IVY

THE SHARP PAIN IN MY STOMACH nearly has me doubling over as I watch Kaiden walk away. I want to follow him, a foreboding sense of dread filling the pit of my stomach.

I clear the negative thoughts. There's no one stupid enough to go up against him, and he's surrounded by his brothers and friends, all of whom are loyal to him and would do anything to see that he's safe.

"You okay?" Clary asks, sidling up to my side.

I glance to the side, nodding. "Just processing," I lie.

She doesn't believe me but doesn't question me either, always giving me that space. I like that about her.

Miss Swansea calls Clary over and she groans. "I'd best go and help her set up like I promised."

I laugh, nudging her shoulder. "She's already done most of it. She just wants you there to greet people."

She looks around like she's only just noticing people arriving. "Shit! My dad's going to be here," she rushes out, before turning to face me, clutching her umbrella. "I'll catch you in the hall."

I nod, waving goodbye. I'm ready to go find Kaiden when Elise, one of Nova's friends from school, calls my name, biting her lip worriedly.

"Hi, Elise," I greet.

"Hello, Ivy. I was wondering if you've seen Nova. She was meant to be here over an hour ago to make sure everything was set up okay, but she hasn't arrived."

I blink in confusion. "That's weird. When I left earlier, she was on her way out. She said she had to pick up a donation before she could get ready."

"When was that?"

I try to think back to when Kaiden picked me up to get ready with Clary. "A little over an hour ago. Have you tried calling her?"

"Yes, but it's going to voicemail. We really need her to get here. The guy from Jet Seas is here. She wanted to get him to donate holidays to families in need in exchange for a place at the school for his son. She wouldn't miss this chance, but he's ready to leave."

"Um, okay," I mumble, looking around for anyone who can help. Nova wouldn't miss today. She's worked hard all week making sure everything goes to plan. The only thing that would stop her is if she had bad news.

I spot Kaiden in the middle of a heated conversation with Rome, and although I know he'd put my needs first, I know he's still got something going on. He thinks he can hide it from me, but I can easily read him now we've opened ourselves up to each other. And not only that, but if the news has something to do with my mum's case, I want to be prepared. Not seeing anyone, I sag with defeat, knowing I'll have to go call a taxi. "I'll go see what's taking her so long. Try to keep him entertained. She's probably got held up in traffic."

"You're a good girl, Ivy," she comments, smiling gratefully.

Ignoring her, I force a smile and head towards the other side of the carpark where the main entrance is.

A car pulls up to a stop in front of me and I drop my phone away from my ear and lean down, smirking at Selina's attire. She looks truly ravished, which explains why she's so late.

"Where are you going?" she asks as she rolls her window down.

Not sure why, but I lie. "I forgot an art piece at home. Can you drop me off?"

She turns to Carter, but before she can ask, he leans over the seat with a smug smile. "Get in."

The rain pelts down against the windows, and as we pass a group of people, I can't help but look back, wishing I had told Kaiden.

I OPEN THE car door but before getting out, I lean between the seats. "I won't be long. If you want, you can go ahead, and I'll catch a ride with Nova."

"We can wait," Carter answers, looking at the house with drawn eyebrows.

I turn to look, and I can see why he looks so freaked. The lights are out, and when a roll of lightening lights up the sky, it makes the manor look like a haunted house.

I nod in acknowledgement before getting out in the pouring rain, ducking my head as I run up the stairs and push open the front door.

The minute I step inside, trepidation slivers down my spine. I close my mouth, unease stopping me from calling out for Nova or Annett.

Something smashes at the top of the stairs, and my feet are moving before I can think to get help. A cry of pain has me moving faster up the winding staircase, the sound coming from my room.

I barrel into the doorframe when the sight of a bloody handprint on the wall outside my room catches me off guard.

It takes me a moment to adjust to what I'm seeing in the dimly lit room. I blink, hoping the sight before me isn't real, that I'm hallucinating all over again.

I'm not.

The sight before me has me rooted to the spot, unable to move or call out for help.

Annett lies diagonally across my bed, beaten and bloody, clothes torn from her body. I gag at the metallic smell of blood that fills the air. It's fresh, not yet dried to the sheets. Her eyes are closed, and with the dim lighting, I'm still unsure as to whether she's alive or not. My heart pounds against my chest as I become unglued and finally register what is happening in the room.

Nova.

Nova and Royce.

"No," I breathe out, watching him tear the deep blue dress from her body. It pools at her feet and my eyes widen at the sight of the angry red blotches already forming on her pale skin.

I black out, and for a moment, I don't see Nova on the floor, fighting with all her strength, but my mum, begging him not to take her innocence.

I scream, charging for him. He doesn't acknowledge the sound, too busy raising his fist to Nova, who is barely keeping her eyes open. I jump on his back, my fist slamming down on any part of him I can reach.

He roars, swinging around to throw me off. I cling to the monster who has haunted my dreams, who destroyed the girl my mum was. Every muscle in my body tenses, desperately trying to cling to him and keep him away from Nova.

He grips my wrist and forcefully yanks on my arm. I cry out, the popping sound making me dizzy as pain like no other vibrates up my arm. My head drops back, smacking against my desk with a *thud*.

"Ivy, run," Nova whispers painfully, trying to get to her knees.

"You!" Royce growls, gripping me by my hair and dragging me into the middle of the floor. He kicks out, landing his foot in the side of my ribs. I roll, breathing heavily as I glare up at him.

When I try to get up, I forget about the pain in my arm and shoulder. I collapse to the floor, my cheek pressed against the carpet as the pressure in my arm builds.

Boots that I vividly remember from the day of the car crash step in front of me. I expected taunts, threats, so when he lifts my head by my hair, smashing my face against the floor, I don't expect it.

I should have got help.

I shouldn't have left Kaiden behind.

He rolls me onto my back and I kick out, screaming at the top of my lungs and praying Carter and Selina will hear me.

"Shut the fuck up," he grits out, the palm of his hand meeting the side of my face. "You couldn't leave well enough alone."

"Fuck you!" I lean up, spitting in his face as I try to get free, jarring my shoulder once again. It becomes too much; the pain, the smell, the overbearing fear. Sweat pours down my face as another wave of dizziness consumes me.

"Oh, I'm going to fuck you. Teach you a lesson, just like I did your slut of a mum."

I whimper, twisting to get out of his grip. He gropes at my dress, and a sickening dread fills the pit of my stomach.

I won't recover.

I've been scared. I've been frightened. But there aren't words to describe how I'm feeling right now.

I want to throw up, especially when Royce mutters, "Fuck it," and lifts up my dress.

I fight. God, do I fight. But the minute he presses his weight over me, digging his palm into my mouth, I come to terms with the fact he's going to rape me. I prepare myself for the worst, yet I don't give up fighting.

He lets go of my good arm that he has pinned down and I reach up, digging my nails into the side of his head, pushing my thumb into his eye.

He falls back, palming his eye, and I use the moment of distraction to push myself away, using my feet.

"No," Nova cries, distracting me.

I glance over, finding her gripping the edge of my desk, blood pouring from her neck before she collapses to her knees again. My eyes widen as I look to the floor, seeing a knife by the end of the bed.

A scream tears from my throat when a hand wraps around my ankle, dragging me along the floor. I reach out, trying to grab onto something, but there's nothing there.

"No," I cry, tears falling down my cheeks.

I lift my leg, kicking him in the chin, fuelling his anger.

"You little slut! You'll like it like your mum did."

"Why?" I scream. "Why did you rape her?"

"Don't be so naïve, girl. You know why," he snaps, but then laughs, his eyes lighting up. "Well, you know the version Neil told."

"What?" I yell, kicking him in the stomach when he reaches for me again.

He lifts up, undoing his belt. "It was true, our dads wanted us to marry into the Kingsley or Monroe empire. It could have been any of them. But your mum? She thought she was too good for us. I wanted her for so long, but she turned me down each and every time. I even dated Nina to make her jealous."

"You're a pig," I scream. "You raped her because she knew what a sleaze you were."

He laughs, pulling his belt free. "And I enjoyed every second of it," he admits, but then his face hardens, a sinister glint to his eye. "But then she had to blackmail me. I couldn't stand for that. I'm not having some washed up whore try to take what I worked hard to achieve."

"What you had handed to you," I retort. "And it didn't stop you from raping her."

"If she hadn't fucked around and tarnished her reputation with drugs and alcohol, I would have fucked her again, made her my wife."

I gag at the delusional prick. "You make me sick."

The belt whistles through the air before coming down across my stomach. The burn and pain has my back arching off the floor.

Another slash to my thighs and my heart shatters into a million pieces, the wave of dizziness blurring my vision.

Another slash across my chest and I fight to stay awake, my entire body trembling in excruciating pain.

My hips are jerked, and moments later, fabric tears. My head tilts to the side, facing the door, and a tear rolls down my cheek.

The last thing I see before I black out is Nova shakily standing behind him, holding something in her hand.

chapter twenty nine

CARTER *(Yes, you've read this right)*

"DID YOU HEAR THAT?" SELINA ASKS, pulling away.

I groan, leaning in to kiss her, but the echo of a scream has me gently pushing her off my lap and into her seat before getting out of the car, letting the rain soak me as I lean back into the car.

"Call the police and don't leave this car."

"No, I'm coming," she tells me, her face pale when another scream erupts from inside.

I shake my head fiercely. "No, Selina. Under no circumstances do you leave this car. I don't care what else you hear. Do you understand?"

She bites her lip, yet thankfully nods, leaning back in her seat. "Please hurry."

I wink, trying to hide the nerves swimming through me. I've never heard anyone scream like that in my life.

And I swear to God, if it turns out she's screaming over a spider or some shit, I'm going to throttle her.

I don't know the chick, but she reminds me so much of my sister, who killed herself a few years ago. My dad had cheated on my mum when I was six and kept his love child a secret. But a year after she was born, we found out and she became my world.

But Dad not acknowledging her and the girls at school bullying her took a toll. She was strong, fierce, and always fought back. But a few years ago, it got too much for her.

I saw that same fierce behaviour and strength in Ivy.

I step inside the darkened house, not knowing where the hell I'm going. I rush towards the sound of whimpers, yet don't get far before I'm falling on the stairs.

Groaning, I push myself up, running up them when I hear another cry, but this one is different. It's more like a battle cry, a cry of strength.

I reach the door, my eyes bugging out at the shit storm going on inside. Nova, Selina's aunt, has a stainless-steel vase in her hand, and before I can stop her, she's smashing it across Royce Kingsley's head. I watch in time to see the creepy bastard fall to the floor, but a hard body barrels into me, pushing me against the wall before I can tell her I'm here.

"I've been waiting for this moment," the deep voice says, holding something sharp against my side. Adrenaline pumps through me and I try to breathe through the haze threatening to consume me. "How does it feel to have your father hand you over to me?"

"What?" I rumble, anger boiling through my veins.

"Don't play coy, Kaiden."

I scrunch my face up in disgust when it registers what he's implying.

"Fuck, what is that?" I ask, hoping to distract him.

It works, and he twists his head in the other direction, giving me the opportunity to jab my elbow in his face.

He staggers back, dropping the knife to the floor. He looks up, shocked to see I'm not Kaiden.

Using the manoeuvres I've been trained to use over the years when I fight, I kick him in the gut, knocking the breath out of him. I don't let him recover, instead stepping forward and headbutting him before I grip his jaw and walk him backwards until he bumps against the wall.

From the corner of my eye, I see his arms lift, and I know he's going to slap his palms over my ears to stun me. It won't work. I've encountered the move many times, and many times my opponent has failed.

I roughly pull him towards me before smashing his head back against the wall. He falls to a heap on the floor, out like a baby.

I rush into the bedroom. Royce is lying sprawled over Ivy, blood pouring from the back of his head. I cringe, stepping forward to see if Ivy's okay, but Nova, who I thought was passed out next to them, reaches up on a cry.

Horrified, I rush forward, but with strength I didn't think she'd have, she stabs the knife into his back, in the nape of his neck.

"What did you do?" I yell, ripping the knife out of his neck. Blood spurts everywhere, the warm liquid flowing through my fingers and onto the ground.

"He can't hurt her again," she whispers, before passing out in front of me.

"Fuck," I yell, going to reach for my phone, coming up empty. I left it in the car.

Noise in the hallway pulls my attention away from Nova and my eyes widen a fraction at the sight of Kaiden tumbling through the door, his gaze behind him at the man I knocked out on the floor.

He turns to us, horrified.

"I didn't do this," I tell him, my voice firm, hard.

He ignores me, falling to his knees beside me. At first, I think he's checking his dad, but he shocks me when he pushes him at me, pulling Ivy out from under him.

"No," he sobs, resting her head in his lap. I look at where he's staring and see welts rising on her thighs.

Vomit rises in my throat when the understanding of what he's breaking over hits me. It's not the marks on her body. It's her knickers, rolled down her thighs. He pulls her dress down, covering her modesty.

"You need to call an ambulance," I tell him gently, but a voice at the door startles me.

"Selina called one, and the police. I'll go check where they are," Grant offers, looking stunned at the scene before him.

Shaking myself out of it, I reach over to check Royce's pulse, my eyes closing when I don't find one.

I look up, watching as Kaiden rocks her back and forth, muttering into her hair.

"Kaiden," I call out, but he's lost in his own mind, so I call out louder, stronger. "Kai?" He looks up, blinking through tears. "I'm sorry, but he's dead."

His gaze doesn't waver, not a flicker of emotion. "Good!"

Shocked at his reaction, I shuffle away from the body and check over Nova, seeing a slash down her neck. She's been beaten pretty badly so it's hard to know if it's superficial or if it's caused damage internally. Her pulse is weak but there, so I get up, moving over to the bed, to the woman who's laying there. I check her pulse first, averting my eyes from her half naked body. It's barely there.

I drag a comforter off the end of the bed and cover her cold body. I gag when I get a glimpse of blood between her legs.

I don't know how long it is before the room fills with police and paramedics. I move off the bed, sitting back against a desk, watching as they first roll out the woman off the bed, followed by Ivy and Nova, leaving Royce to lie there with a blanket over his face.

What happened here tonight is going to impact those involved, and not just those who were in this room.

This is what nightmares stem from.

A night not one of them will fully recover from.

And I sit, feeling useless.

Useless for not walking Ivy in.

Useless for not sensing something beforehand.

Useless for not stopping Nova before she killed a man, even if he did deserve it.

And useless for not being able to help them.

"Sir," a woman calls, bending down in front of me. I raise my head from my bent knees and stare blankly at her. "We need to check you out."

I shake my head. "It's not my blood," I croak out.

She looks confused for a moment, before placing her warm hand over mine. "You've got blood running down your side."

What?

I glance down to my side, numb at the sight of blood and a small tear in my shirt.

"It's okay. Let's get you checked over," she whispers, helping me to my feet.

I look around the room, feeling dizzy at the sight of blood around me. The little amount of time I've been in here feels like hours. I can't imagine how long it felt to the women attacked tonight.

Or how they'll recover.

epilogue

IVY

I'M NOT LEAVING, NO MATTER HOW MANY times the doctors, nurses or Kaiden ask me to. They want me to rest, to recover, however, all I want to do is stay by Nova's side, which is why I'm walking back in her room, Kaiden beside me.

"Ivy, you need to rest," Sam orders, but I ignore him, sitting down on the sofa in Nova's room.

I continue to ignore him, keeping my focus on her sleeping in the bed as Kaiden throws a blanket on me.

It has been two days since the attack and emotions are high. Kaiden has hardly spoken and I'm giving him time to process what happened, to process the death of his father.

I grit my teeth at the thought of him. I don't care that he's dead. I only care about Kaiden and how he's feeling. And he's yet to express any kind of emotion towards it. Even the twins didn't know how to react, or how to feel, and I can't blame them. They're in the middle of a shitty situation.

"Will they move Annette in yet?" I ask, closing my eyes when the image of her on the bed flashes through my mind.

She's awake and alert and had informed the police of what she remembered. Royce had beat her when she wouldn't tell him where I was. He had just penetrated her when Nova walked in and attacked him. It didn't matter how long it lasted or if they penetrated a person or not. Rape was rape and the police are treating it as such. The rest the police can't puzzle together until Nova is awake, as Annette had passed out the second Nova entered the room.

My gaze goes to Sam when he doesn't answer. His expression softens. He's going to tell me no. I can read it on his face. Tears pool in my eyes because they should be together. We all should.

"The police would like to question Nova first," he explains. "And Annette needs privacy. It's unfair to her to force her to be around everyone."

I grit my teeth when he briefly looks to Kaiden. "I'd never hurt her," Kaiden growls, speaking to someone other than me for the first time.

"I know," Sam tells him, sighing.

Nova woke up this morning, briefly, before passing back out. She's going to make a full recovery medically speaking. Mentally is another story. We have a lot to work through. She killed a man.

They aren't charging her, not yet, and Sullivan doesn't think there will be a case. She was fighting for her life. For mine.

She saved me from being raped.

Tears pool in my eyes as I pull the blanket tighter around me. Kaiden wraps his arm around my shoulders, kissing the top of my head.

I watch as Sam lovingly caresses her head, sadness pouring from him. "You love her," I state.

He smiles down at Nova, unable to take his eyes off her. "I never stopped. She was my world. What happened with your mum was a mistake. One I can't regret now that I've got you. I was a coward, riddled with guilt over what happened to your mum that night. I should have done something. I screwed up more than your mum's life that night. I ruined mine. I lost out on watching my daughter grow up. And I lost the love of my life. The woman I wanted to grow old with."

"There's still time," I remind him gently.

He looks over at me. "I know. And I should have fought harder back then. Maybe we wouldn't be here now. I don't know. I just know I'm not leaving her."

"Why don't you go get a coffee," I tell him, seeing how worn out he is. He's stayed by her side from the moment I woke up and told him to watch over her, unaware at the time that Royce was dead. "You look worn out."

"I will," he replies, getting up and stretching his back. "Would you two like me to bring you anything?"

"We're good."

The room is silent when he leaves, and the silence is awkward. My mind runs through ways to get Kaiden to open up to me. He's stuck in the nightmare of that night. He needs dragging out of it so he can process it. His dad has just died, and although I won't shed a tear over the loss, I want to be there to support Kaiden and the twins.

As for me, I'm alive. I passed out that night thinking it would be my last moment, and although it will take me a while to be okay again, I'm not going to let it destroy me. We have a mountain to climb, but I'll exhaust every inch of my body to get over it.

My concern is more for Anette and Nova. The mental scars are going to be a lot harder to move forward from. They have a long road of recovery, and I plan on being there every step of the way. And that's only if Annette ever wants to come back to the house.

Twisting in the seat without jarring my shoulder is hard. I have to have it in a sling for a while since Royce had dislocated my shoulder.

I study Kaiden, trying to get a read on him, but I'm coming up blank. His gaze is fixated on Nova. There's no anger, no sadness, or a mixture of both. There's nothing. If it wasn't for the relief and pain and love I saw in him when I woke up, I would think he wasn't in his body at all.

"Kaiden, talk to me," I whisper, placing my hand over his. He doesn't. He stays unmoving as he continues to stare at Nova.

An unnerving thought hits me. What if he blames me for his dad's death?

I twist my neck so fast I wince, letting out a tiny puff of air. I close my eyes, waiting for the pain to subside.

Hearing me, he glances over with concern, scanning me from head to toe. "You need to go back to bed. You should be resting," he croaks, his voice raw.

Tears pool in my eyes. "Do you blame me for your dad's death?"

Unable to look at him, I concentrate on Nova, yet I don't really see, lost in my own head.

The touch of his hand slipping out from under mine startles me, and I jerk to glance at him again. "No. Never."

I sag with relief. "I need you to talk to me, Kai. You seem so lost, and I don't know what to do. I don't know what to say to make you feel better. I'm not going to pretend that I'm sad that he's dead. It might sound callous, but I'll only ever be honest with you. I'll do my best to support you," I ramble, taking a deep breath. "Who am I kidding? Maybe I'm not the best person to be with you right now."

"Will you shut up now," he orders bluntly.

My mouth falls open in shock. "Wha—"

"No, I need you to listen," he orders. My heart races and I dread the worst as I give him a firm nod. "Under no circumstances do I blame you or anyone other than my father for what happened that night. His death? It's a blessing. Yeah, I'm going to miss the absence of a father, but I've been feeling that loss my whole life. I'm not going to lie and say I don't care, because when the anger wears off, I might feel something." He shrugs, rubbing a hand over his unshaven jaw. He tilts his head until his eyes meet mine. "I nearly lost you. Again."

"I have a death curse," I tease, trying to lighten the mood, but he doesn't laugh.

"I've never in all my life been scared to lose anything or anyone, but I was—am—terrified of losing you, and I nearly did. Three times.

"But I'm okay. You can see that, right?" I ask gently.

"Yeah."

"Why do I feel like there's a *but* on the end of that sentence?"

Rubbing a hand down his face, he turns away, staring straight ahead. "There's always a *but* in life, no matter how much you pretend there isn't. You're happy, *but*; you got a promotion, *but*; you're pregnant, *but*…" He sighs, shaking his head. "I'm happy you're all okay, exhilarated that you are alive and that I didn't lose you, *but*… all I can feel is guilt. Guilt that my father did this, guilt for the promise I didn't keep and guilt for not being able to stop him. It's eating away at me, and all I can do is think, what if. What if Nova didn't find the strength to hit my dad? He would have…" He gulps, paling. Taking a deep breath, he shakes himself out of it. "He would have raped you. He raped Annette. He beat you all."

"But you didn't do any of those things, Kai."

"I didn't stop it either," he yells, breathing heavily. "I'm sorry."

"It's okay to be angry, Kai."

"How can you even look at me after what he's done?" he asks quietly.

"Because it wasn't you in that room. Because his actions don't reflect on you or who you are as a human being. Because I love you."

"I love you too." His posture is still stiff, but now I know what the issue is, I'll make sure he knows this wasn't his fault and that he has nothing to feel guilty about. "And I'm sorry. They seem like pointless words in light of what's happened, but it's all I have, Ivy. It's all I have right now."

I can't stand to see him so broken. It's not the Kaiden I know. He's ruthless and a fighter. I rest my head on his shoulder, wishing I knew how to comfort him. "You have nothing to be sorry for."

"There's something else you should know. In the midst of what's happened, it seems irrelevant."

"What is it?"

"Hackett has been fired, and the proof of what he was doing has been sent to the police."

"Good," I whisper, a shiver running through my spine as I think of what a creep he was. "Actually, there's something I was meant to speak to you about."

"Yeah?"

"Clary came to visit me when you went to see what was taking the doctor so long this morning. She said Danielle's home has been burnt down."

He shrugs. "I didn't think Rome would continue with the plan. But if you want to know if it was us, then yes. Her dad is fighting tooth and nail to get her released until the court date. He's going to keep fighting and he's made a good argument to get her released and let off from all charges."

"Really?" I ask, stunned she'd get away with it. And kind of pissed off.

"Don't worry, her dad has already started to liquidate his businesses over here and move overseas to do business. We won't be seeing her again."

There's a knock on the door when I go to reply, and we both turn to see Carter walking in. "Carter," I call out, surprised to see him. And thankful. He did save my life. Again.

"Hey," he greets, his gaze flicking to Nova before coming back to us. "I need to speak to you. Alone."

I glance at Kaiden, my brows scrunched together. "Um, sure."

He pointedly looks at Kaiden. He grunts beside me. "I'm not leaving, Remington, so spit it out."

"Fuck it. Just remember I saved your girl. Three times."

Kaiden tenses beside me and I grab his hand, squeezing it. "Go on, Carter," I order, keeping my voice low.

His gaze flicks back to the bed before he walks over, sitting on the edge of the coffee table. He looks wary as he scrubs a hand over his face, looking tired and worn out.

"Whatever it is, it can't be worse than what happened the other night," Kaiden warns him, and there's frustration in his voice.

Carter's jaw clenches as he narrows his eyes on him. "Dickhead." He takes a moment, sorting through his words. "That night, it's burned into my memory. Nova was hitting Royce with a stainless-steel vase when I reached the room. He was out cold."

I close my eyes, trying to picture the vase in my mind, and the only one I can come up with is the rose gold vase that was on my desk. It weighed a ton. Vomit rises in my throat and I open my eyes to glare at Carter.

"Why are you telling us this?"

He swallows, looking nervous. "Because I had a friend look through the autopsy. Royce died from the stab wound to the back of his neck. She hit his left vertebral artery. That is what caused his death."

"I know," Kaiden grits out.

"Fuck," Carter curses, pulling his hair. "I'm telling you now, if you repeat the wrong thing, I'll end you. There are people worth protecting and those who aren't. Your father wasn't one worth spitting on. So, what I'm about to tell you stays between us."

"Okay," Kaiden confirms, sitting up straighter, sensing the tension coming in waves.

"Nova stabbed him when he was out cold. There was no way he was waking up. I told the police she tried hitting him with the vase, but he went at her again, so she reached for the knife and stabbed him in the back of the neck. I don't know what she'll remember when she wakes up. She'll be better off not knowing. But if she does, she doesn't deserve to go to prison. Feed her the story I told the police and she should be okay."

I look to Kaiden with wide eyes, not knowing how he'll take it, and in fear of possibly losing Nova.

Kaiden's quiet for a few moments before he nods. "We'll let Sam know. If there's a chance she wakes when we aren't here, it's best that Sam can fill her in. You're right, she doesn't deserve to go to prison."

Carter stands, looking shaky on his feet. "I'll give you some privacy."

"Wait," I call out when he reaches the door. "Aren't you admitted?"

Carter chuckles, shrugging. "I released myself this morning. If one more person fusses over me I'm going to lose my shit."

"Thank you," I tell him, forcing a smile at his confused expression. "For saving my life."

He looks to Nova, wonder in his eyes. "As much as I'd like to give it to Kaiden about saving you for a third time, it was all her. She was barely breathing yet found the strength to fight him off and win."

I shiver with trepidation. Kaiden shuffles closer, wrapping his arm around my waist. I curl into him, resting my head on his shoulder. "She was a warrior."

He leaves and a few moments later, the door opens again. Instead of Sam, who I thought it would be, a tall, slender woman walks in wearing business attire. She's beautiful.

"Mum," Kaiden splutters.

She smiles, dropping her bag near the door. "Well, aren't you going to come give your mother a kiss and a hug?"

He slowly gets up, and I watch in shock as he pulls her into his arms, shoving his face into her neck.

Her face softens as she runs a hand over his back. "My handsome boy."

"When did you get back?"

"Just. I came straight here from the airport. I heard what happened with your father and got the next plane home."

She looks over at Nova, tears gathering in her eyes before turning to me, a gentle smile reaching her lips. "And you must be Ivy." I go to get up, feeling awkward sitting down, but she waves me off. "Don't get up. You need to rest."

"Okay," I whisper, unsure of how to act. I inwardly groan, and if it wasn't for the fact Kaiden looks as shocked as me, I'd go back to my room for making an arse out of myself.

"I've been wanting to meet you again."

"Again?" I ask, looking up at Kaiden, but he seems as shocked as I do. He walks back over, sitting down next to me.

"What do you mean again?" he asks.

"I was there when your mum gave birth."

"You were?"

She nods. "There's something I need to tell you."

I sit up, squeezing Kaiden's hand. A while back he said his mum had something she wanted to tell me about mine. And as much as I hid it, I desperately wanted to know.

"After your mum left, I had her followed. I went to where my PI told me to and found her pregnant and in desperate need of help. She said Nova had tried, but she couldn't look at her, couldn't look at herself for what she had done to her. She begged me to get her help. She didn't want you growing up with a druggie for a mother."

"She did?" I choke out, losing my voice.

"She did. She loved you and wanted a better life for you. She didn't want you to grow up in a world where rape was passed off as excusable behaviour. She blamed her grandparents for forcing her parents' hand over not taking it further, for forcing them not to fight for you. They all had a part to play. They lived in a world where they had their own code. We set out to change it; me and Flora. We believed your mum. But Cara didn't accept our help. She couldn't look in the mirror, let alone at us, especially after she revealed everything the way she did. The night Flora died, we were leaving to set things right. We were going to tell Nova the whole truth. I met your mum outside of the manors and she was distraught, sobbing over what she had become and what she had done to her sister. I told her our plan, but she told us it was too late. She had ruined any kind of life at Cheshire Grove. I planned to follow her, but I got the phone call from Sam's parents informing me of Flora's passing."

"Why didn't you tell Nova after, so she could mend the rift between her and my mum?"

Nina smiles, her expression softening. "Because the man she loved had just cheated on her with her sister. As much as she thinks she would have, I knew she wouldn't have seen reason."

"Why didn't you still leave after?" Kaiden asks, wiping his palm down his leg.

"Because I was scared. Scared of what he'd do if I didn't do it right. Neil knew Flora was leaving him and he messed with her car. Royce made sure that I knew and promised me something much worse. He beat me so bad that night I ended up in hospital. The doctors gave me pain meds to help with the pain. It worked. It numbed me, and the second they wore off, I craved that numbness again. I chased it. Which is where my problem started. It didn't stop me from hoping, from planning. I did. But the pretending…" she states, closing her eyes like it pains her. "It was too much and that's when the drinking began. And then that became my life. Whenever I got clean, I started planning again, wanting to destroy your father in a way he'd never recover from, and he knew. He was one step ahead from the get-go, no matter how hard I tried. He would drug me. He would force me to have a drink. And an addict is always an addict, no matter how long they've been clean." She wipes at the tears falling down her cheeks, looking regretful when she turns her attention to her son. "I'll always be sorry for what I've put you and your brothers through. It's one of my greatest regrets, not being stronger."

"It will be okay, Mum. We can get through it."

I clear my throat, nervously twisting my fingers together. "You said Mum got clean?"

"She did. She loved you. You were her whole world. Her strength inspired me. Her hopes and dreams were ones that could only come from a loving mother."

"So, what happened?" I ask, swallowing past the lump in my throat.

All these years I believed she didn't feel anything for me. I didn't know what to do or how to feel.

"Royce happened," she states.

"What did he do?" I spit, my heart racing.

"He found her. He blamed her for ruining all our lives, forcing her to believe that we hated her. He said they would kill her if she didn't disappear. I'm not sure if Nova had found her or not before or after this. He told her the minute she was happy he would rip her world apart again, taking you away and using you as his own toy to play with."

I gag. I cover my mouth with my hand and breathe through my nose.

"Mum," Kaiden whispers.

I look up through tears, staring at his mum. "So, she spent my life pretending to not feel anything for me?"

Nina nods slowly. "She did. I spoke to her before she died. She told me she had the proof to ruin Royce, and it was time to use it. She wanted to get clean. To be a mum. I asked what made her change her mind and she said it was you. One of the men was standing above you while you were sleeping, and the look in his eyes was the same look Royce and Neil had that night. It flicked a switch inside her, and she needed help. She was angry she let Royce get to her that much she turned her back on her own child."

"What about the drugs? She didn't care about me. She cared about them."

"Drugs always come first with an addict. Your mum had relied on them for a long time, Ivy, and I'm not making excuses here. She made her own. She had a life filled with people who let her down. Drugs, to her, didn't come with emotional attachments. They hadn't let her down. In fact, they made her forget. You're a completely different person to what you are sober."

"And I wasn't enough," I finish, my stomach bottoming out.

"She was scared of being happy. Scared of losing you. In her own way, she would rather have you hate her and still have you in her life, than to love you and have him rip you away."

"It was a no-win situation," I whisper, looking down to the floor.

"I know it doesn't give you any closure. It doesn't make up for the years of neglect. But I needed you to know that there was a time she loved you. And a part of Cara who was still inside the druggie, loved you. She was protecting you in her way."

I fall into Kaiden, not caring about my shoulder, the bruises or the pain. I sob into his chest, gripping the back of his T-shirt.

"There's one more thing before I leave to go see my other two boys." I sniffle, tears blurring my vision, and turn to her. "When Cara called me and told me what she had done, she knew there was a possibility that he'd kill her. She said to make sure Nova found you, that she would love and take care of you."

"But she knew Nova lived next door to Royce," I state, confused.

"No, back then, Nova and Sam were staying there whilst their home was built. She didn't know. It would have been you dealing with your mum's debts or have you living next door to a monster. I made sure to keep Royce busy at work and spent a fortune on gathering information to get him locked away for good. I'm sorry you got hurt. I'm sorry Annette and Nova got hurt. I should have warned her who he was, but I didn't want to put her in danger."

I nod, watching her stand. "I need to go see my sons. I hope I've answered all your questions, and if you have any more, I will try to answer them."

"Thank you for coming to tell me," I whisper.

She nods, stepping forward to lean down and kiss Kaiden on the forehead. She surprises me by running her hand over the top of my head. "Take care of each other."

When the door clicks shut, Kaiden leans back to look at me. "How are you doing?"

"Honestly?" I ask, and he nods. "I don't know. She's not here to answer questions only she can really know the answers to. It's a lot to take in. She loved me, Kai. Loved me. And although I never witnessed that love, it's still nice to know I had it."

"Are you going to be okay?"

I look up into his loving eyes and smile. "It's a new beginning, a new chapter, and the more pages that turn, the more memories I'll make. And the best thing about it is I get to do it surrounded by people who love me and who I love."

He smiles, leaning in to kiss me, mindful of my cut lip. He pulls back a little, his eyes sparkling. "To making memories with the person you love."

I smile, closing my eyes to soak in this moment. "I love you."

"You too, baby."

I lean into him, relief consuming me. We might have a dark cloud still hanging above us, but the storm of it all has finally passed.

And together, we'll get through it.

I arrived at Cheshire Grove with an empty heart, no hope, and a man out to end me. But I sit here today, alive, wanted, loved, and that is more than I could ever have wished for.

Money doesn't make you rich.

It's the people.

Family.

And for me.

Kaiden.

And although this is how chapter one of our story ends, we still have a lifetime of more, and I'm excited to experience every second of them.

Love has changed me. Changed us.

And I don't regret a moment.

THE END

AUTHOR'S NOTE.

GUYS! We're finally here. It's the end. And although I do plan on adding more books in the future, using some of your favourite characters from the series, this is the end for Kaiden and Ivy's story.

I'm sorry for the delay on the release of Crowd of Lies. It was never my intention for you all to wait this long, so I hope you enjoyed it and that the wait was worth it.

Wrong Crowd had been in my notes since 2014 yet went in a new direction and I ended up writing Malik instead.

Inspiration came to me as I was writing Landon and I knew I had to get Wrong Crowd written. I wanted to make a replica of Landon, but without that Carter family bond and morals. I wanted someone who was ruthless, cunning and didn't care what people thought. And although I wrote the book, it doesn't mean I condone Kaiden's behaviour in book one or any of the male characters who sexually exploited Ivy.

It's been a long journey getting the duet completed. I've faced so much this year and completing book two has felt like a massive achievement, and one I've loved sharing with my readers.

Thank you for the continuous support. You guys rock!!

And as long as you keep reading, I'll keep writing.

In all my books I give out special announcements, whether it's bloggers, my beta team, or readers. I do it.

It's hard to put into words just how much I've appreciated the support this year. How much love I've felt from people I've never even met before yet who openly shared their support and understanding every day.

That's how incredible this book community can be. Forget about the drama, about who said what or what someone said you did. It's not about popularity or what someone can do for another.

It's about a group of avid readers from all over the world coming together and sharing something beautiful.

And knowing my words are something you all share, it's beyond any feeling you can imagine.

I work hard, but it's you who keep me going, who give me a reason to keep writing.

And I have so many to thank, so I'm sorry if I miss anyone.

As many of you would agree, Cassy at Pink Ink Designs did a fantastic job with the cover. She never fails to impress me. Thank you, Cassy, for bringing the book colour and life.

Rachel Osbourne, for keeping my readers group going and continuously being there if I need help. For being the friend that notices you've disappeared off Facebook and messages you to find out why. You are awesome.

To my readers in my group or on Instagram that messaged support through Rachel or Stephanie. They sent every single comment to let me know you were there. Thank you. Thank you for being an amazing group of women. It's been wonderful getting to know you all.

But my biggest thank you, my most heartfelt dedication, is to Stephanie Farrant. Her support holds no bounds. There are no strings or ulterior motives. She is pure and selfless to those she considers a friend.

She gave me advice and direction through the hardest time in my writing career, and I wouldn't have made it through without her.

Thank you for not only being a friend, but for working as hard as you do to complete my books.

I lurves you, my psycho midget, and wouldn't change you for the world. You are small, but you are mighty. And I think this should be your tagline.

Other books by Lisa Helen Gray

A Carter Brother Series

Malik – Book One
Mason – Book Two
Myles – Book Three
Evan Book 3.5
Max – Book Four
Maverick – Book Five

A Next Generation Carter Brother Novel

Faith – Book One
Aiden – Book Two
Landon – Book Three
(Read Soul of my Soul next)
Hayden – Coming soon

Take A Chance

Soul of my Soul

I Wish

If I could I'd Wish it all Away
Wishing For A Happily Ever After

Forgotten Series

Better Left Forgotten – Book One
Obsession – Book Two
Forgiven – Book Three

Whithall University

Foul Play – Book One
Game Over – Book Two
Almost Three – Book Three

Kingsley Academy

Wrong Crowd – Book One
Crowd of Lies – Now available

Printed in Poland
by Amazon Fulfillment
Poland Sp. z o.o., Wrocław